The Mysterious Mr Quin

HarperCollins*Publishers*

HarperCollins*Publishers*
1 London Bridge Street
London SE1 9GF
www.harpercollins.co.uk

HarperCollins*Publishers*
1st Floor, Watermarque Building, Ringsend Road
Dublin 4, Ireland

This paperback edition 2017

11

First published in Great Britain by
Collins 1930

A catalogue record for this book is available from the British Library

ISBN 978-0-00-819641-7 (PB)
ISBN 978-0-00-825623-4 (POD PB)

Set in Sabon LT Std by Palimpsest Book Production Limited,
Falkirk, Stirlingshire
Printed and bound in the UK using 100% renewable electricity at
CPI Group (UK) Ltd

MIX
Paper from
responsible sources
FSC™
www.fsc.org
FSC® C007454

To Harlequin the Invisible

Foreword

The Mr Quin stories were not written as a series. They were written one at a time at rare intervals. Mr Quin, I consider, is an epicure's taste.

A set of Dresden figures on my mother's mantelpiece fascinated me as a child and afterwards. They represented the Italian *commedia dell'arte*: Harlequin, Columbine, Pierrot, Pierette, Punchinello, and Punchinella. As a girl I wrote a series of poems about them, and I rather think that one of the poems, *Harlequin's Song*, was my first appearance in print. It was in the *Poetry Review*, and I got a guinea for it!

After I turned from poetry and ghost stories to crime, Harlequin finally reappeared; a figure invisible except when he chose, not quite human, yet concerned with the affairs of human beings and particularly of lovers. He is also the advocate for the dead.

Though each story about him is quite separate, yet the collection, written over a considerable period of years, outlines in the end of the story of Harlequin himself.

Agatha Christie

With Mr Quin there has been created little Mr Satterthwaite, Mr Quin's friend in this mortal world: Mr Satterthwaite, the gossip, the looker-on at life, the little man who without ever touching the depths of joy and sorrow himself, recognizes drama when he sees it, and is conscious that he has a part to play.

Of the Mr Quin stories, my favourites are: *The World's End*, *The Man from the Sea*, and *Harlequin's Lane*.

Agatha Christie

Contents

CHAPTER 1

The Coming of Mr Quin

It was New Year's Eve.

The elder members of the house party at Royston were assembled in the big hall.

Mr Satterthwaite was glad that the young people had gone to bed. He was not fond of young people in herds. He thought them uninteresting and crude. They lacked subtlety and as life went on he had become increasingly fond of subtleties.

Mr Satterthwaite was sixty-two—a little bent, dried-up man with a peering face oddly elflike, and an intense and inordinate interest in other people's lives. All his life, so to speak, he had sat in the front row of the stalls watching various dramas of human nature unfold before him. His role had always been that of the onlooker. Only now, with old age holding him in its clutch, he found himself increasingly critical of the drama submitted to him. He demanded now something a little out of the common.

There was no doubt that he had a flair for these things. He knew instinctively when the elements of drama were at hand. Like a war horse, he sniffed the scent. Since his arrival at Royston this afternoon, that strange inner sense of his had stirred and bid him be ready. Something interesting was happening or going to happen.

The house party was not a large one. There was Tom Evesham, their genial good-humoured host, and his serious political wife who had been before her marriage Lady Laura Keene. There was Sir Richard Conway, soldier, traveller and sportsman, there were six or seven young people whose names Mr Satterthwaite had not grasped and there were the Portals.

It was the Portals who interested Mr Satterthwaite.

He had never met Alex Portal before, but he knew all about him. Had known his father and his grandfather. Alex Portal ran pretty true to type. He was a man of close on forty, fair-haired, and blue-eyed like all the Portals, fond of sport, good at games, devoid of imagination. Nothing unusual about Alex Portal. The usual good sound English stock.

But his wife was different. She was, Mr Satterthwaite knew, an Australian. Portal had been out in Australia two years ago, had met her out there and had married her and brought her home. She had never been to England previous to her marriage. All the same, she wasn't at all like any other Australian woman Mr Satterthwaite had met.

He observed her now, covertly. Interesting woman—very. So still, and yet so—alive. Alive! That was just it! Not exactly beautiful—no, you wouldn't call her beautiful, but there was a kind of calamitous magic about her that you couldn't miss—that no man could miss. The masculine side of Mr Satterthwaite spoke there, but the feminine side (for Mr Satterthwaite had a large share of femininity) was equally interested in another question. *Why did Mrs Portal dye her hair?*

No other man would probably have known that she dyed her hair, but Mr Satterthwaite knew. He knew all those things. And it puzzled him. Many dark women dye their hair blonde; he had never before come across a fair woman who dyed her hair black.

Everything about her intrigued him. In a queer intuitive way, he felt certain that she was either very happy or very unhappy—but he didn't know which, and it annoyed him not to know. Furthermore there was the curious effect she had upon her husband.

'He adores her,' said Mr Satterthwaite to himself, 'but sometimes he's—yes, afraid of her! That's very interesting. That's uncommonly interesting.'

Portal drank too much. That was certain. And he had a curious way of watching his wife when she wasn't looking.

'Nerves,' said Mr Satterthwaite. 'The fellow's all nerves. She knows it too, but she won't do anything about it.'

He felt very curious about the pair of them. Something was going on that he couldn't fathom.

He was roused from his meditations on the subject by the solemn chiming of the big clock in the corner.

'Twelve o'clock,' said Evesham. 'New Year's Day. Happy New Year—everybody. As a matter of fact that clock's five minutes fast . . . I don't know why the children wouldn't wait up and see the New Year in?'

'I don't suppose for a minute they've really gone to bed,'

said his wife placidly. 'They're probably putting hairbrushes or something in our beds. That sort of thing does so amuse them. I can't think why. We should never have been allowed to do such a thing in my young days.'

'*Autre temps, autres moeurs*,' said Conway, smiling.

He was a tall soldierly-looking man. Both he and Evesham were much of the same type—honest upright kindly men with no great pretensions to brains.

'In my young days we all joined hands in a circle and sang "Auld Lang Syne",' continued Lady Laura. '"Should auld acquaintance be forgot"—so touching, I always think the words are.'

Evesham moved uneasily.

'Oh! drop it, Laura,' he muttered. '*Not here.*'

He strode across the wide hall where they were sitting, and switched on an extra light.

'Very stupid of me,' said Lady Laura, *sotto voce*. 'Reminds him of poor Mr Capel, of course. My dear, is the fire too hot for you?'

Eleanor Portal made a brusque movement.

'Thank you. I'll move my chair back a little.'

What a lovely voice she had—one of those low murmuring echoing voices that stay in your memory, thought Mr Satterthwaite. Her face was in shadow now. What a pity.

From her place in the shadow she spoke again.

'Mr—Capel?'

'Yes. The man who originally owned this house. He shot himself you know—oh! very well, Tom dear, I won't speak of it unless you like. It was a great shock for Tom, of

4

course, because he was here when it happened. So were you, weren't you, Sir Richard?'

'Yes, Lady Laura.'

An old grandfather clock in the corner groaned, wheezed, snorted asthmatically, and then struck twelve.

'Happy New Year, Tom,' grunted Evesham perfunctorily.

Lady Laura wound up her knitting with some deliberation.

'Well, we've seen the New Year in,' she observed, and added, looking towards Mrs Portal, 'What do you think, my dear?'

Eleanor Portal rose quickly to her feet.

'Bed, by all means,' she said lightly.

'She's very pale,' thought Mr Satterthwaite, as he too rose, and began busying himself with candlesticks. 'She's not usually as pale as that.'

He lighted her candle and handed it to her with a funny little old-fashioned bow. She took it from him with a word of acknowledgment and went slowly up the stairs.

Suddenly a very odd impulse swept over Mr Satterthwaite. He wanted to go after her—to reassure her—he had the strangest feeling that she was in danger of some kind. The impulse died down, and he felt ashamed. *He* was getting nervy too.

She hadn't looked at her husband as she went up the stairs, but now she turned her head over her shoulder and gave him a long searching glance which had a queer intensity in it. It affected Mr Satterthwaite very oddly.

He found himself saying goodnight to his hostess in quite a flustered manner.

'I'm sure I hope it *will* be a happy New Year,' Lady Laura was saying. 'But the political situation seems to me to be fraught with grave uncertainty.'

'I'm sure it is,' said Mr Satterthwaite earnestly. 'I'm sure it is.'

'I only hope,' continued Lady Laura, without the least change of manner, 'that it will be a dark man who first crosses the threshold. You know that superstition, I suppose, Mr Satterthwaite? No? You surprise me. To bring luck to the house it must be a dark man who first steps over the door step on New Year's Day. Dear me, I hope I shan't find anything *very* unpleasant in my bed. I never trust the children. They have such very high spirits.'

Shaking her head in sad foreboding, Lady Laura moved majestically up the staircase.

With the departure of the women, chairs were pulled in closer round the blazing logs on the big open hearth.

'Say when,' said Evesham, hospitably, as he held up the whisky decanter.

When everybody had said when, the talk reverted to the subject which had been tabooed before.

'You knew Derek Capel, didn't you, Satterthwaite?' asked Conway.

'Slightly—yes.'

'And you, Portal?'

'No, I never met him.'

So fiercely and defensively did he say it, that Mr Satterthwaite looked up in surprise.

'I always hate it when Laura brings up the subject,' said Evesham slowly. 'After the tragedy, you know, this place was sold to a big manufacturer fellow. He cleared out after a year—didn't suit him or something. A lot of tommy rot was talked about the place being haunted of course, and it gave the house a bad name. Then, when Laura got me to stand for West Kidleby, of course it meant living up in these parts, and it wasn't so easy to find a suitable house. Royston was going cheap, and—well, in the end I bought it. Ghosts are all tommy rot, but all the same one doesn't exactly care to be reminded that you're living in a house where one of your own friends shot himself. Poor old Derek—we shall never know why he did it.'

'He won't be the first or the last fellow who's shot himself without being able to give a reason,' said Alex Portal heavily.

He rose and poured himself out another drink, splashing the whisky in with a liberal hand.

'There's something very wrong with him,' said Mr Satterthwaite, to himself. 'Very wrong indeed. I wish I knew what it was all about.'

'Gad!' said Conway. 'Listen to the wind. It's a wild night.'

'A good night for ghosts to walk,' said Portal with a reckless laugh. 'All the devils in Hell are abroad tonight.'

'According to Lady Laura, even the blackest of them would bring us luck,' observed Conway, with a laugh. 'Hark to that!'

The wind rose in another terrific wail, and as it died away there came three loud knocks on the big nailed doorway.

Everyone started.

'Who on earth can that be at this time of night?' cried Evesham.

They stared at each other.

'I will open it,' said Evesham. 'The servants have gone to bed.'

He strode across to the door, fumbled a little over the heavy bars, and finally flung it open. An icy blast of wind came sweeping into the hall.

Framed in the doorway stood a man's figure, tall and slender. To Mr Satterthwaite, watching, he appeared by some curious effect of the stained glass above the door, to be dressed in every colour of the rainbow. Then, as he stepped forward, he showed himself to be a thin dark man dressed in motoring clothes.

'I must really apologize for this intrusion,' said the stranger, in a pleasant level voice. 'But my car broke down. Nothing much, my chauffeur is putting it to rights, but it will take half an hour or so, and it is so confoundedly cold outside—'

He broke off, and Evesham took up the thread quickly.

'I should think it was. Come in and have a drink. We can't give you any assistance about the car, can we?'

'No, thanks. My man knows what to do. By the way, my name is Quin—Harley Quin.'

'Sit down, Mr Quin,' said Evesham. 'Sir Richard Conway, Mr Satterthwaite. My name is Evesham.'

Mr Quin acknowledged the introductions, and dropped into the chair that Evesham had hospitably pulled forward. As he sat, some effect of the firelight threw a bar of shadow across his face which gave almost the impression of a mask.

Evesham threw a couple more logs on the fire.

'A drink?'

'Thanks.'

Evesham brought it to him and asked as he did so:

'So you know this part of the world well, Mr Quin?'

'I passed through it some years ago.'

'Really?'

'Yes—This house belonged then to a man called Capel.'

'Ah! yes,' said Evesham. 'Poor Derek Capel. You knew him?'

'Yes, I knew him.'

Evesham's manner underwent a faint change, almost imperceptible to one who had not studied the English character. Before, it had contained a subtle reserve, now this was laid aside. Mr Quin had known Derek Capel. He was the friend of a friend, and, as such, was vouched for and fully accredited.

'Astounding affair, that,' he said confidentially. 'We were just talking about it. I can tell you, it went against the grain, buying this place. If there had been anything else suitable, but there wasn't you see. I was in the house the night he shot himself—so was Conway, and upon my word, I've always expected his ghost to walk.'

'A very inexplicable business,' said Mr Quin, slowly and deliberately, and he paused with the air of an actor who has just spoken an important cue.

'You may well say inexplicable,' burst in Conway. 'The thing's a black mystery—always will be.'

'I wonder,' said Mr Quin, non-committally. 'Yes, Sir Richard, you were saying?'

'Astounding—that's what it was. Here's a man in the prime of life, gay, light-hearted, without a care in the world.

Five or six old pals staying with him. Top of his spirits at dinner, full of plans for the future. And from the dinner table he goes straight upstairs to his room, takes a revolver from a drawer and shoots himself. Why? Nobody ever knew. Nobody ever will know.'

'Isn't that rather a sweeping statement, Sir Richard?' asked Mr Quin, smiling.

Conway stared at him.

'What d'you mean? I don't understand.'

'A problem is not necessarily unsolvable because it has remained unsolved.'

'Oh! Come, man, if nothing came out at the time, it's not likely to come out now—ten years afterwards?'

Mr Quin shook his head gently.

'I disagree with you. The evidence of history is against you. The contemporary historian never writes such a true history as the historian of a later generation. It is a question of getting the true perspective, of seeing things in proportion. If you like to call it so, it is, like everything else, a question of relativity.'

Alex Portal leant forward, his face twitching painfully.

'You are right, Mr Quin,' he cried, 'you are right. Time does not dispose of a question—it only presents it anew in a different guise.'

Evesham was smiling tolerantly.

'Then you mean to say, Mr Quin, that if we were to hold, let us say, a Court of Inquiry tonight, into the circumstances of Derek Capel's death, we are as likely to arrive at the truth as we should have been at the time?'

'*More* likely, Mr Evesham. The personal equation has

largely dropped out, and you will remember facts as facts without seeking to put your own interpretation upon them.'

Evesham frowned doubtfully.

'One must have a starting point, of course,' said Mr Quin in his quiet level voice. 'A starting point is usually a theory. One of you must have a theory, I am sure. How about you, Sir Richard?'

Conway frowned thoughtfully.

'Well, of course,' he said apologetically, 'we thought— naturally we all thought—that there must be a woman in it somewhere. It's usually either that or money, isn't it? And it certainly wasn't money. No trouble of that description. So—what else could it have been?'

Mr Satterthwaite started. He had leant forward to contribute a small remark of his own and in the act of doing so, he had caught sight of a woman's figure crouched against the balustrade of the gallery above. She was huddled down against it, invisible from everywhere but where he himself sat, and she was evidently listening with strained attention to what was going on below. So immovable was she that he hardly believed the evidence of his own eyes.

But he recognized the pattern of the dress easily enough— an old-world brocade. It was Eleanor Portal.

And suddenly all the events of the night seemed to fall into pattern—Mr Quin's arrival, no fortuitous chance, but the appearance of an actor when his cue was given. There was a drama being played in the big hall at Royston tonight—a drama none the less real in that one of the actors was dead. Oh! yes, Derek Capel had a part in the play. Mr Satterthwaite was sure of that.

And, again suddenly, a new illumination came to him. This was Mr Quin's doing. It was he who was staging the play—was giving the actors their cues. He was at the heart of the mystery pulling the strings, making the puppets work. He knew everything, even to the presence of the woman crouched against the woodwork upstairs. Yes, he knew.

Sitting well back in his chair, secure in his role of audience, Mr Satterthwaite watched the drama unfold before his eyes. Quietly and naturally, Mr Quin was pulling the strings, setting his puppets in motion.

'A woman—yes,' he murmured thoughtfully. 'There was no mention of any woman at dinner?'

'Why, of course,' cried Evesham. 'He announced his engagement. That's just what made it seem so absolutely mad. Very bucked about it he was. Said it wasn't to be announced just yet—but gave us the hint that he was in the running for the Benedick stakes.'

'Of course we all guessed who the lady was,' said Conway. 'Marjorie Dilke. Nice girl.'

It seemed to be Mr Quin's turn to speak, but he did not do so, and something about his silence seemed oddly provocative. It was as though he challenged the last statement. It had the effect of putting Conway in a defensive position.

'Who else could it have been? Eh, Evesham?'

'I don't know,' said Tom Evesham slowly. 'What did he say exactly now? Something about being in the running for the Benedick stakes—that he couldn't tell us the lady's name till he had her permission—it wasn't to be announced

12

yet. He said, I remember, that he was a damned lucky fellow. That he wanted his two old friends to know that by that time next year he'd be a happy married man. Of course, we assumed it was Marjorie. They were great friends and he'd been about with her a lot.'

'The only thing—' began Conway and stopped.

'What were you going to say, Dick?'

'Well, I mean, it was odd in a way, if it were Marjorie, that the engagement shouldn't be announced at once. I mean, why the secrecy? Sounds more as though it were a married woman—you know, someone whose husband had just died, or who was divorcing him.'

'That's true,' said Evesham. 'If that were the case, of course, the engagement couldn't be announced at once. And you know, thinking back about it, I don't believe he had been seeing much of Marjorie. All that was the year before. I remember thinking things seemed to have cooled off between them.'

'Curious,' said Mr Quin.

'Yes—looked almost as though someone had come between them.'

'Another woman,' said Conway thoughtfully.

'By jove,' said Evesham. 'You know, there was something almost indecently hilarious about old Derek that night. He looked almost drunk with happiness. And yet—I can't quite explain what I mean—but he looked oddly defiant too.'

'Like a man defying Fate,' said Alex Portal heavily.

Was it of Derek Capel he was speaking—or was it of himself? Mr Satterthwaite, looking at him, inclined to the latter view. Yes, that was what Alex Portal represented—a man defying Fate.

His imagination, muddled by drink, responded suddenly to that note in the story which recalled his own secret preoccupation.

Mr Satterthwaite looked up. She was still there. Watching, listening—still motionless, frozen—like a dead woman.

'Perfectly true,' said Conway. 'Capel *was* excited—curiously so. I'd describe him as a man who had staked heavily and won against well nigh overwhelming odds.'

'Getting up courage, perhaps, for what he's made up his mind to do?' suggested Portal.

And as though moved by an association of ideas, he got up and helped himself to another drink.

'Not a bit of it,' said Evesham sharply. 'I'd almost swear nothing of that kind was in his mind. Conway's right. A successful gambler who has brought off a long shot and can hardly believe in his own good fortune. That was the attitude.'

Conway gave a gesture of discouragement.

'And yet,' he said. 'Ten minutes later—'

They sat in silence. Evesham brought his hand down with a bang on the table.

'Something must have happened in that ten minutes,' he cried. 'It must! But what? Let's go over it carefully. We were all talking. In the middle of it Capel got up suddenly and left the room—'

'Why?' said Mr Quin.

The interruption seemed to disconcert Evesham.

'I beg your pardon?'

'I only said: Why?' said Mr Quin.

Evesham frowned in an effort of memory.

'It didn't seem vital—at the time—Oh! of course—the Post. Don't you remember that jangling bell, and how excited we were. We'd been snowed up for three days, remember. Biggest snowstorm for years and years. All the roads were impassable. No newspapers, no letters. Capel went out to see if something had come through at last, and got a great pile of things. Newspapers and letters. He opened the paper to see if there was any news, and then went upstairs with his letters. Three minutes afterwards, we heard a shot . . . Inexplicable—absolutely inexplicable.'

'That's not inexplicable,' said Portal. 'Of course the fellow got some unexpected news in a letter. Obvious, I should have said.'

'Oh! Don't think we missed anything so obvious as that. It was one of the Coroner's first questions. *But Capel never opened one of his letters.* The whole pile lay unopened on his dressing-table.'

Portal looked crestfallen.

'You're sure he didn't open just one of them? He might have destroyed it after reading it?'

'No, I'm quite positive. Of course, that would have been the natural solution. No, every one of the letters was unopened. Nothing burnt—nothing torn up—There was no fire in the room.'

Portal shook his head.

'Extraordinary.'

'It was a ghastly business altogether,' said Evesham in a

15

low voice. 'Conway and I went up when we heard the shot, and found him—It gave me a shock, I can tell you.'

'Nothing to be done but telephone for the police, I suppose?' said Mr Quin.

'Royston wasn't on the telephone then. I had it put in when I bought the place. No, luckily enough, the local constable happened to be in the kitchen at the time. One of the dogs—you remember poor old Rover, Conway?— had strayed the day before. A passing carter had found it half buried in a snowdrift and had taken it to the police station. They recognized it as Capel's, and a dog he was particularly fond of, and the constable came up with it. He'd just arrived a minute before the shot was fired. It saved us some trouble.'

'Gad, that was a snowstorm,' said Conway reminiscently. 'About this time of year, wasn't it? Early January.'

'February, I think. Let me see, we went abroad soon afterwards.'

'I'm pretty sure it was January. My hunter Ned—you remember Ned?—lamed himself the end of January. That was just after this business.'

'It must have been quite the end of January then. Funny how difficult it is to recall dates after a lapse of years.'

'One of the most difficult things in the world,' said Mr Quin, conversationally. 'Unless you can find a landmark in some big public event—an assassination of a crowned head, or a big murder trial.'

'Why, of course,' cried Conway, 'it was just before the Appleton case.'

'Just after, wasn't it?'

'No, no, don't you remember—Capel knew the Appletons—he'd stayed with the old man the previous Spring—just a week before he died. He was talking of him one night—what an old curmudgeon he was, and how awful it must have been for a young and beautiful woman like Mrs Appleton to be tied to him. There was no suspicion then that she had done away with him.'

'By jove, you're right. I remember reading the paragraph in the paper saying an exhumation order had been granted. It would have been that same day—I remember only seeing it with half my mind, you know, the other half wondering about poor old Derek lying dead upstairs.'

'A common, but very curious phenomenon, that,' observed Mr Quin. 'In moments of great stress, the mind focuses itself upon some quite unimportant matter which is remembered long afterwards with the utmost fidelity, driven in, as it were, by the mental stress of the moment. It may be some quite irrelevant detail, like the pattern of a wallpaper, but it will never be forgotten.'

'Rather extraordinary, your saying that, Mr Quin,' said Conway. 'Just as you were speaking, I suddenly felt myself back in Derek Capel's room—with Derek lying dead on the floor—I saw as plainly as possible the big tree outside the window, and the shadow it threw upon the snow outside. Yes, the moonlight, the snow, and the shadow of the tree—I can see them again this minute. By Gad, I believe I could draw them, and yet I never realized I was looking at them at the time.'

'His room was the big one over the porch, was it not?' asked Mr Quin.

'Yes, and the tree was the big beech, just at the angle of the drive.'

Mr Quin nodded, as though satisfied. Mr Satterthwaite was curiously thrilled. He was convinced that every word, every inflection of Mr Quin's voice, was pregnant with purpose. He was driving at something—exactly what Mr Satterthwaite did not know, but he was quite convinced as to whose was the master hand.

There was a momentary pause, and then Evesham reverted to the preceding topic.

'That Appleton case, I remember it very well now. What a sensation it made. She got off, didn't she? Pretty woman, very fair—remarkably fair.'

Almost against his will, Mr Satterthwaite's eyes sought the kneeling figure up above. Was it his fancy, or did he see it shrink a little as though at a blow? Did he see a hand slide upwards to the table cloth—and then pause?

There was a crash of falling glass. Alex Portal, helping himself to whisky, had let the decanter slip.

'I say—sir, damn' sorry. Can't think what came over me.'

Evesham cut short his apologies.

'Quite all right. Quite all right, my dear fellow. Curious— That smash reminded me. That's what she did, didn't she? Mrs Appleton? Smashed the port decanter?'

'Yes. Old Appleton had his glass of port—only one—each night. The day after his death, one of the servants saw her take the decanter out and smash it deliberately. That set them talking, of course. They all knew she had been perfectly wretched with him. Rumour grew and grew, and in the end, months later, some of his relatives applied for an exhumation order. And sure enough, the old fellow had been poisoned. Arsenic, wasn't it?'

'No—strychnine, I think. It doesn't much matter. Well, of course, there it was. Only one person was likely to have done it. Mrs Appleton stood her trial. She was acquitted more through lack of evidence against her than from any overwhelming proof of innocence. In other words, she was lucky. Yes, I don't suppose there's much doubt she did it right enough. What happened to her afterwards?'

'Went out to Canada, I believe. Or was it Australia? She had an uncle or something of the sort out there who offered her a home. Best thing she could do under the circumstances.'

Mr Satterthwaite was fascinated by Alex Portal's right hand as it clasped his glass. How tightly he was gripping it.

'You'll smash that in a minute or two, if you're not careful,' thought Mr Satterthwaite. 'Dear me, how interesting all this is.'

Evesham rose and helped himself to a drink.

'Well, we're not much nearer to knowing why poor Derek Capel shot himself,' he remarked. 'The Court of Inquiry hasn't been a great success, has it, Mr Quin?'

Mr Quin laughed . . .

It was a strange laugh, mocking—yet sad. It made everyone jump.

'I beg your pardon,' he said. 'You are still living in the past, Mr Evesham. You are still hampered by your preconceived notion. But I—the man from outside, the stranger passing by, see only—facts!'

'Facts?'

19

'Yes—facts.'

'What do you mean?' said Evesham.

'I see a clear sequence of facts, outlined by yourselves but of which you have not seen the significance. Let us go back ten years and look at what we see—untrammelled by ideas or sentiment.'

Mr Quin had risen. He looked very tall. The fire leaped fitfully behind him. He spoke in a low compelling voice.

'You are at dinner. Derek Capel announces his engagement. You think then it was to Marjorie Dilke. You are not so sure now. He has the restlessly excited manner of a man who has successfully defied Fate—who, in your own words, has pulled off a big coup against overwhelming odds. Then comes the clanging of the bell. He goes out to get the long overdue mail. He doesn't open his letters, but you mention yourselves that *he opened the paper to glance at the news*. It is ten years ago—so we cannot know what the news was that day—a far-off earthquake, a near at hand political crisis? The only thing we do know about the contents of that paper is that it contained one small paragraph—*a paragraph stating that the Home Office had given permission to exhume* the body of Mr Appleton three days ago.'

'What?'

Mr Quin went on.

'Derek Capel goes up to his room, and there he sees something out of the window. Sir Richard Conway has told us that the curtain was not drawn across it and further that it gave on to the drive. What did he see? What could he have seen that forced him to take his life?'

'What do you mean? What did he see?'

'I think,' said Mr Quin, 'that he saw a policeman. A policeman who had come about a dog—But Derek Capel didn't know that—he just saw—a policeman.'

There was a long silence—as though it took some time to drive the inference home.

'My God!' whispered Evesham at last. 'You can't mean that? Appleton? But he wasn't there at the time Appleton died. The old man was alone with his wife—'

'But he may have been there a week earlier. Strychnine is not very soluble unless it is in the form of hydrochloride. The greater part of it, put into the port, would be taken in the last glass, perhaps a week after he left.'

Portal sprung forward. His voice was hoarse, his eyes bloodshot.

'Why did she break the decanter?' he cried. 'Why did she break the decanter? Tell me that!'

For the first time that evening, Mr Quin addressed himself to Mr Satterthwaite.

'You have a wide experience of life, Mr Satterthwaite. Perhaps you can tell us that.'

Mr Satterthwaite's voice trembled a little. His cue had come at last. He was to speak some of the most important lines in the play. He was an actor now—not a looker-on.

'As I see it,' he murmured modestly. 'She—cared for Derek Capel. She was, I think, a good woman—and she had sent him away. When her husband—died, she suspected the truth. And so, to save the man she loved, she tried to destroy the evidence against him. Later, I think, he persuaded her that her suspicions were unfounded, and she consented

21

to marry him. But even then, she hung back—women, I fancy, have a lot of instinct.'

Mr Satterthwaite had spoken his part.

Suddenly a long trembling sigh filled the air.

'My God!' cried Evesham, starting, 'what was that?'

Mr Satterthwaite could have told him that it was Eleanor Portal in the gallery above, but he was too artistic to spoil a good effect.

Mr Quin was smiling.

'My car will be ready by now. Thank you for your hospitality, Mr Evesham. I have, I hope, done something for my friend.'

They stared at him in blank amazement.

'That aspect of the matter has not struck you? He loved this woman, you know. Loved her enough to commit murder for her sake. When retribution overtook him, as he mistakenly thought, he took his own life. But unwittingly, he left her to face the music.'

'She was acquitted,' muttered Evesham.

'Because the case against her could not be proved. I fancy—it may be only a fancy—that she is still—facing the music.'

Portal had sunk into a chair, his face buried in his hands.

Quin turned to Satterthwaite.

'Goodbye, Mr Satterthwaite. You are interested in the drama, are you not?'

Mr Satterthwaite nodded—surprised.

'I must recommend the Harlequinade to your attention. It is dying out nowadays—but it repays attention, I assure you. Its symbolism is a little difficult to follow—but the

22

immortals are always immortal, you know. I wish you all goodnight.'

They saw him stride out into the dark. As before, the coloured glass gave the effect of motley . . .

Mr Satterthwaite went upstairs. He went to draw down his window, for the air was cold. The figure of Mr Quin moved down the drive, and from a side door came a woman's figure, running. For a moment they spoke together, then she retraced her steps to the house. She passed just below the window, and Mr Satterthwaite was struck anew by the vitality of her face. She moved now like a woman in a happy dream.

'Eleanor!'

Alex Portal had joined her.

'Eleanor, forgive me—forgive me—You told me the truth, but God forgive me—I did not quite believe . . .'

Mr Satterthwaite was intensely interested in other people's affairs, but he was also a gentleman. It was borne in upon him that he must shut the window. He did so.

But he shut it very slowly.

He heard her voice, exquisite and indescribable.

'I know—I know. You have been in hell. So was I once. Loving—yet alternately believing and suspecting—thrusting aside one's doubts and having them spring up again with leering faces . . . I know, Alex, I know . . . But there is a worse hell than that, the hell I have lived in with you. I have seen your doubt—your fear of me . . . poisoning all our love. That man—that chance passer by, saved me. I could bear it no longer, you understand. Tonight—tonight I was going to kill myself . . . Alex . . . Alex . . .'

CHAPTER 2

The Shadow on the Glass

'Listen to this,' said Lady Cynthia Drage.

She read aloud from the journal she held in her hand.

'Mr and Mrs Unkerton are entertaining a party at Greenways House this week. Amongst the guests are Lady Cynthia Drage, Mr and Mrs Richard Scott, Major Porter, D.S.O., Mrs Staverton, Captain Allenson and Mr Satterthwaite.'

'It's as well,' remarked Lady Cynthia, casting away the paper, 'to know what we're in for. But they *have* made a mess of things!'

Her companion, that same Mr Satterthwaite whose name figured at the end of the list of guests, looked at her interrogatively. It had been said that if Mr Satterthwaite were found at the houses of those rich who had newly arrived, it was a sign either that the cooking was unusually good, or that a drama of human life was to be enacted there. Mr Satterthwaite was abnormally interested in the comedies and tragedies of his fellow men.

Lady Cynthia, who was a middle-aged woman, with a hard face and a liberal allowance of make-up, tapped him

24

smartly with the newest thing in parasols which lay rakishly
across her knee.

'Don't pretend you don't understand me. You do
perfectly. What's more I believe you're here on purpose to
see the fur fly!'

Mr Satterthwaite protested vigorously. He didn't know
what she was talking about.

'I'm talking about Richard Scott. Do you pretend you've
never heard of him?'

'No, of course not. He's the Big Game man, isn't he?'

'That's it—"Great big bears and tigers, etc." as the song
says. Of course, he's a great lion himself just now—the
Unkertons would naturally be mad to get hold of him—*and*
the bride! A charming child—oh! quite a charming child—
but so naïve, only twenty, you know, and he must be at
least forty-five.'

'Mrs Scott seems to be very charming,' said Mr
Satterthwaite sedately.

'Yes, poor child.'

'Why poor child?'

Lady Cynthia cast him a look of reproach, and went on
approaching the point at issue in her own manner.

'Porter's all right—a dull dog, though—another of these
African hunters, all sunburnt and silent. Second fiddle to
Richard Scott and always has been—life-long friends and
all that sort of thing. When I come to think of it, I believe
they were together on that trip—'

'Which trip?'

'*The* trip. The Mrs Staverton trip. You'll be saying next
you've never heard of Mrs Staverton.'

'I *have* heard of Mrs Staverton,' said Mr Satterthwaite, almost with unwillingness.

And he and Lady Cynthia exchanged glances.

'It's so exactly like the Unkertons,' wailed the latter, 'they are absolutely hopeless—socially, I mean. The idea of asking those two together! Of course they'd heard that Mrs Staverton was a sportswoman and a traveller and all that, and about her book. People like the Unkertons don't even begin to realize what pitfalls there are! I've been running them, myself, for the last year, and what I've gone through nobody knows. One has to be constantly at their elbow. "Don't do that! You can't do this!" Thank goodness, I'm through with it now. Not that we've quarrelled—oh! no, I never quarrel, but somebody else can take on the job. As I've always said, I can put up with vulgarity, but I can't stand meanness!'

After this somewhat cryptic utterance, Lady Cynthia was silent for a moment, ruminating on the Unkertons' meanness as displayed to herself.

'If I'd still been running the show for them,' she went on presently, 'I should have said quite firmly and plainly: "You can't ask Mrs Staverton with the Richard Scotts. She and he were once—"'

She stopped eloquently.

'But were they once?' asked Mr Satterthwaite.

'My dear man! It's well known. That trip into the Interior! I'm surprised the woman had the face to accept the invitation.'

'Perhaps she didn't know the others were coming?' suggested Mr Satterthwaite.

'Perhaps she did. That's far more likely.'

'You think—?'

'She's what I call a dangerous woman—the sort of woman who'd stick at nothing. I wouldn't be in Richard Scott's shoes this week-end.'

'And his wife knows nothing, you think?'

'I'm certain of it. But I suppose some kind friend will enlighten her sooner or later. Here's Jimmy Allenson. Such a nice boy. He saved my life in Egypt last winter—I was so bored, you know. Hullo, Jimmy, come here at once.'

Captain Allenson obeyed, dropping down on the turf beside her. He was a handsome young fellow of thirty, with white teeth and an infectious smile.

'I'm glad somebody wants me,' he observed. 'The Scotts are doing the turtle dove stunt, two required, not three, Porter's devouring the *Field*, and I've been in mortal danger of being entertained by my hostess.'

He laughed. Lady Cynthia laughed with him. Mr Satterthwaite, who was in some ways a little old-fashioned, so much so that he seldom made fun of his host and hostess until after he had left their house, remained grave.

'Poor Jimmy,' said Lady Cynthia.

'Mine not to reason why, mine but to swiftly fly. I had a narrow escape of being told the family ghost story.'

'An Unkerton ghost,' said Lady Cynthia. 'How screaming.'

'Not an Unkerton ghost,' said Mr Satterthwaite. 'A Greenways ghost. They bought it with the house.'

'Of course,' said Lady Cynthia. 'I remember now. But it doesn't clank chains, does it? It's only something to do with a window.'

Jimmy Allenson looked up quickly.

'A window?'

But for the moment Mr Satterthwaite did not answer. He was looking over Jimmy's head at three figures approaching from the direction of the house—a slim girl between two men. There was a superficial resemblance between the men, both were tall and dark with bronzed faces and quick eyes, but looked at more closely the resemblance vanished. Richard Scott, hunter and explorer, was a man of extraordinarily vivid personality. He had a manner that radiated magnetism. John Porter, his friend and fellow hunter, was a man of squarer build with an impassive, rather wooden face, and very thoughtful grey eyes. He was a quiet man, content always to play second fiddle to his friend.

And between these two walked Moira Scott who, until three months ago, had been Moira O'Connell. A slender figure, big wistful brown eyes, and golden red hair that stood out round her small face like a saint's halo.

'That child mustn't be hurt,' said Mr Satterthwaite to himself. 'It would be abominable that a child like that should be hurt.'

Lady Cynthia greeted the newcomers with a wave of the latest thing in parasols.

'Sit down, and don't interrupt,' she said. 'Mr Satterthwaite is telling us a ghost story.'

'I love ghost stories,' said Moira Scott. She dropped down on the grass.

'The ghost of Greenways House?' asked Richard Scott.

'Yes. You know about it?'

Scott nodded.

'I used to stay here in the old days,' he explained. 'Before the Elliots had to sell up. The Watching Cavalier, that's it, isn't it?'

'The Watching Cavalier,' said his wife softly. 'I like that. It sounds interesting. Please go on.'

But Mr Satterthwaite seemed somewhat loath to do so. He assured her that it was not really interesting at all.

'Now you've done it, Satterthwaite,' said Richard Scott sardonically. 'That hint of reluctance clinches it.'

In response to popular clamour, Mr Satterthwaite was forced to speak.

'It's really very uninteresting,' he said apologetically. 'I believe the original story centres round a Cavalier ancestor of the Elliot family. His wife had a Roundhead lover. The husband was killed by the lover in an upstairs room, and the guilty pair fled, but as they fled, they looked back at the house, and saw the face of the dead husband at the window, watching them. That is the legend, but the ghost story is only concerned with a pane of glass in the window of that particular room on which is an irregular stain, almost imperceptible from near at hand, but which from far away certainly gives the effect of a man's face looking out.'

'Which window is it?' asked Mrs Scott, looking up at the house.

'You can't see it from here,' said Mr Satterthwaite. 'It is round the other side but was boarded up from the inside some years ago—forty years ago, I think, to be accurate.'

'What did they do that for? I thought you said the ghost didn't walk.'

'It doesn't,' Mr Satterthwaite assured her. 'I suppose— well, I suppose there grew to be a superstitious feeling about it, that's all.'

Then, deftly enough, he succeeded in turning the conversation. Jimmy Allenson was perfectly ready to hold forth upon Egyptian sand diviners.

'Frauds, most of them. Ready enough to tell you vague things about the past, but won't commit themselves as to the future.'

'I should have thought it was usually the other way about,' remarked John Porter.

'It's illegal to tell the future in this country, isn't it?' said Richard Scott. 'Moira persuaded a gypsy into telling her fortune, but the woman gave her her shilling back, and said there was nothing doing, or words to that effect.'

'Perhaps she saw something so frightful that she didn't like to tell it me,' said Moira.

'Don't pile on the agony, Mrs Scott,' said Allenson lightly. 'I, for one, refuse to believe that an unlucky fate is hanging over you.'

'I wonder,' thought Mr Satterthwaite to himself. 'I wonder . . .'

Then he looked up sharply. Two women were coming from the house, a short stout woman with black hair, inappropriately dressed in jade green, and a tall slim figure in creamy white. The first woman was his hostess, Mrs Unkerton, the second was a woman he had often heard of, but never met.

'Here's Mrs Staverton,' announced Mrs Unkerton, in a tone of great satisfaction. 'All friends here, I think.'

'These people have an uncanny gift for saying just the most awful things they can,' murmured Lady Cynthia, but Mr Satterthwaite was not listening. He was watching Mrs Staverton.

Very easy—very natural. Her careless 'Hullo! Richard, ages since we met. Sorry I couldn't come to the wedding. Is this your wife? You must be tired of meeting all your husband's weather-beaten old friends.' Moira's response—suitable, rather shy. The elder woman's swift appraising glance that went on lightly to another old friend.

'Hullo, John!' The same easy tone, but with a subtle difference in it—a warming quality that had been absent before.

And then that sudden smile. It transformed her. Lady Cynthia had been quite right. A dangerous woman! Very fair—deep blue eyes—not the traditional colouring of the siren—a face almost haggard in repose. A woman with a slow dragging voice and a sudden dazzling smile.

Iris Staverton sat down. She became naturally and inevitably the centre of the group. So you felt it would always be.

Mr Satterthwaite was recalled from his thoughts by Major Porter's suggesting a stroll. Mr Satterthwaite, who was not as a general rule much given to strolling, acquiesced. The two men sauntered off together across the lawn.

'Very interesting story of yours just now,' said the Major.

'I will show you the window,' said Mr Satterthwaite.

He led the way round to the west side of the house. Here there was a small formal garden—the Privy Garden, it was always called, and there was some point in the name, for it was surrounded by high holly hedges, and even the entrance to it ran zigzag between the same high prickly hedges.

Once inside, it was very charming with an old-world charm of formal flower beds, flagged paths and a low stone seat, exquisitely carved. When they had reached the centre of the garden, Mr Satterthwaite turned and pointed up at the house. The length of Greenways House ran north and south. In this narrow west wall there was only one window, a window on the first floor, almost overgrown by ivy, with grimy panes, and which you could just see was boarded up on the inside.

'There you are,' said Mr Satterthwaite.

Craning his neck a little, Porter looked up.

'H'm, I can see a kind of discolouration on one of the panes, nothing more.'

'We're too near,' said Mr Satterthwaite. 'There's a clearing higher up in the woods where you get a really good view.'

He led the way out of the Privy Garden, and turning sharply to the left, struck into the woods. A certain enthusiasm of showmanship possessed him, and he hardly noticed that the man at his side was absent and inattentive.

'They had, of course, to make another window, when they boarded up this one,' he explained. 'The new one faces south overlooking the lawn where we were sitting just now. I rather fancy the Scotts have the room in question. That is why I didn't want to pursue the subject. Mrs Scott might have felt nervous if she had realized that she was sleeping in what might be called the haunted room.'

'Yes. I see,' said Porter.

Mr Satterthwaite looked at him sharply, and realized that the other had not heard a word of what he was saying.

'Very interesting,' said Porter. He slashed with his stick at some tall foxgloves, and, frowning, he said: 'She ought not to have come. She ought never to have come.'

People often spoke after this fashion to Mr Satterthwaite. He seemed to matter so little, to have so negative a personality. He was merely a glorified listener.

'No,' said Porter, 'she ought never to have come.'

Mr Satterthwaite knew instinctively that it was not of Mrs Scott he spoke.

'You think not?' he asked.

Porter shook his head as though in foreboding.

'I was on that trip,' he said abruptly. 'The three of us went. Scott and I and Iris. She's a wonderful woman—and a damned fine shot.' He paused. 'What made them ask her?' he finished abruptly.

Mr Satterthwaite shrugged his shoulders.

'Ignorance,' he said.

'There's going to be trouble,' said the other. 'We must stand by—and do what we can.'

'But surely Mrs Staverton—?'

'I'm talking of Scott.' He paused. 'You see—there's Mrs Scott to consider.'

Mr Satterthwaite had been considering her all along, but he did not think it necessary to say so, since the other man had so clearly forgotten her until this minute.

'How did Scott meet his wife?' he asked.

'Last winter, in Cairo. A quick business. They were engaged in three weeks, and married in six.'

'She seems to me very charming.'

'She is, no doubt about it. And he adores her—but that will make no difference.' And again Major Porter repeated to himself, using the pronoun that meant to him one person only: 'Hang it all, she shouldn't have come . . .'

Just then they stepped out upon a high grassy knoll at some little distance from the house. With again something of the pride of the showman, Mr Satterthwaite stretched out his arm.

'Look,' he said.

It was fast growing dusk. The window could still be plainly descried, and apparently pressed against one of the panes was a man's face surmounted by a plumed Cavalier's hat.

'Very curious,' said Porter. 'Really very curious. What will happen when that pane of glass gets smashed some day?'

Mr Satterthwaite smiled.

'That is one of the most interesting parts of the story. That pane of glass has been replaced to my certain know-ledge at least eleven times, perhaps oftener. The last time was twelve years ago when the then owner of the house determined to destroy the myth. But it's always the same. *The stain reappears*—not all at once, the discolouration spreads gradually. It takes a month or two as a rule.'

For the first time, Porter showed signs of real interest. He gave a sudden quick shiver.

'Damned odd, these things. No accounting for them. What's the real reason of having the room boarded up inside?'

'Well, an idea got about that the room was—unlucky. The Eveshams were in it just before the divorce. Then Stanley and his wife were staying here, and had that room when he ran off with his chorus girl.'

Porter raised his eyebrows.

'I see. Danger, not to life, but to morals.'

'And now,' thought Mr Satterthwaite to himself, 'the Scotts have it . . . I wonder . . .'

They retraced their steps in silence to the house. Walking almost noiselessly on the soft turf, each absorbed in his own thoughts, they became unwittingly eavesdroppers.

They were rounding the corner of the holly hedge when they heard Iris Staverton's voice raised fierce and clear from the depths of the Privy Garden.

'You shall be sorry—sorry—for this!'

Scott's voice answered low and uncertain, so that the words could not be distinguished, and then the woman's voice rose again, speaking words that they were to remember later.

'Jealousy—it drives one to the Devil—it *is* the Devil! It can drive one to black murder. Be careful, Richard, for God's sake, be careful!'

And then on that she had come out of the Privy Garden ahead of them, and on round the corner of the house without seeing them, walking swiftly, almost running, like a woman hag-ridden and pursued.

Mr Satterthwaite thought again of Lady Cynthia's words. A dangerous woman. For the first time, he had a premonition of tragedy, coming swift and inexorable, not to be gainsaid.

Yet that evening he felt ashamed of his fears. Everything seemed normal and pleasant. Mrs Staverton, with her easy insouciance, showed no sign of strain. Moira Scott was her charming, unaffected self. The two women appeared to be getting on very well. Richard Scott himself seemed to be in boisterous spirits.

The most worried looking person was stout Mrs Unkerton. She confided at length in Mr Satterthwaite.

'Think it silly or not, as you like, there's something giving me the creeps. And I'll tell you frankly, I've sent for the glazier unbeknown to Ned.'

'The glazier?'

'To put a new pane of glass in that window. It's all very well. Ned's proud of it—says it gives the house a tone. I don't like it. I tell you flat. We'll have a nice plain modern pane of glass, with no nasty stories attached to it.'

'You forget,' said Mr Satterthwaite, 'or perhaps you don't know. The stain comes back.'

'That's as it may be,' said Mrs Unkerton. 'All I can say is if it does, it's against nature!'

Mr Satterthwaite raised his eyebrows, but did not reply.

'And what if it does?' pursued Mrs Unkerton defiantly. 'We're not so bankrupt, Ned and I, that we can't afford a new pane of glass every month—or every week if need be for the matter of that.'

Mr Satterthwaite did not meet the challenge. He had seen too many things crumple and fall before the power of money to believe that even a Cavalier ghost could put up a successful fight. Nevertheless, he was interested by Mrs Unkerton's manifest uneasiness. Even she was not exempt from the tension in the atmosphere—only she attributed it to an attenuated ghost story, not to the clash of personalities amongst her guests.

Mr Sattherwaite was fated to hear yet another scrap of conversation which threw light upon the situation. He was going up the wide staircase to bed, John Porter and Mrs Staverton were sitting together in an alcove of the big hall. She was speaking with a faint irritation in her golden voice.

'I hadn't the least idea the Scotts were going to be here. I daresay, if I had known, I shouldn't have come, but I can assure you, my dear John, that now I am here, I'm not going to run away—'

Mr Satterthwaite passed on up the staircase out of earshot. He thought to himself: 'I wonder now—How much of that is true? Did she know? I wonder—what's going to come of it?'

He shook his head.

In the clear light of the morning he felt that he had perhaps been a little melodramatic in his imaginings of the evening before. A moment of strain—yes, certainly—inevitable under the circumstances—but nothing more. People adjusted themselves. His fancy that some great catastrophe was pending was nerves—pure nerves—or possibly liver. Yes, that was it, liver. He was due at Carlsbad in another fortnight.

On his own account he proposed a little stroll that evening just as it was growing dusk. He suggested to Major Porter that they should go up to the clearing and see if Mrs Unkerton had been as good as her word, and had a new pane of glass put in. To himself, he said: 'Exercise, that's what I need. Exercise.'

The two men walked slowly through the words. Porter, as usual, was taciturn.

'I can't help feeling,' said Mr Satterthwaite loquaciously, 'that we were a little foolish in our imaginings yesterday. Expecting—er—trouble, you know. After all, people have to behave themselves—swallow their feelings and that sort of thing.'

'Perhaps,' said Porter. After a minute or two he added: 'Civilized people.'

'You mean—?'

'People who've lived outside civilization a good deal sometimes go back. Revert. Whatever you call it.'

They emerged on to the grassy knoll. Mr Satterthwaite was breathing rather fast. He never enjoyed going up hill.

He looked towards the window. The face was still there, more life-like than ever.

'Our hostess has repented, I see.'

Porter threw it only a cursory glance.

'Unkerton cut up rough, I expect,' he said indifferently. 'He's the sort of man who is willing to be proud of another family's ghost, and who isn't going to run the risk of having it driven away when he's paid spot cash for it.'

He was silent a minute or two, staring, not at the house, but at the thick undergrowth by which they were surrounded.

'Has it ever struck you,' he said, 'that civilization's damned dangerous?'

'Dangerous?' Such a revolutionary remark shocked Mr Satterthwaite to the core.

'Yes. There are no safety valves, you see.'

He turned abruptly, and they descended the path by which they had come.

'I really am quite at a loss to understand you,' said Mr Satterthwaite, pattering along with nimble steps to keep up with the other's strides. 'Reasonable people—'

Porter laughed. A short disconcerting laugh. Then he looked at the correct little gentleman by his side.

'You think it's all bunkum on my part, Mr Satterthwaite? But there are people, you know, who can tell you when a storm's coming. They feel it beforehand in the air. And other people can foretell trouble. There's trouble coming now, Mr Satterthwaite, big trouble. It may come any minute. It may—'

He stopped dead, clutching Mr Satterthwaite's arm. And in that tense minute of silence it came—the sound of two shots and following them a cry—a cry in a woman's voice.

'My god!' cried Porter, 'it's come.'

He raced down the path, Mr Satterthwaite panting behind him. In a minute they came out on to the lawn, close by the hedge of the Privy Garden. At the same time, Richard Scott and Mr Unkerton came round the opposite corner of the house. They halted, facing each other, to left and right of the entrance to the Privy Garden.

'It—it came from in there,' said Unkerton, pointing with a flabby hand.

'We must see,' said Porter. He led the way into the enclosure. As he rounded the last bend of the holly hedge, he stopped dead. Mr Satterthwaite peered over his shoulder. A loud cry burst from Richard Scott.

There were three people in the Privy Garden. Two of them lay on the grass near the stone seat, a man and a woman. The third was Mrs Staverton. She was standing quite close to them by the holly hedge, gazing with horror-stricken eyes, and holding something in her right hand.

'Iris,' cried Porter. 'Iris. For God's sake! What's that you've got in your hand?'

She looked down at it then—with a kind of wonder, an unbelievable indifference.

'It's a pistol,' she said wonderingly. And then—after what seemed an interminable time, but was in reality only a few seconds, 'I—picked it up.'

Mr Satterthwaite had gone forward to where Unkerton and Scott were kneeling on the turf.

'A doctor,' the latter was murmuring. 'We must have a doctor.'

But it was too late for any doctor. Jimmy Allenson who had complained that the sand diviners hedged about the future, and Moira Scott to whom the gypsy had returned a shilling, lay there in the last great stillness.

It was Richard Scott who completed a brief examination. The iron nerve of the man showed in this crisis. After the first cry of agony, he was himself again.

He laid his wife gently down again.

'Shot from behind,' he said briefly. 'The bullet has passed right through her.'

Then he handled Jimmy Allenson. The wound here was in the breast and the bullet was lodged in the body.

John Porter came towards them.

'Nothing should be touched,' he said sternly. 'The police must see it all exactly as it is now.'

'The police,' said Richard Scott. His eyes lit up with a sudden flame as he looked at the woman standing by the holly hedge. He made a step in that direction, but at the same time John Porter also moved, so as to bar his way. For a moment it seemed as though there was a duel of eyes between the two friends.

Porter very quietly shook his head.

'No, Richard,' he said. 'It looks like it—but you're wrong.'

Richard Scott spoke with difficulty, moistening his dry lips.

'Then why—has she got that in her hand?'

And again Iris Staverton said in the same lifeless tone: 'I—picked it up.'

'The police,' said Unkerton rising. 'We must send for the police—at once. You will telephone perhaps, Scott? Someone should stay here—yes, I am sure someone should stay here.'

In his quiet gentlemanly manner, Mr Satterthwaite

offered to do so. His host accepted the offer with manifest relief.

'The ladies,' he explained. 'I must break the news to the ladies, Lady Cynthia and my dear wife.'

Mr Satterthwaite stayed in the Privy Garden looking down on the body of that which had once been Moira Scott.

'Poor child,' he said to himself. 'Poor child . . .'

He quoted to himself the tag about the evil men do living after them. For was not Richard Scott in a way responsible for his innocent wife's death? They would hang Iris Staverton, he supposed, not that he liked to think of it, but was not it at least a part of the blame he laid at the man's door? The evil that men do—

And the girl, the innocent girl, had paid.

He looked down at her with a very deep pity. Her small face, so white and wistful, a half smile on the lips still. The ruffled golden hair, the delicate ear. There was a spot of blood on the lobe of it. With an inner feeling of being something of a detective, Mr Satterthwaite deduced an ear-ring, torn away in her fall. He craned his neck forward. Yes, he was right, there was a small pearl drop hanging from the other ear.

Poor child, poor child.

'And now, sir,' said Inspector Winkfield.

They were in the library. The Inspector, a shrewd-looking forceful man of forty odd, was concluding his investigations. He had questioned most of the guests, and had by now pretty well made up his mind on the case. He was listening to what Major Porter and Mr Satterthwaite had to say. Mr Unkerton sat heavily in a chair, staring with protruding eyes at the opposite wall.

'As I understand it, gentlemen,' said the Inspector, 'you'd been for a walk. You were returning to the house by a path that winds round the left side of what they call the Privy Garden. Is that correct?'

'Quite correct, Inspector.'

'You heard two shots, and a woman's scream?'

'Yes.'

'You then ran as fast as you could, emerged from the woods and made your way to the entrance of the Privy Garden. If anybody had left that garden, they could only do so by one entrance. The holly bushes are impassable. If anyone had run out of the garden and turned to the right, he would have been met by Mr Unkerton and Mr Scott. If he had turned to the left, he could not have done so without being seen by you. Is that right?'

'That is so,' said Major Porter. His face was very white.

'That seems to settle it,' said the Inspector. 'Mr and Mrs Unkerton and Lady Cynthia Drage were sitting on the lawn, Mr Scott was in the Billiard Room which opens on to that lawn. At ten minutes past six, Mrs Staverton came out of the house, spoke a word or two to those sitting there, and went round the corner of the house towards the Privy Garden. Two minutes later the shots were heard. Mr Scott rushed out of the house and together with Mr Unkerton ran to the Privy Garden. At the same time you and Mr—er—Satterthwaite arrived from the

opposite direction. Mrs Staverton was in the Privy Garden
with a pistol in her hand from which two shots had been
fired. As I see it, she shot the lady first from behind as
she was sitting on the bench. Then Captain Allenson
sprang up and went for her, and she shot him in the chest
as he came towards her. I understand that there had been
a—er—previous attachment between her and Mr Richard
Scott—'

'That's a damned lie,' said Porter.

His voice rang out hoarse and defiant. The Inspector
said nothing, merely shook his head.

'What is her own story?' asked Mr Satterthwaite.

'She says that she went into the Privy Garden to be
quiet for a little. Just before she rounded the last hedge,
she heard the shots. She came round the corner, saw the
pistol lying at her feet, and picked it up. No one passed
her, and she saw no one in the garden but the two victims.'
The Inspector gave an eloquent pause. 'That's what she
says—and although I cautioned her, she insisted on making
a statement.'

'If she said that,' said Major Porter, and his face was
still deadly white, 'she was speaking the truth. I know Iris
Staverton.'

'Well, sir,' said the Inspector, 'there'll be plenty of time
to go into all that later. In the meantime, I've got my duty
to do.'

With an abrupt movement, Porter turned to Mr
Satterthwaite.

'You! Can't you help? Can't *you* do something?'

Mr Satterthwaite could not help feeling immensely

flattered. He had been appealed to, he, most insignificant of men, and by a man like John Porter.

He was just about to flutter out a regretful reply, when the butler, Thompson, entered, with a card upon a salver which he took to his master with an apologetic cough. Mr Unkerton was still sitting huddled up in a chair, taking no part in the proceedings.

'I told the gentleman you would probably not be able to see him, sir,' said Thompson. 'But he insisted that he had an appointment and that it was most urgent.'

Unkerton took the card.

'Mr Harley Quin,' he read. 'I remember, he was to see me about a picture. I did make an appointment, but as things are—'

But Mr Satterthwaite had started forward.

'Mr Harley Quin, did you say?' he cried. 'How extraordinary, how very extraordinary. Major Porter, you asked me if I could help you. I think I can. This Mr Quin is a friend—or I should say, an acquaintance of mine. He is a most remarkable man.'

'One of these amateur solvers of crime, I suppose,' remarked the Inspector disparagingly.

'No,' said Mr Satterthwaite. 'He is not that kind of man at all. But he has a power—an almost uncanny power—of showing you what you have seen with your own eyes, of making clear to you what you have heard with your own ears. Let us, at any rate, give him an outline of the case, and hear what he has to say.'

Mr Unkerton glanced at the Inspector, who merely snorted and looked at the ceiling. Then the former gave a short nod to Thompson, who left the room and returned ushering in a tall, slim stranger.

'Mr Unkerton?' The stranger shook him by the hand. 'I am sorry to intrude upon you at such a time. We must leave our little picture chat until another time. Ah! my friend, Mr Satterthwaite. Still as fond of the drama as ever?'

A faint smile played for a minute round the stranger's lips as he said these last words.

'Mr Quin,' said Mr Satterthwaite impressively, 'we have a drama here, we are in the midst of one, I should like, and my friend, Major Porter, would like, to have your opinion of it.'

Mr Quin sat down. The red-shaded lamp threw a broad band of coloured light over the checked pattern of his overcoat, and left his face in shadow almost as though he wore a mask.

Succinctly, Mr Satterthwaite recited the main points of the tragedy. Then he paused, breathlessly awaiting the words of the oracle.

But Mr Quin merely shook his head.

'A sad story,' he said. 'A very sad and shocking tragedy. The lack of motive makes it very intriguing.'

Unkerton stared at him.

'You don't understand,' he said. 'Mrs Staverton was heard to threaten Richard Scott. She was bitterly jealous of his wife. Jealousy—'

'I agree,' said Mr Quin. 'Jealousy or Demoniac Possession. It's all the same. But you misunderstand me. I was not referring to the murder of Mrs Scott, but to that of Captain Allenson.'

'You're right,' cried Porter, springing forward. 'There's a flaw there. If Iris had ever contemplated shooting Mrs Scott, she'd have got her alone somewhere. No, we're on the wrong tack. And I think I see another solution. Only those three people went into the Privy Garden. That is indisputable and I don't intend to dispute it. But I reconstruct the tragedy differently. Supposing Jimmy Allenson shoots first Mrs Scott and then himself. That's possible, isn't it? He flings the pistol from him as he falls—Mrs Staverton finds it lying on the ground and picks it up just as she said. How's that?'

The Inspector shook his head.

'Won't wash, Major Porter. If Captain Allenson had fired that shot close to his body, the cloth would have been singed.'

'He might have held the pistol at arm's length.'

'Why should he? No sense in it. Besides, there's no motive.'

'Might have gone off his head suddenly,' muttered Porter, but without any great conviction. He fell to silence again, suddenly rousing himself to say defiantly: 'Well, Mr Quin?'

The latter shook his head.

'I'm not a magician. I'm not even a criminologist. But I will tell you one thing—I believe in the value of impressions. In any time of crisis, there is always one moment that stands out from all the others, one picture that remains when all else has faded. Mr Satterthwaite is, I think, likely to have been the most unprejudiced observer of those present. Will you cast your mind back, Mr Satterthwaite, and tell us the moment that made the strongest impression on you? Was it when you heard the shots? Was it when you first saw the dead bodies? Was it when you first observed the pistol in Mrs Staverton's hand? Clear your mind of any preconceived standard of values, and tell us.'

Mr Satterthwaite fixed his eyes on Mr Quin's face, rather as a schoolboy might repeat a lesson of which he was not sure.

'No,' he said slowly. 'It was not any of those. The moment that I shall always remember was when I stood alone by the bodies—afterwards—looking down on Mrs Scott. She was lying on her side. Her hair was ruffled. There was a spot of blood on her little ear.'

And instantly, as he said it, he felt that he had said a terrific, a significant thing.

'Blood on her ear? Yes, I remember,' said Unkerton slowly.

'Her ear-ring must have been torn out when she fell,' explained Mr Satterthwaite.

But it sounded a little improbable as he said it.

'She was lying on her left side,' said Porter. 'I suppose it was that ear?'

'No,' said Mr Satterthwaite quickly. 'It was her right ear.'

The Inspector coughed.

'I found this in the grass,' he vouchsafed. He held up a loop of gold wire.

'But my God, man,' cried Porter. 'The thing can't have been wrenched to pieces by a mere fall. It's more as though it had been shot away by a bullet.'

'So it was,' cried Mr Satterthwaite. 'It was a bullet. It must have been.'

'There were only two shots,' said the Inspector. 'A shot can't have grazed her ear and shot her in the back as well. And if one shot carried away the ear-ring, and the second shot killed her, it can't have killed Captain Allenson as well—not unless he was standing close in front of her— very close—facing her as it might be. Oh! no, not even then, unless, that is—'

'Unless she was in his arms, you were going to say,' said Mr Quin, with a queer little smile. 'Well, why not?'

Everyone stared at each other. The idea was so vitally strange to them—Allenson and Mrs Scott—Mr Unkerton voiced the same feeling.

'But they hardly knew each other,' he said.

'I don't know,' said Mr Satterthwaite thoughtfully. 'They might have known each other better than we thought. Lady Cynthia said he saved her from being bored in Egypt last winter, and you'—he turned to Porter—'you told me that Richard Scott met his wife in Cairo last winter. They might have known each other very well indeed out there . . .'

'They didn't seem to be together much,' said Unkerton.

'No—they rather avoided each other. It was almost unnatural, now I come to think of it—'

They all looked at Mr Quin, as if a little startled at the conclusions at which they had arrived so unexpectedly.

Mr Quin rose to his feet.

'You see,' he said, 'what Mr Satterthwaite's impression has done for us.' He turned to Unkerton. 'It is your turn now.'

'Eh? I don't understand you.'

'You were very thoughtful when I came into this room. I should like to know exactly what thought it was that obsessed you. Never mind if it has nothing to do with the tragedy. Never mind if it seems to you—superstitious—' Mr Unkerton started, ever so slightly. 'Tell us.'

'I don't mind telling you,' said Unkerton. 'Though it's nothing to do with the business, and you'll probably laugh at me into the bargain. I was wishing that my Missus had left well alone and not replaced that pane of glass in the haunted window. I feel as though doing that has maybe brought a curse upon us.'

He was unable to understand why the two men opposite him stared so.

'But she hasn't replaced it yet,' said Mr Satterthwaite at last.

'Yes, she has. Man came first thing this morning.'

'My God!' said Porter, 'I begin to understand. That room, it's panelled, I supposed, not papered?'

'Yes, but what does that—?'

But Porter had swung out of the room. The others followed him. He went straight upstairs to the Scotts' bedroom. It was a charming room, panelled in cream with two windows facing south. Porter felt with his hands along the panels on the western wall.

'There's a spring somewhere—must be. Ah!' There was a click, and a section of the panelling rolled back. It disclosed the grimy panes of the haunted window. One pane of glass was clean and new. Porter stooped quickly and picked up something. He held it out on the palm of his hand. It was a fragment of ostrich feather. Then he looked at Mr Quin. Mr Quin nodded.

He went across to the hat cupboard in the bedroom. There were several hats in it—the dead woman's hats. He took out one with a large brim and curling feathers—an elaborate Ascot hat.

Mr Quin began speaking in a gentle, reflective voice.

'Let us suppose,' said Mr Quin, 'a man who is by nature intensely jealous. A man who has stayed here in bygone years and knows the secret of the spring in the panelling. To amuse himself he opens it one day, and looks out over the Privy Garden. There, secure as they think from being overlooked, he sees his wife and another man. There can be no possible doubt in his mind as to the relations between them. He is mad with rage. What shall he do? An idea comes to him. He goes to the cupboard and puts on the hat with the brim and feathers. It is growing dusk, and he remembers the story of the stain on the glass. Anyone looking up at the window will see as they think the Watching Cavalier. Thus secure he watches them, and at the moment they are clasped in each other's arms, he shoots. He is a good shot—a wonderful shot. As they fall, he fires once more—that shot carries away the ear-ring. He flings the pistol out of the window into the Privy Garden, rushes downstairs and out through the billiard room.'

Porter took a step towards him.

'But he let her be accused!' he cried. 'He stood by and let her be accused. Why? Why?'

'I think I know why,' said Mr Quin. 'I should guess—it's

51

only guess-work on my part, mind—that Richard Scott was once madly in love with Iris Staverton—so madly that even meeting her years afterwards stirred up the embers of jealousy again. I should say that Iris Staverton once fancied that she might love him, that she went on a hunting trip with him and another—and that she came back in love with the better man.'

'The better man,' muttered Porter, dazed. 'You mean—?'

'Yes,' said Mr Quin, with a faint smile. 'I mean you.' He paused a minute, and then said: 'If I were you—I should go to her now.'

'I will,' said Porter.

He turned and left the room.

CHAPTER 3

At the 'Bells and Motley'

Mr Satterthwaite was annoyed. Altogether it had been an unfortunate day. They had started late, there had been two punctures already, finally they had taken the wrong turning and lost themselves amidst the wilds of Salisbury Plain. Now it was close on eight o'clock, they were still a matter of forty miles from Marswick Manor whither they were bound, and a third puncture had supervened to render matters still more trying.

Mr Satterthwaite, looking like some small bird whose plumage had been ruffled, walked up and down in front of the village garage whilst his chauffeur conversed in hoarse undertones with the local expert.

'Half an hour at least,' said that worthy, pronouncing judgment.

'And lucky at that,' supplemented Masters, the chauffeur. 'More like three quarters if you ask me.'

'What is this—place, anyway?' demanded Mr Satterthwaite fretfully. Being a little gentleman considerate of the feelings of others, he substituted the word 'place' for 'God-forsaken hole' which had first risen to his lips.

'Kirtlington Mallet.'

Mr Satterthwaite was not much wiser, and yet a faint familiarity seemed to linger round the name. He looked round him disparagingly. Kirtlington Mallet seemed to consist of one straggling street, the garage and the post office on one side of it balanced by three indeterminate shops on the other side. Farther down the road, however, Mr Satterthwaite perceived something that creaked and swung in the wind, and his spirits rose ever so slightly.

'There's an inn here, I see,' he remarked.

'"Bells and Motley",' said the garage man. 'That's it—yonder.'

'If I might make a suggestion, sir,' said Masters, 'why not try it? They would be able to give you some sort of a meal, no doubt—not, of course, what you are accustomed to.' He paused apologetically, for Mr Satterthwaite was accustomed to the best cooking of continental chefs, and had in his own service a *cordon bleu* to whom he paid a fabulous salary.

'We shan't be able to take the road again for another three quarters of an hour, sir. I'm sure of that. And it's already past eight o'clock. You could ring up Sir George Foster, sir, from the Inn, and acquaint him with the cause of our delay.'

'You seem to think you can arrange everything, Masters,' said Mr Satterthwaite snappily.

Masters, who did think so, maintained a respectful silence.

Mr Satterthwaite, in spite of his earnest wish to discountenance any suggestion that might possibly be made to him—he was in that mood—nevertheless looked down the road towards the creaking inn sign with faint inward approval. He was a man of birdlike appetite, an epicure, but even such men can be hungry.

'The "Bells and Motley",' he said thoughtfully. 'That's an odd name for an Inn. I don't know that I ever heard it before.'

'There's odd folks come to it by all account,' said the local man.

He was bending over the wheel, and his voice came muffled and indistinct.

'Odd folks?' queried Mr Satterthwaite. 'Now what do you mean by that?'

The other hardly seemed to know what he meant.

'Folks that come and go. That kind,' he said vaguely.

Mr Satterthwaite reflected that people who come to an inn are almost of necessity those who 'come and go'. The definition seemed to him to lack precision. But nevertheless his curiosity was stimulated. Somehow or other he had got to put in three quarters of an hour. The 'Bells and Motley' would be as good as anywhere else.

With his usual small mincing steps he walked away down the road. From afar there came a rumble of thunder. The mechanic looked up and spoke to Masters.

'There's a storm coming over. Thought I could feel it in the air.'

'Crikey,' said Masters. 'And forty miles to go.'

'Ah!' said the other. 'There's no need to be hurrying over this job. You'll not be wanting to take the road till the storm's passed over. That little boss of yours doesn't look as though he'd relish being out in thunder and lightning.'

'Hope they'll do him well at that place,' muttered the chauffeur. 'I'll be pushing along there for a bite myself presently.'

'Billy Jones is all right,' said the garage man. 'Keeps a good table.'

Mr William Jones, a big burly man of fifty and landlord of the 'Bells and Motley', was at this minute beaming ingratiatingly down on little Mr Satterthwaite.

'Can do you a nice steak, sir—*and* fried potatoes, and as good a cheese as any gentleman could wish for. This way, sir, in the coffee-room. We're not very full at present, the last of the fishing gentlemen just gone. A little later we'll be full again for the hunting. Only one gentleman here at present, name of Quin—'

Mr Satterthwaite stopped dead.

'Quin?' he said excitedly. 'Did you say Quin?'

'That's the name, sir. Friend of yours perhaps?'

'Yes, indeed. Oh! yes, most certainly.' Twittering with excitement, Mr Satterthwaite hardly realized that the world might contain more than one man of that name. He had no doubts at all. In an odd way, the information fitted in with what the man at the garage had said. 'Folks that come and go . . .' a very apt description of Mr Quin. And the name of the inn, too, seemed a peculiarly fitting and appropriate one.

'Dear me, dear me,' said Mr Satterthwaite. 'What a *very* odd thing. That we should meet like this! Mr Harley Quin, is it not?'

'That's right, sir. This is the coffee-room, sir. Ah! here is the gentleman.'

Tall, dark, smiling, the familiar figure of Mr Quin rose from the table at which he was sitting, and the well-remembered voice spoke.

'Ah! Mr Satterthwaite, we meet again. An unexpected meeting!'

Mr Satterthwaite was shaking him warmly by the hand.

'Delighted. Delighted, I'm sure. A lucky breakdown for me. My car, you know. And you are staying here? For long?'

'One night only.'

'Then I am indeed fortunate.'

Mr Satterthwaite sat down opposite his friend with a little sigh of satisfaction, and regarded the dark, smiling face opposite him with a pleasurable expectancy.

The other man shook his head gently.

'I assure you,' he said, 'that I have not a bowl of goldfish or a rabbit to produce from my sleeve.'

'Too bad,' cried Mr Satterthwaite, a little taken aback. 'Yes, I must confess—I do rather adopt that attitude towards you. A man of magic. Ha, ha. That is how I regard you. A man of magic.'

'And yet,' said Mr Quin, 'it is you who do the conjuring tricks, not I.'

'Ah!' said Mr Satterthwaite eagerly. 'But I cannot do them without you. I lack—shall we say—inspiration?'

Mr Quin smilingly shook his head.

'That is too big a word. I speak the cue, that is all.'

The landlord came in at that minute with bread and a

slab of yellow butter. As he set the things on the table there was a vivid flash of lightning, and a clap of thunder almost overhead.

'A wild night, gentlemen.'

'On such a night—' began Mr Satterthwaite, and stopped.

'Funny now,' said the landlord, unconscious of the question, 'if those weren't just the words I was going to use myself. It was just such a night as this when Captain Harwell brought his bride home, the very day before he disappeared for ever.'

'Ah!' cried Mr Satterthwaite suddenly. 'Of course!'

He had got the clue. He knew now why the name Kirtlington Mallet was familiar. Three months before he had read every detail of the astonishing disappearance of Captain Richard Harwell. Like other newspaper readers all over Great Britain he had puzzled over the details of the disappearance, and, also like every other Briton, had evolved his own theories.

'Of course,' he repeated. 'It was at Kirtlington Mallet it happened.'

'It was at this house he stayed for the hunting last winter,' said the landlord. 'Oh! I knew him well. A main handsome young gentleman and not one that you'd think had a care on his mind. He was done away with—that's my belief. Many's the time I've seen them come riding home together—he and Miss Le Couteau, and all the village saying there'd be a match come of it—and sure enough, so it did. A very beautiful young lady, and well thought of, for all she was a Canadian and a stranger. Ah! there's some dark mystery there. We'll never know the rights of it. It broke her heart, it did, sure enough. You've heard as she's sold the place up and gone abroad, couldn't bear to go on here with everyone staring and pointing after her—through no fault of her own, poor young dear! A black mystery, that's what it is.'

He shook his head, then suddenly recollecting his duties, hurried from the room.

'A black mystery,' said Mr Quin softly.

His voice was provocative in Mr Satterthwaite's ears.

'Are you pretending that we can solve the mystery where Scotland Yard failed?' he asked sharply.

The other made a characteristic gesture.

'Why not? Time has passed. Three months. That makes a difference.'

'That is a curious idea of yours,' said Mr Satterthwaite slowly. 'That one sees things better afterwards than at the time.'

'The longer the time that has elapsed, the more things fall into proportion. One sees them in their true relationship to one another.'

There was a silence which lasted for some minutes.

'I am not sure,' said Mr Satterthwaite, in a hesitating voice, 'that I remember the facts clearly by now.'

'I think you do,' said Mr Quin quietly.

It was all the encouragement Mr Satterthwaite needed. His general role in life was that of listener and looker-on. Only in the company of Mr Quin was the position reversed. There Mr Quin was the appreciative listener, and Mr Satterthwaite took the centre of the stage.

'It was just over a year ago,' he said, 'that Ashley Grange

passed into the possession of Miss Eleanor Le Couteau. It is a beautiful old house, but it had been neglected and allowed to remain empty for many years. It could not have found a better chatelaine. Miss Le Couteau was a French Canadian, her forebears were *émigrés* from the French Revolution, and had handed down to her a collection of almost priceless French relics and antiques. She was a buyer and a collector also, with a very fine and discriminating taste. So much so, that when she decided to sell Ashley Grange and everything it contained after the tragedy, Mr Cyrus G. Bradburn, the American millionaire, made no bones about paying the fancy price of sixty thousand pounds for the Grange as it stood.'

Mr Satterthwaite paused.

'I mention these things,' he said apologetically, 'not because they are relevant to the story—strictly speaking, they are not—but to convey an atmosphere, the atmosphere of young Mrs Harwell.'

Mr Quin nodded.

'Atmosphere is always valuable,' he said gravely.

'So we get a picture of this girl,' continued the other. 'Just twenty-three, dark, beautiful, accomplished, nothing crude and unfinished about her. And rich—we must not forget that. She was an orphan. A Mrs St Clair, a lady of unimpeachable breeding and social standing, lived with her as duenna. But Eleanor Le Couteau had complete control of her own fortune. And fortune-hunters are never hard to seek. At least a dozen impecunious young men were to be found dangling round her on all occasions, in the hunting field, in the ballroom, wherever she went. Young Lord

Leccan, the most eligible *parti* in the country, is reported to have asked her to marry him, but she remained heart free. That is, until the coming of Captain Richard Harwell.

'Captain Harwell had put up at the local inn for the hunting. He was a dashing rider to hounds. A handsome, laughing daredevil of a fellow. You remember the old saying, Mr Quin? "Happy the wooing that's not long doing." The adage was carried out at least in part. At the end of two months, Richard Harwell and Eleanor Le Couteau were engaged.

'The marriage followed three months afterwards. The happy pair went abroad for a two weeks' honeymoon, and then returned to take up their residence at Ashley Grange. The landlord has just told us that it was on a night of storm such as this that they returned to their home. An omen, I wonder? Who can tell? Be that as it may, the following morning very early—about half-past seven, Captain Harwell was seen walking in the garden by one of the gardeners, John Mathias. He was bareheaded, and was whistling. We have a picture there, a picture of light-heartedness, of careless happiness. And yet from that minute, as far as we know, no one ever set eyes on Captain Richard Harwell again.'

Mr Satterthwaite paused, pleasantly conscious of a dramatic moment. The admiring glance of Mr Quin gave him the tribute he needed, and he went on.

'The disappearance was remarkable—unaccountable. It was not till the following day that the distracted wife called in the police. As you know, they have not succeeded in solving the mystery.'

'There have, I suppose, been theories?' asked Mr Quin.

'Oh! theories, I grant you. Theory No. 1, that Captain Harwell had been murdered, done away with. But if so, where was the body? It could hardly have been spirited away. And besides, what motive was there? As far as was known, Captain Harwell had not an enemy in the world.'

He paused abruptly, as though uncertain. Mr Quin leaned forward.

'You are thinking,' he said softly, 'of young Stephen Grant.'

'I am,' admitted Mr Satterthwaite. 'Stephen Grant, if I remember rightly, had been in charge of Captain Harwell's horses, and had been discharged by his master for some trifling offence. On the morning after the homecoming, very early, Stephen Grant was seen in the vicinity of Ashley Grange, and could give no good account of his presence there. He was detained by the police as being concerned in the disappearance of Captain Harwell, but nothing could be proved against him, and he was eventually discharged. It is true that he might be supposed to bear a grudge against Captain Harwell for his summary dismissal, but the motive was undeniably of the flimsiest. I suppose the police felt they must do something. You see, as I said just now, Captain Harwell had not an enemy in the world.'

'As far as was known,' said Mr Quin reflectively . . .

Mr Satterthwaite nodded appreciatively.

'We are coming to that. What, after all, *was* known of Captain Harwell? When the police came to look into his antecedents they were confronted with a singular paucity of material. Who was Richard Harwell? Where did he come from? He had appeared, literally out of the blue as it seemed. He was a magnificent rider, and apparently well off. Nobody in Kirtlington Mallet had bothered to inquire further. Miss Le Couteau had had no parents or guardians to make inquiries into the prospects and standing of her fiancé. She was her own mistress. The police theory at this point was clear enough. A rich girl and an impudent impostor. The old story!

'But it was not quite that. True, Miss Le Couteau had no parents or guardians, but she had an excellent firm of solicitors in London who acted for her. Their evidence made the mystery deeper. Eleanor Le Couteau had wished to settle a sum outright upon her prospective husband, but he had refused. He himself was well off, he declared. It was proved conclusively that Harwell never had a penny of his wife's money. Her fortune was absolutely intact.

'He was, therefore, no common swindler, but was his object a refinement of the art? Did he propose blackmail at some future date if Eleanor Harwell should wish to marry some other man? I will admit that something of that kind seemed to me the most likely solution. It had always seemed so to me—until tonight.'

Mr Quin leaned forward, prompting him.

'Tonight?'

'Tonight. I am not satisfied with that. How did he manage to disappear so suddenly and completely—at that hour in the morning, with every labourer bestirring himself and tramping to work? Bareheaded, too.'

'There is no doubt about the latter point—since the gardener saw him?'

'Yes—the gardener—John Mathias. Was there anything there, I wonder?'

'The police would not overlook him,' said Mr Quin.

'They questioned him closely. He never wavered in his statement. His wife bore him out. He left his cottage at seven to attend to the greenhouses, he returned at twenty minutes to eight. The servants in the house heard the front door slam at about a quarter after seven. That fixes the time when Captain Harwell left the house. Ah! yes, I know what you are thinking.'

'Do you, I wonder?' said Mr Quin.

'I fancy so. Time enough for Mathias to have made away with his master. But why, man, why? And if so, where did he hide the body?'

The landlord came in bearing a tray.

'Sorry to have kept you so long, gentlemen.'

He set upon the table a mammoth steak and beside it a dish filled to overflowing with crisp brown potatoes. The odour from the dishes was pleasant to Mr Satterthwaite's nostrils. He felt gracious.

'This looks excellent,' he said. 'Most excellent. We have been discussing the disappearance of Captain Harwell. What became of the gardener, Mathias?'

'Took a place in Essex, I believe. Didn't care to stay hereabouts. There were some as looked askance at him, you understand. Not that I ever believe he had anything to do with it.'

Mr Satterthwaite helped himself to steak. Mr Quin followed suit. The landlord seemed disposed to linger and chat. Mr Satterthwaite had no objection, on the contrary.

'This Mathias now,' he said. 'What kind of a man was he?'

'Middle-aged chap, must have been a powerful fellow once but bent and crippled with rheumatism. He had that mortal bad, was laid up many a time with it, unable to do any work. For my part, I think it was sheer kindness on Miss Eleanor's part to keep him on. He'd outgrown his usefulness as a gardener, though his wife managed to make herself useful up at the house. Been a cook she had, and always willing to lend a hand.'

'What sort of a woman was she?' asked Mr Satterthwaite, quickly.

The landlord's answer disappointed him.

'A plain body. Middle-aged, and dour like in manner. Deaf, too. Not that I ever knew much of them. They'd only been here a month, you understand, when the thing happened. They say he'd been a rare good gardener in his time, though. Wonderful testimonials Miss Eleanor had with him.'

'Was she interested in gardening?' asked Mr Quin, softly.

'No, sir, I couldn't say that she was, not like some of the ladies round here who pay good money to gardeners and spend the whole of their time grubbing about on their knees as well. Foolishness I call it. You see, Miss Le Couteau wasn't here very much except in the winter for hunting. The rest of the time she was up in London and away in those foreign seaside places where they say the French ladies don't so much as put a toe into the water for fear of spoiling their costumes, or so I've heard.'

Mr Satterthwaite smiled.

'There was no—er—woman of any kind mixed up with Captain Harwell?' he asked.

Though his first theory was disposed of, he nevertheless clung to his idea.

Mr William Jones shook his head.

'Nothing of that sort. Never a whisper of it. No, it's a dark mystery, that's what it is.'

'And your theory? What do you yourself think?' persisted Mr Satterthwaite.

'What do I think?'

'Yes.'

'Don't know what to think. It's my belief as how he was done in, but who by I can't say. I'll fetch you gentlemen the cheese.'

He stumped from the room bearing empty dishes. The storm, which had been quietening down, suddenly broke out with redoubled vigour. A flash of forked lightning and a great clap of thunder close upon each other made little Mr Satterthwaite jump, and before the last echoes of the thunder had died away, a girl came into the room carrying the advertised cheese.

She was tall and dark, and handsome in a sullen fashion of her own. Her likeness to the landlord of the 'Bells and Motley' was apparent enough to proclaim her his daughter.

'Good evening, Mary,' said Mr Quin. 'A stormy night.'

She nodded.

'I hate these stormy nights,' she muttered.

'You are afraid of thunder, perhaps?' said Mr Satterthwaite kindly.

'Afraid of thunder? Not me! There's little that I'm afraid of. No, but the storm sets them off. Talking, talking, the same thing over and over again, like a lot of parrots. Father begins it. "It reminds me, this does, of the night poor Captain Harwell . . ." And so on, and so on.' She turned on Mr Quin. 'You've heard how he goes on. What's the sense of it? Can't anyone let past things be?'

'A thing is only past when it is done with,' said Mr Quin.

'Isn't this done with? Suppose he wanted to disappear? These fine gentlemen do sometimes.'

'You think he disappeared of his own free will?'

'Why not? It would make better sense than to suppose a kind-hearted creature like Stephen Grant murdered him. What should he murder him for, I should like to know? Stephen had had a drop too much one day and spoke to him saucy like, and got the sack for it. But what of it? He got another place just as good. Is that a reason to murder a man in cold blood?'

'But surely,' said Mr Satterthwaite, 'the police were quite satisfied of his innocence?'

'The police! What do the police matter? When Stephen comes into the bar of an evening, every man looks at him queer like. They don't really believe he murdered Harwell, but they're not sure, and so they look at him sideways and edge away. Nice life for a man, to see people shrink away from you, as though you were something different from the rest of folks. Why won't Father hear of our getting married, Stephen and I? "You can take your pigs to a better market, my girl. I've nothing against Stephen, but—well, we don't know, do we?"'

She stopped, her breast heaving with the violence of her resentment.

'It's cruel, cruel, that's what it is,' she burst out. 'Stephen, that wouldn't hurt a fly! And all through life there'll be people who'll think he did. It's turning him queer and bitter like. I don't wonder, I'm sure. And the more he's like that, the more people think there must have been something in it.'

Again she stopped. Her eyes were fixed on Mr Quin's face, as though something in it was drawing this outburst from her.

'Can nothing be done?' said Mr Satterthwaite.

He was genuinely distressed. The thing was, he saw, inevitable. The very vagueness and unsatisfactoriness of the evidence against Stephen Grant made it the more difficult for him to disprove the accusation.

The girl whirled round on him.

'Nothing but the truth can help him,' she cried. 'If Captain Harwell were to be found, if he was to come back. If the true rights of it were only known—'

She broke off with something very like a sob, and hurried quickly from the room.

'A fine-looking girl,' said Mr Satterthwaite. 'A sad case altogether. I wish—I very much wish that something could be done about it.'

His kind heart was troubled.

'We are doing what we can,' said Mr Quin. 'There is still nearly half an hour before your car can be ready.'

Mr Satterthwaite stared at him.

'You think we can come at the truth just by—talking it over like this?'

'You have seen much of life,' said Mr Quin gravely. 'More than most people.'

'Life has passed me by,' said Mr Satterthwaite bitterly.

'But in so doing has sharpened your vision. Where others are blind you can see.'

'It is true,' said Mr Satterthwaite. 'I am a great observer.'

He plumed himself complacently. The moment of bitterness was passed.

'I look at it like this,' he said after a minute or two. 'To get at the cause for a thing, we must study the effect.'

'Very good,' said Mr Quin approvingly.

'The effect in this case is that Miss Le Couteau—Mrs Harwell, I mean, is a wife and yet not a wife. She is not free—she cannot marry again. And look at it as we will, we see Richard Harwell as a sinister figure, a man from nowhere with a mysterious past.'

'I agree,' said Mr Quin. 'You see what all are bound to see, what cannot be missed, Captain Harwell in the limelight, a suspicious figure.'

Mr Satterthwaite looked at him doubtfully. The words seemed somehow to suggest a faintly different picture to his mind.

'We have studied the effect,' he said. 'Or call it the *result*. We can now pass—'

Mr Quin interrupted him.

'You have not touched on the result on the strictly material side.'

'You are right,' said Mr Satterthwaite, after a moment or two for consideration. 'One should do the thing thoroughly. Let us say then that the result of the tragedy is that Mrs Harwell is a wife and not a wife, unable to marry again, that Mr Cyrus Bradburn has been able to buy Ashley Grange and its contents for—sixty thousand pounds, was it?—and that somebody in Essex has been able to secure John Mathias as a gardener! For all that we do not suspect "somebody in Essex" or Mr Cyrus Bradburn of having engineered the disappearance of Captain Harwell.'

'You are sarcastic,' said Mr Quin.

Mr Satterthwaite looked sharply at him.

'But surely you agree—?'

'Oh! I agree,' said Mr Quin. 'The idea is absurd. What next?'

'Let us imagine ourselves back on the fatal day. The disappearance has taken place, let us say, this very morning.'

'No, no,' said Mr Quin, smiling. 'Since, in our imagination, at least, we have power over time, let us turn it the other way. Let us say the disappearance of Captain Harwell took place a hundred years ago. That we, in the year two thousand twenty-five are looking back.'

'You are a strange man,' said Mr Satterthwaite slowly. 'You believe in the past, not the present. Why?'

'You used, not long ago, the word atmosphere. There is no atmosphere in the present.'

'That is true, perhaps,' said Mr Satterthwaite thoughtfully. 'Yes, it is true. The present is apt to be—parochial.'

'A good word,' said Mr Quin.

Mr Satterthwaite gave a funny little bow.

'You are too kind,' he said.

70

'Let us take—not this present year, that would be too difficult, but say—last year,' continued the other. 'Sum it up for me, you who have the gift of the neat phrase.'

Mr Satterthwaite thought for a minute. He was jealous of his reputation.

'A hundred years ago we have the age of powder and patches,' he said. 'Shall we say that 1924 was the age of Crossword Puzzles and Cat Burglars?'

'Very good,' approved Mr Quin. 'You mean that nationally, not internationally, I presume?'

'As to Crossword Puzzles, I must confess that I do not know,' said Mr Satterthwaite. 'But the Cat Burglar had a great innings on the Continent. You remember that series of famous thefts from French châteaux? It is surmised that one man alone could not have done it. The most miraculous feats were performed to gain admission. There was a theory that a troupe of acrobats were concerned—the Clondinis. I once saw their performance—truly masterly. A mother, son and daughter. They vanished from the stage in a rather mysterious fashion. But we are wandering from our subject.'

'Not very far,' said Mr Quin. 'Only across the Channel.'

'Where the French ladies will not wet their toes, according to our worthy host,' said Mr Satterthwaite, laughing.

There was a pause. It seemed somehow significant.

'Why did he disappear?' cried Mr Satterthwaite. 'Why? Why? It is incredible, a kind of conjuring trick.'

'Yes,' said Mr Quin. 'A conjuring trick. That describes it exactly. Atmosphere again, you see. And wherein does the essence of a conjuring trick lie?'

71

'The quickness of the hand deceives the eye,' quoted Mr Satterthwaite glibly.

'That is everything, is it not? To deceive the eye? Sometimes by the quickness of the hand, sometimes—by other means. There are many devices, the pistol shot, the waving of a red handkerchief, something that seems important, but in reality is not. The eye is diverted from the real business, it is caught by the spectacular action that means nothing—nothing at all.'

Mr Satterthwaite leant forward, his eyes shining.

'There is something in that. It is an idea.'

He went on softly. 'The pistol shot. What was the pistol shot in the conjuring trick we were discussing? What is the spectacular moment that holds the imagination?'

He drew in his breath sharply.

'The disappearance,' breathed Mr Satterthwaite. 'Take that away, and it leaves nothing.'

'Nothing? Suppose things took the same course without that dramatic gesture?'

'You mean—supposing Miss Le Couteau were still to sell Ashley Grange and leave—for no reason?'

'Well.'

'Well, why not? It would have aroused talk, I suppose, there would have been a lot of interest displayed in the value of the contents in—Ah! wait!'

He was silent a minute, then burst out.

'You are right, there is too much limelight, the limelight on Captain Harwell. And because of that, *she* has been in shadow. *Miss Le Couteau!* Everyone asking "Who was Captain Harwell? Where did he come from?" But because she is the injured party, no one makes inquiries about her. Was she really a French Canadian? Were those wonderful heirlooms really handed down to her? You were right when you said just now that we had not wandered far from our subject—*only across the Channel*. Those so-called heirlooms were stolen from the French châteaux, most of them valuable *objets d'art*, and in consequence difficult to dispose of. She buys the house—for a mere song, probably. Settles down there and pays a good sum to an irreproachable English woman to chaperone her. Then *he* comes. The plot is laid beforehand. The marriage, the disappearance and the nine days' wonder! What more natural than that a broken-hearted woman should want to sell everything that reminds her of her past happiness. The American is a connoisseur, the things are genuine and beautiful, some of them beyond price. He makes an offer, she accepts it. She leaves the neighbourhood, a sad and tragic figure. The great *coup* has come off. The eye of the public has been deceived by the quickness of the hand and the spectacular nature of the trick.'

Mr Satterthwaite paused, flushed with triumph.

'But for you, I should never have seen it,' he said with sudden humility. 'You have a most curious effect upon me. One says things so often without even seeing what they really mean. You have the knack of showing one. But it is still not quite clear to me. It must have been most difficult for Harwell to disappear as he did. After all, the police all over England were looking for him.'

'They were probably looking,' said Mr Quin, 'all over England.'

'It would have been simplest to remain hidden at the Grange,' mused Mr Satterthwaite. 'If it could be managed.'

'He was, I think, very near the Grange,' said Mr Quin.

His look of significance was not lost on Mr Satterthwaite.

'Mathias' cottage?' he exclaimed. 'But the police must have searched it?'

'Repeatedly, I should imagine,' said Mr Quin.

'Mathias,' said Mr Satterthwaite, frowning.

'And Mrs Mathias,' said Mr Quin.

Mr Satterthwaite stared hard at him.

'If that gang was really the Clondinis,' he said dreamily, 'there were three of them in it. The two young ones were Harwell and Eleanor Le Couteau. The mother now, was she Mrs Mathias? But in that case . . .'

'Mathias suffered from rheumatism, did he not?' said Mr Quin innocently.

'Oh!' cried Mr Satterthwaite. 'I have it. But could it be done? I believe it could. Listen. Mathias was there a month. During that time, Harwell and Eleanor were away for a fortnight on a honeymoon. For the fortnight before the wedding, they were supposedly in town. A clever man could have doubled the parts of Harwell and Mathias. When Harwell was at Kirtlington Mallet, Mathias was conveniently laid up with rheumatism, with Mrs Mathias to sustain the fiction. Her part was very necessary. Without her, someone might have suspected the truth. As you say, Harwell was hidden in Mathias' cottage. He *was* Mathias. When at last the plans matured, and Ashley Grange was sold, he and his wife gave out that they were taking a place in Essex. Exit John Mathias and his wife—for ever.'

There was a knock at the coffee-room door, and Masters entered. 'The car is at the door, sir,' he said.

Mr Satterthwaite rose. So did Mr Quin, who went across to the window, pulling the curtains. A beam of moonlight streamed into the room.

'The storm is over,' he said.

Mr Satterthwaite was pulling on his gloves.

'The Commissioner is dining with me next week,' he said importantly. 'I shall put my theory—ah!—before him.'

'It will be easily proved or disproved,' said Mr Quin. 'A comparison of the objects at Ashley Grange with a list supplied by the French police—!'

'Just so,' said Mr Satterthwaite. 'Rather hard luck on Mr Bradburn, but—well—'

'He can, I believe, stand the loss,' said Mr Quin.

Mr Satterthwaite held out his hand.

'Goodbye,' he said. 'I cannot tell you how much I have appreciated this unexpected meeting. You are leaving here tomorrow, I think you said?'

'Possibly tonight. My business here is done . . . I come and go, you know.'

Mr Satterthwaite remembered hearing those same words earlier in the evening. Rather curious.

He went out to the car and the waiting Masters. From the open door into the bar the landlord's voice floated out, rich and complacent.

'A dark mystery,' he was saying. 'A dark mystery, that's what it is.'

But he did not use the word 'dark'. The word he used suggested quite a different colour. Mr William Jones was a man of discrimination who suited his adjectives to his company. The company in the bar liked their adjectives full flavoured.

Mr Satterthwaite reclined luxuriously in the comfortable limousine. His breast was swelled with triumph. He saw the girl Mary come out on the steps and stand under the creaking inn sign.

'She little knows,' said Mr Satterthwaite to himself. 'She little knows what *I* am going to do!'

The sign of the 'Bells and Motley' swayed gently in the wind.

CHAPTER 4

The Sign in the Sky

The Judge was finishing his charge to the jury.

'Now, gentlemen, I have almost finished what I want to say to you. There is evidence for you to consider as to whether this case is plainly made out against this man so that you may say he is guilty of the murder of Vivien Barnaby. You have had the evidence of the servants as to the time the shot was fired. They have one and all agreed upon it. You have had the evidence of the letter written to the defendant by Vivien Barnaby on the morning of that same day, Friday, September 13th—a letter which the defence has not attempted to deny. You have had evidence that the prisoner first denied having been at Deering Hill, and later, after evidence had been given by the police, admitted he had. You will draw your own conclusions from that denial. This is not a case of direct evidence. You will have to come to your own conclusions on the subject of motive—of means, of opportunity. The contention of the defence is that some person unknown entered the music room after the defendant had left it, and shot Vivien

Barnaby with the gun which, by strange forgetfulness, the defendant had left behind him. You have heard the defendant's story of the reason it took him half an hour to get home. If you disbelieve the defendant's story and are satisfied, beyond any reasonable doubt, that the defendant did, upon Friday, September 13th, discharge his gun at close quarters to Vivien Barnaby's head with intent to kill her, then, gentlemen, your verdict must be Guilty. If, on the other hand, you have any reasonable doubt, it is your duty to acquit the prisoner. I will now ask you to retire to your room and consider and let me know when you have arrived at a conclusion.'

The jury were absent a little under half an hour. They returned the verdict that to everyone had seemed a foregone conclusion, the verdict of 'Guilty'.

Mr Satterthwaite left the court after hearing the verdict, with a thoughtful frown on his face.

A mere murder trial as such did not attract him. He was of too fastidious a temperament to find interest in the sordid details of the average crime. But the Wylde case had been different. Young Martin Wylde was what is termed a gentleman—and the victim, Sir George Barnaby's young wife, had been personally known to the elderly gentleman.

He was thinking of all this as he walked up Holborn, and then plunged into a tangle of mean streets leading in the direction of Soho. In one of these streets there was a small restaurant, known only to the few, of whom Mr Satterthwaite was one. It was not cheap—it was, on the contrary, exceedingly expensive, since it catered exclusively for the palate of the jaded *gourmet*. It was quiet—no strains of jazz were allowed to disturb the hushed atmosphere—it was rather dark, waiters appeared soft-footed out of the twilight, bearing silver dishes with the air of participating in some holy rite. The name of the restaurant was Arlecchino.

Still thoughtful, Mr Satterthwaite turned into the Arlecchino and made for his favourite table in a recess in the far corner. Owing to the twilight before mentioned, it was not until he was quite close to it that he saw it was already occupied by a tall dark man who sat with his face in shadow, and with a play of colour from a stained window turning his sober garb into a kind of riotous motley.

Mr Satterthwaite would have turned back, but just at that moment the stranger moved slightly and the other recognized him.

'God bless my soul,' said Mr Satterthwaite, who was given to old-fashioned expressions. 'Why, it's Mr Quin!'

Three times before he had met Mr Quin, and each time the meeting had resulted in something a little out of the ordinary. A strange person, this Mr Quin, with a knack of showing you the things you had known all along in a totally different light.

At once Mr Satterthwaite felt excited—pleasurably excited. His role was that of the looker-on, and he knew it, but sometimes when in the company of Mr Quin he had the illusion of being an actor—and the principal actor at that.

'This is very pleasant,' he said, beaming all over his dried-up little face. 'Very pleasant indeed. You've no objection to my joining you, I hope?'

'I shall be delighted,' said Mr Quin. 'As you see, I have not yet begun my meal.'

A deferential head waiter hovered up out of the shadows. Mr Satterthwaite, as befitted a man with a seasoned palate, gave his whole mind to the task of selection. In a few minutes, the head waiter, a slight smile of approbation on his lips, retired, and a young satellite began his ministrations. Mr Satterthwaite turned to Mr Quin.

'I have just come from the Old Bailey,' he began. 'A sad business, I thought.'

'He was found guilty?' said Mr Quin.

'Yes, the jury were out only half an hour.'

Mr Quin bowed his head.

'An inevitable result—on the evidence,' he said.

'And yet,' began Mr Satterthwaite—and stopped.

Mr Quin finished the sentence for him.

'And yet your sympathies were with the accused? Is that what you were going to say?'

'I suppose it was. Martin Wylde is a nice-looking young fellow—one can hardly believe it of him. All the same, there have been a good many nice-looking young fellows lately who have turned out to be murderers of a particularly cold-blooded and repellent type.'

'Too many,' said Mr Quin quietly.

'I beg your pardon?' said Mr Satterthwaite, slightly startled.

'Too many for Martin Wylde. There has been a tendency from the beginning to regard this as just one more of a series of the same type of crime—a man seeking to free himself from one woman in order to marry another.'

'Well,' said Mr Satterthwaite doubtfully. 'On the evidence—'

'Ah!' said Mr Quin quickly. 'I am afraid I have not followed all the evidence.'

Mr Satterthwaite's self-confidence came back to him with a rush. He felt a sudden sense of power. He was tempted to be consciously dramatic.

'Let me try and show it to you. I have met the Barnabys, you understand. I know the peculiar circumstances. With me, you will come behind the scenes—you will see the thing from inside.'

Mr Quin leant forward with his quick encouraging smile.

'If anyone can show me that, it will be Mr Satterthwaite,' he murmured.

Mr Satterthwaite gripped the table with both hands. He was uplifted, carried out of himself. For the moment, he was an artist pure and simple—an artist whose medium was words.

Swiftly, with a dozen broad strokes, he etched in the picture of life at Deering Hill. Sir George Barnaby, elderly, obese, purse-proud. A man perpetually fussing over the little things of life. A man who wound up his clocks every Friday afternoon, and who paid his own house-keeping books every Tuesday morning, and who always saw to the locking of his own front door every night. A careful man.

And from Sir George he went on to Lady Barnaby. Here his touch was gentler, but none the less sure. He had seen her but once, but his impression of her was definite and lasting. A vivid defiant creature—pitifully young. A trapped child, that was how he described her.

AgathaChristie

'She hated him, you understand? She had married him before she knew what she was doing. And now—'

She was desperate—that was how he put it. Turning this way and that. She had no money of her own, she was entirely dependent on this elderly husband. But all the same she was a creature at bay—still unsure of her own powers, with a beauty that was as yet more promise than actuality. And she was greedy. Mr Satterthwaite affirmed that definitely. Side by side with defiance there ran a greedy streak—a clasping and a clutching at life.

'I never met Martin Wylde,' continued Mr Satterthwaite. 'But I heard of him. He lived less than a mile away. Farming, that was his line. And she took an interest in farming—or pretended to. If you ask me, it was pretending. I think that she saw in him her only way of escape—and she grabbed at him, greedily, like a child might have done. Well, there could only be one end to that. We know what that end was, because the letters were read out in court. He kept her letters—she didn't keep his, but from the text of hers one can see that he was cooling off. He admits as much. There was the other girl. She also lived in the village of Deering Vale. Her father was the doctor there. You saw her in court, perhaps? No, I remember, you were not there, you said. I shall have to describe her to you. A fair girl—very fair. Gentle. Perhaps—yes, perhaps a tiny bit stupid. But very restful, you know. And loyal. Above all, loyal.'

He looked at Mr Quin for encouragement, and Mr Quin gave it him by a slow appreciative smile. Mr Satterthwaite went on.

'You heard that last letter read—you must have seen it, in the papers, I mean. The one written on the morning of Friday, September 13th. It was full of desperate reproaches and vague threats, and it ended by begging Martin Wylde to come to Deering Hill that same evening at six o'clock. "*I will leave the side door open for you, so that no one need know you have been here. I shall be in the music room.*" It was sent by hand.'

Mr Satterthwaite paused for a minute or two.

'When he was first arrested, you remember, Martin Wylde denied that he had been to the house at all that evening. His statement was that he had taken his gun and gone out shooting in the woods. But when the police brought forward their evidence, that statement broke down. They had found his finger-prints, you remember, both on the wood of the side door and on one of the two cocktail glasses on the table in the music room. He admitted then that he had come to see Lady Barnaby, that they had had a stormy interview, but that it had ended in his having managed to soothe her down. He swore that he left his gun outside leaning against the wall near the door, and that he left Lady Barnaby alive and well, the time being then a minute or two after a quarter past six. He went straight home, he says. But evidence was called to show that he did not reach his farm until a quarter to seven, and as I have just mentioned, it is barely a mile away. It would not take half an hour to get there. He forgot all about his gun, he declares. Not a very likely statement—and yet—'

'And yet?' queried Mr Quin.

'Well,' said Mr Satterthwaite slowly, 'it's a possible one, isn't it? Counsel ridiculed the supposition, of course, but I think he was wrong. You see, I've known a good many young men, and these emotional scenes upset them very much—especially the dark, nervous type like Martin Wylde. Women now, can go through a scene like that and feel positively better for it afterwards, with all their wits about them. It acts like a safety valve for them, steadies their nerves down and all that. But I can see Martin Wylde going away with his head in a whirl, sick and miserable, and without a thought of the gun he had left leaning up against the wall.'

He was silent for some minutes before he went on.

'Not that it matters. For the next part is only too clear, unfortunately. It was exactly twenty minutes past six when the shot was heard. All the servants heard it, the cook, the kitchen-maid, the butler, the housemaid and Lady Barnaby's own maid. They came rushing to the music room. She was lying huddled over the arm of her chair. The gun had been discharged close to the back of her head, so that the shot hadn't a chance to scatter. At least two of them penetrated the brain.'

He paused again and Mr Quin asked casually:

'The servants gave evidence, I suppose?'

Mr Satterthwaite nodded.

'Yes. The butler got there a second or two before the others, but their evidence was practically a repetition of each other's.'

'So they *all* gave evidence,' said Mr Quin musingly. 'There were no exceptions?'

'Now I remember it,' said Mr Satterthwaite, 'the house-maid was only called at the inquest. She's gone to Canada since, I believe.'

'I see,' said Mr Quin.

There was a silence, and somehow the air of the little restaurant seemed to be charged with an uneasy feeling. Mr Satterthwaite felt suddenly as though he were on the defensive.

'Why shouldn't she?' he said abruptly.

'Why should she?' said Mr Quin with a very slight shrug of the shoulders.

Somehow, the question annoyed Mr Satterthwaite. He wanted to shy away from it—to get back on familiar ground.

'There couldn't be much doubt who fired the shot. As a matter of fact the servants seemed to have lost their heads a bit. There was no one in the house to take charge. It was some minutes before anyone thought of ringing up the police, and when they did so they found that the telephone was out of order.'

'Oh!' said Mr Quin. 'The telephone was out of order.'

'It was,' said Mr Satterthwaite—and was struck suddenly by the feeling that he had said something tremendously important. 'It might, of course, have been done on purpose,' he said slowly. 'But there seems no point in that. Death was practically instantaneous.'

Mr Quin said nothing, and Mr Satterthwaite felt that his explanation was unsatisfactory.

'There was absolutely no one to suspect but young Wylde,' he went on. 'By his own account, even, he was only out of

85

the house three minutes before the shot was fired. And
who else could have fired it? Sir George was at a bridge
party a few houses away. He left there at half-past six and
was met just outside the gate by a servant bringing him
the news. The last rubber finished at half-past six exactly—
no doubt about that. Then there was Sir George's secretary,
Henry Thompson. He was in London that day, and actually
at a business meeting at the moment the shot was fired.
Finally, there is Sylvia Dale, who after all, had a perfectly
good motive, impossible as it seems that she should have
had anything to do with such a crime. She was at the
station of Deering Vale seeing a friend off by the 6.28 train.
That lets her out. Then the servants. What earthly motive
could any one of them have? Besides they all arrived on
the spot practically simultaneously. No, it must have been
Martin Wylde.'

But he said it in a dissatisfied kind of voice.

They went on with their lunch. Mr Quin was not in a
talkative mood, and Mr Satterthwaite had said all he had
to say. But the silence was not a barren one. It was filled
with the growing dissatisfaction of Mr Satterthwaite,
heightened and fostered in some strange way by the mere
acquiescence of the other man.

Mr Satterthwaite suddenly put down his knife and fork
with a clatter.

'Supposing that that young man is really innocent,' he
said. 'He's going to be hanged.'

He looked very startled and upset about it. And still Mr
Quin said nothing.

'It's not as though—' began Mr Satterthwaite, and

stopped. 'Why shouldn't the woman go to Canada?' he ended inconsequently.

Mr Quin shook his head.

'I don't even know what part of Canada she went to,' continued Mr Satterthwaite peevishly.

'Could you find out?' suggested the other.

'I suppose I could. The butler, now. He'd know. Or possibly Thompson, the secretary.'

He paused again. When he resumed speech, his voice sounded almost pleading.

'It's not as though it were anything to do with me?'

'That a young man is going to be hanged in a little over three weeks?'

'Well, yes—if you put it that way, I suppose. Yes, I see what you mean. Life and death. And that poor girl, too. It's not that I'm hard-headed—but, after all—what good will it do? Isn't the whole thing rather fantastic? Even if I found out where the woman's gone in Canada—why, it would probably mean that I should have to go out there myself.'

Mr Satterthwaite looked seriously upset.

'And I was thinking of going to the Riviera next week,' he said pathetically.

And his glance towards Mr Quin said as plainly as it could be said, 'Do let me off, won't you?'

'You have never been to Canada?'

'Never.'

'A very interesting country.'

Mr Satterthwaite looked at him undecidedly.

'You think I ought to go?'

Mr Quin leaned back in his chair and lighted a cigarette. Between puffs of smoke, he spoke deliberately.

'You are, I believe, a rich man, Mr Satterthwaite. Not a millionaire, but a man able to indulge a hobby without counting the expense. You have looked on at the dramas of other people. Have you never contemplated stepping in and playing a part? Have you never seen yourself for a minute as the arbiter of other people's destinies—standing in the centre of the stage with life and death in your hands?'

Mr Satterthwaite leant forward. The old eagerness surged over him.

'You mean—if I go on this wild-goose chase to Canada—?'

Mr Quin smiled.

'Oh! it was your suggestion, going to Canada, not mine,' he said lightly.

'You can't put me off like that,' said Mr Satterthwaite earnestly. 'Whenever I have come across you—' He stopped.

'Well?'

'There is something about you I do not understand. Perhaps I never shall. The last time I met you—'

'On Midsummer's Eve.'

Mr Satterthwaite was startled, as though the words held a clue that he did not quite understand.

'Was it Midsummer's Eve?' he asked confusedly.

'Yes. But let us not dwell on that. It is unimportant, is it not?'

'Since you say so,' said Mr Satterthwaite courteously. He felt that elusive clue slipping through his fingers. 'When I come back from Canada'—he paused a little awkwardly—'I—I—should much like to see you again.'

'I am afraid I have no fixed address for the moment,' said Mr Quin regretfully. 'But I often come to this place. If you also frequent it, we shall no doubt meet before very long.'

They parted pleasantly.

Mr Satterthwaite was very excited. He hurried round to Cook's and inquired about boat sailings. Then he rang up Deering Hill. The voice of a butler, suave and deferential, answered him.

'My name is Satterthwaite. I am speaking for a—er—firm of solicitors. I wished to make a few inquiries about a young woman who was recently housemaid in your establishment.'

'Would that be Louisa, sir? Louisa Bullard?'

'That is the name,' said Mr Satterthwaite, very pleased to be told it.

'I regret she is not in this country, sir. She went to Canada six months ago.'

'Can you give me her present address?'

The butler was afraid he couldn't. It was a place in the mountains she had gone to—a Scotch name—ah! Banff, that was it. Some of the other young women in the house had been expecting to hear from her, but she had never written or given them any address.

Mr Satterthwaite thanked him and rang off. He was still undaunted. The adventurous spirit was strong in his breast. He would go to Banff. If this Louisa Bullard was there, he would track her down somehow or other.

To his own surprise, he enjoyed the trip greatly. It was many years since he had taken a long sea voyage. The

Riviera, Le Touquet and Deauville, and Scotland had been his usual round. The feeling that he was setting off on an impossible mission added a secret zest to his journey. What an utter fool these fellow travellers of his would think him did they but know the object of his quest! But then—they were not acquainted with Mr Quin.

In Banff he found his objective easily attained. Louisa Bullard was employed in the large hotel there. Twelve hours after his arrival he was standing face to face with her.

She was a woman of about thirty-five, anaemic looking, but with a strong frame. She had pale brown hair inclined to curl, and a pair of honest brown eyes. She was, he thought, slightly stupid, but very trustworthy.

She accepted quite readily his statement that he had been asked to collect a few further facts from her about the tragedy at Deering Hill.

'I saw in the paper that Mr Martin Wylde had been convicted, sir. Very sad, it is, too.'

She seemed, however, to have no doubt as to his guilt.

'A nice young gentleman gone wrong. But though I wouldn't speak ill of the dead, it was her ladyship what led him on. Wouldn't leave him alone, she wouldn't. Well, they've both got their punishment. There's a text used to hang on my wall when I was a child, "God is not mocked," and it's very true. I knew something was going to happen that very evening—and sure enough it did.'

'How was that?' said Mr Satterthwaite.

'I was in my room, sir, changing my dress, and I happened to glance out of the window. There was a train going along, and the white smoke of it rose up in the air, and if you'll believe me it formed itself into the sign of a gigantic hand. A great white hand against the crimson of the sky. The fingers were crooked like, as though they were reaching out for something. It fair gave me a turn. "Did you ever now?" I said to myself. "That's a sign of something coming"—and sure enough at that very minute I heard the shot. "It's come," I said to myself, and I rushed downstairs and joined Carrie and the others who were in the hall, and we went into the music room and there she was, shot through the head—and the blood and everything. Horrible! I spoke up, I did, and told Sir George how I'd seen the sign beforehand, but he didn't seem to think much of it. An unlucky day, that was, I'd felt it in my bones from early in the morning. Friday, and the 13th—what could you expect?'

She rambled on. Mr Satterthwaite was patient. Again and again he took her back to the crime, questioning her closely. In the end he was forced to confess defeat. Louisa Bullard had told all she knew, and her story was perfectly simple and straightforward.

Yet he did discover one fact of importance. The post in question had been suggested to her by Mr Thompson, Sir George's secretary. The wages attached were so large that she was tempted, and accepted the job, although it involved her leaving England very hurriedly. A Mr Denman had made all the arrangements this end and had also warned her not to write to her fellow-servants in England, as this might 'get her into trouble with the immigration authorities', which statement she had accepted in blind faith.

The amount of wages, casually mentioned by her, was indeed so large that Mr Satterthwaite was startled. After some hesitation he made up his mind to approach this Mr Denman.

He found very little difficulty in inducing Mr Denman to tell all he knew. The latter had come across Thompson in London and Thompson had done him a good turn. The secretary had written to him in September saying that for personal reasons Sir George was anxious to get this girl out of England. Could he find her a job? A sum of money had been sent to raise the wages to a high figure.

'Usual trouble, I guess,' said Mr Denman, leaning back nonchalantly in his chair. 'Seems a nice quiet girl, too.'

Mr Satterthwaite did not agree that this was the usual trouble. Louisa Bullard, he was sure, was not a cast-off fancy of Sir George Barnaby's. For some reason it had been vital to get her out of England. But why? And who was at the bottom of it? Sir George himself, working through Thompson? Or the latter working on his own initiative, and dragging in his employer's name?

Still pondering over these questions, Mr Satterthwaite made the return journey. He was cast down and despondent. His journey had done no good.

Smarting under a sense of failure, he made his way to the *Arlecchino* the day after his return. He hardly expected to be successful the first time, but to his satisfaction the familiar figure was sitting at the table in the recess, and the dark face of Mr Harley Quin smiled a welcome.

'Well,' said Mr Satterthwaite as he helped himself to a pat of butter, 'you sent me on a nice wild-goose chase.'

Mr Quin raised his eyebrows.

'I sent you?' he objected. 'It was your own idea entirely.'

'Whosever idea it was, it's not succeeded. Louisa Bullard has nothing to tell.'

Thereupon Mr Satterthwaite related the details of his conversation with the housemaid and then went on to his interview with Mr Denman. Mr Quin listened in silence.

'In one sense, I was justified,' continued Mr Satterthwaite. 'She was deliberately got out of the way. But why? I can't see it.'

'No?' said Mr Quin, and his voice was, as ever, provocative.

Mr Satterthwaite flushed.

'I dare say you think I might have questioned her more adroitly. I can assure you that I took her over the story again and again. It was not my fault that I did not get what we want.'

'Are you sure,' said Mr Quin, 'that you did not get what you want?'

Mr Satterthwaite looked up at him in astonishment, and met that sad, mocking gaze he knew so well.

The little man shook his head, slightly bewildered.

There was a silence, and then Mr Quin said, with a total change of manner:

'You gave me a wonderful picture the other day of the people in this business. In a few words you made them stand out as clearly as though they were etched. I wish you would do something of that kind for the place—you left that in shadow.'

Mr Satterthwaite was flattered.

'The place? Deering Hill? Well, it's a very ordinary sort of house nowadays. Red brick, you know, and bay windows. Quite hideous outside, but very comfortable inside. Not a very large house. About two acres of ground. They're all much the same, those houses round the links. Built for rich men to live in. The inside of the house is reminiscent of a hotel—the bedrooms are like hotel suites. Baths and hot and cold basins in all the bedrooms and a good many gilded electric-light fittings. All wonderfully comfortable, but not very country-like. You can tell that Deering Vale is only nineteen miles from London.'

Mr Quin listened attentively.

'The train service is bad, I have heard,' he remarked.

'Oh! I don't know about that,' said Mr Satterthwaite, warming to his subject. 'I was down there for a bit last summer. I found it quite convenient for town. Of course the trains only go every hour. Forty-eight minutes past the hour from Waterloo—up to 10.48.'

'And how long does it take to Deering Vale?'

'Just about three quarters of an hour. Twenty-eight minutes past the hour at Deering Vale.'

'Of course,' said Mr Quin with a gesture of vexation. 'I should have remembered. Miss Dale saw someone off by the 6.28 that evening, didn't she?'

Mr Satterthwaite did not reply for a minute or two. His mind had gone back with a rush to his unsolved problem. Presently he said:

'I wish you would tell me what you meant just now when you asked me if I was sure I had not got what I wanted?'

It sounded rather complicated, put that way, but Mr Quin made no pretence of not understanding.

'I just wondered if you weren't being a little too exacting. After all, you found out that Louisa Bullard was deliberately got out of the country. That being so, there must be a reason. And the reason must lie in what she said to you.'

'Well,' said Mr Satterthwaite argumentatively. 'What did she say? If she'd given evidence at the trial, what could she have said?'

'She might have told what she saw,' said Mr Quin.

'What did she see?'

'A sign in the sky.'

Mr Satterthwaite stared at him.

'Are you thinking of *that* nonsense? That superstitious notion of its being the hand of God?'

'Perhaps,' said Mr Quin, 'for all you and I know it may have been the hand of God, you know.'

The other was clearly puzzled at the gravity of his manner.

'Nonsense,' he said. 'She said herself it was the smoke of the train.'

'An up train or a down train, I wonder?' murmured Mr Quin.

'Hardly an up train. They go at ten minutes to the hour. It must have been a down train—the 6.28—no, that won't do. She said the shot came immediately afterwards, and we know the shot was fired at twenty minutes past six. The train couldn't have been ten minutes early.'

'Hardly, on that line,' agreed Mr Quin.

Mr Satterthwaite was staring ahead of him.

'Perhaps a goods train,' he murmured. 'But surely, if so—'

'There would have been no need to get her out of England. I agree,' said Mr Quin.

Mr Satterthwaite gazed at him, fascinated.

'The 6.28,' he said slowly. 'But if so, if the shot was fired then, why did everyone say it was earlier?'

'Obvious,' said Mr Quin. 'The clocks must have been wrong.'

'All of them?' said Mr Satterthwaite doubtfully. 'That's a pretty tall coincidence, you know.'

'I wasn't thinking of it as a coincidence,' said the other. 'I was thinking it was Friday.'

'Friday?' said Mr Satterthwaite.

'You did tell me, you know, that Sir George always wound the clocks on a Friday afternoon,' said Mr Quin apologetically.

'He put them back ten minutes,' said Mr Satterthwaite, almost in a whisper, so awed was he by the discoveries he was making. 'Then he went out to bridge. I think he must have opened the note from his wife to Martin Wylde that morning—yes, decidedly he opened it. He left his bridge party at 6.30, found Martin's gun standing by the side door, and went in and shot her from behind. Then he went out again, threw the gun into the bushes where it was found later, and was apparently just coming out of the neighbour's gate when someone came running to fetch him. But the telephone—what about the telephone? Ah! yes, I see. He disconnected it so that a summons could not be sent to the police that way—they might have noted the time it was received. And Wylde's story works out now. The real time he left was five and twenty minutes past six. Walking slowly, he would reach home about a quarter to seven. Yes, I see it all. Louisa was the only danger with her endless talk about her superstitious fancies. Someone might realize the significance of the train and then—goodbye to that excellent *alibi*.'

'Wonderful,' commented Mr Quin.

Mr Satterthwaite turned to him, flushed with success.

'The only thing is—how to proceed now?'

'I should suggest Sylvia Dale,' said Mr Quin.

Mr Satterthwaite looked doubtful.

'I mentioned to you,' he said, 'she seemed to me a little—er—stupid.'

'She has a father and brothers who will take the necessary steps.'

'That is true,' said Mr Satterthwaite, relieved.

A very short time afterwards he was sitting with the girl telling her the story. She listened attentively. She put no questions to him but when he had done she rose.

'I must have a taxi—at once.'

'My dear child, what are you going to do?'

'I am going to Sir George Barnaby.'

'Impossible. Absolutely the wrong procedure. Allow me to—'

He twittered on by her side. But he produced no impression. Sylvia Dale was intent on her own plans. She allowed him to go with her in the taxi, but to all his remonstrances she addressed a deaf ear. She left him in the taxi while she went into Sir George's city office.

It was half an hour later when she came out. She looked exhausted, her fair beauty drooping like a waterless flower. Mr Satterthwaite received her with concern.

'I've won,' she murmured, as she leant back with half-closed eyes.

'What?' He was startled. 'What did you do? What did you say?'

She sat up a little.

'I told him that Louisa Bullard had been to the police with her story. I told him that the police had made inquiries and that he had been seen going into his own grounds and out again a few minutes after half-past six. I told him that the game was up. He—he went to pieces. I told him that there was still time for him to get away, that the police weren't coming for another hour to arrest him. I told him that if he'd sign a confession that he'd killed Vivien I'd do nothing, but that if he didn't I'd scream and tell the whole building the truth. He was so panicky that he didn't know what he was doing. He signed the paper without realizing what he was doing.'

She thrust it into his hands.

'Take it—take it. You know what to do with it so that they'll set Martin free.'

'He actually signed it,' cried Mr Satterthwaite, amazed.

'He is a little stupid, you know,' said Sylvia Dale. 'So am I,' she added as an afterthought. 'That's why I know how stupid people behave. We get rattled, you know, and then we do the wrong thing and are sorry afterwards.'

She shivered and Mr Satterthwaite patted her hand.

'You need something to pull you together,' he said. 'Come,

we are close to a very favourite resort of mine—the *Arlecchino*. Have you ever been there?'

She shook her head.

Mr Satterthwaite stopped the taxi and took the girl into the little restaurant. He made his way to the table in the recess, his heart beating hopefully. But the table was empty.

Sylvia Dale saw the disappointment in his face.

'What is it?' she asked.

'Nothing,' said Mr Satterthwaite. 'That is, I half expected to see a friend of mine here. It doesn't matter. Some day, I expect, I shall see him again . . .'

CHAPTER 5

The Soul of the Croupier

Mr Satterthwaite was enjoying the sunshine on the terrace at Monte Carlo.

Every year regularly on the second Sunday in January, Mr Satterthwaite left England for the Riviera. He was far more punctual than any swallow. In the month of April he returned to England, May and June he spent in London, and had never been known to miss Ascot. He left town after the Eton and Harrow match, paying a few country house visits before repairing to Deauville or Le Touquet. Shooting parties occupied most of September and October, and he usually spent a couple of months in town to wind up the year. He knew everybody and it may safely be said that everybody knew him.

This morning he was frowning. The blue of the sea was admirable, the gardens were, as always, a delight, but the people disappointed him—he thought them an ill-dressed, shoddy crowd. Some, of course, were gamblers, doomed souls who could not keep away. Those Mr Satterthwaite tolerated. They were a necessary background. But he missed the usual leaven of the *élite*—his own people.

'It's the exchange,' said Mr Satterthwaite gloomily. 'All sorts of people come here now who could never have afforded it before. And then, of course, I'm getting old . . . All the young people—the people coming on—they go to these Swiss places.'

But there were others that he missed, the well-dressed Barons and Counts of foreign diplomacy, the Grand Dukes and the Royal Princes. The only Royal Prince he had seen so far was working a lift in one of the less well-known hotels. He missed, too, the beautiful and expensive ladies. There was still a few of them, but not nearly as many as there used to be.

Mr Satterthwaite was an earnest student of the drama called Life, but he liked his material to be highly coloured. He felt discouragement sweep over him. Values were changing—and he—was too old to change.

It was at that moment that he observed the Countess Czarnova coming towards him.

Mr Satterthwaite had seen the Countess at Monte Carlo for many seasons now. The first time he had seen her she had been in the company of a Grand Duke. On the next occasion she was with an Austrian Baron. In successive years her friends had been of Hebraic extraction wearing rather flamboyant jewellery. For the last year or two she was much seen with very young men, almost boys.

She was walking with a very young man now. Mr Satterthwaite happened to know him, and he was sorry.

Franklin Rudge was a young American, a typical product of one of the Middle West States, eager to register impression, crude, but loveable, a curious mixture of native shrewdness and idealism. He was in Monte Carlo with a party of other young Americans of both sexes, all much of the same type. It was their first glimpse of the Old World and they were outspoken in criticism and in appreciation.

On the whole they disliked the English people in the hotel, and the English people disliked them. Mr Satterthwaite, who prided himself on being a cosmopolitan, rather liked them. Their directness and vigour appealed to him, though their occasional solecisms made him shudder.

It occurred to him that the Countess Czarnova was a most unsuitable friend for young Franklin Rudge.

He took off his hat politely as they came abreast of him, and the Countess gave him a charming bow and smile.

She was a very tall woman, superbly made. Her hair was black, so were her eyes, and her eyelashes and eyebrows were more superbly black than any Nature had ever fashioned.

Mr Satterthwaite, who knew far more of feminine secrets than it is good for any man to know, rendered immediate homage to the art with which she was made up. Her complexion appeared to be flawless, of a uniform creamy white. The very faint bistre shadows under her eyes were most effective. Her mouth was neither crimson nor scarlet, but a subdued wine colour. She was dressed in a very daring creation of black and white and carried a parasol of the shade of pinky red which is most helpful to the complexion.

Franklin Rudge was looking happy and important.

'There goes a young fool,' said Mr Satterthwaite to himself. 'But I suppose it's no business of mine and anyway he wouldn't listen to me. Well, well, I've bought experience myself in my time.'

But he still felt rather worried, because there was a very attractive little American girl in the party, and he was sure that she would not like Franklin Rudge's friendship with the Countess at all.

He was just about to retrace his steps in the opposite direction when he caught sight of the girl in question coming up one of the paths towards him. She wore a well-cut tailor-made 'suit' with a white muslin shirt waist, she had on good, sensible walking shoes, and carried a guide-book. There are some Americans who pass through Paris and emerge clothed as the Queen of Sheba, but Elizabeth Martin was not one of them. She was 'doing Europe' in a stern, conscientious spirit. She had high ideas of culture and art and she was anxious to get as much as possible for her limited store of money.

It is doubtful if Mr Satterthwaite thought of her as either cultured or artistic. To him she merely appeared very young.

'Good morning, Mr Satterthwaite,' said Elizabeth. 'Have you seen Franklin—Mr Rudge—anywhere about?'

'I saw him just a few minutes ago.'

'With his friend the Countess, I suppose,' said the girl sharply.

'Er—with the Countess, yes,' admitted Mr Satterthwaite.

'That Countess of his doesn't cut any ice with me,' said

the girl in a rather high, shrill voice. 'Franklin's just crazy about her. *Why* I can't think.'

'She's got a very charming manner, I believe,' said Mr Satterthwaite cautiously.

'Do you know her?'

'Slightly.'

'I'm right down worried about Franklin,' said Miss Martin. 'That boy's got a lot of sense as a rule. You'd never think he'd fall for this sort of siren stuff. And he won't hear a thing, he gets madder than a hornet if anyone tries to say a word to him. Tell me, anyway—is she a real Countess?'

'I shouldn't like to say,' said Mr Satterthwaite. 'She may be.'

'That's the real Ha Ha English manner,' said Elizabeth with signs of displeasure. 'All I can say is that in Sargon Springs—that's our home town, Mr Satterthwaite—that Countess would look a mighty queer bird.'

Mr Satterthwaite thought it possible. He forebore to point out that they were not in Sargon Springs but in the principality of Monaco, where the Countess happened to synchronize with her environment a great deal better than Miss Martin did.

He made no answer and Elizabeth went on towards the Casino. Mr Satterthwaite sat on a seat in the sun, and was presently joined by Franklin Rudge.

Rudge was full of enthusiasm.

'I'm enjoying myself,' he announced with naïve enthusiasm. 'Yes, sir! This is what I call seeing life—rather a different kind of life from what we have in the States.'

The elder man turned a thoughtful face to him.

'Life is lived very much the same everywhere,' he said rather wearily. 'It wears different clothes—that's all.'

Franklin Rudge stared.

'I don't get you.'

'No,' said Mr Satterthwaite. 'That's because you've got a long way to travel yet. But I apologize. No elderly man should permit himself to get into the habit of preaching.'

'Oh! that's all right.' Rudge laughed, displaying the beautiful teeth of all his countrymen. 'I don't say, mind you, that I'm not disappointed in the Casino. I thought the gambling would be different—something much more feverish. It seems just rather dull and sordid to me.'

'Gambling is life and death to the gambler, but it has no great spectacular value,' said Mr Satterthwaite. 'It is more exciting to read about than to see.'

The young man nodded his agreement.

'You're by way of being rather a big bug socially, aren't you?' he asked with a diffident candour that made it impossible to take offence. 'I mean, you know all the Duchesses and Earls and Countesses and things.'

'A good many of them,' said Mr Satterthwaite. 'And also the Jews and the Portuguese and the Greeks and the Argentines.'

'Eh?' said Mr Rudge.

'I was just explaining,' said Mr Satterthwaite, 'that I move in English society.'

Franklin Rudge meditated for a moment or two.

'You know the Countess Czarnova, don't you?' he said at length.

'Slightly,' said Mr Satterthwaite, making the same answer he had made to Elizabeth.

'Now there's a woman whom it's been very interesting to meet. One's inclined to think that the aristocracy of Europe is played out and effete. That may be true of the men, but the women are different. Isn't it a pleasure to meet an exquisite creature like the Countess? Witty, charming, intelligent, generations of civilization behind her, an aristocrat to her finger-tips!'

'Is she?' asked Mr Satterthwaite.

'Well, isn't she? You know what her family are?'

'No,' said Mr Satterthwaite. 'I'm afraid I know very little about her.'

'She was a Radzynski,' explained Franklin Rudge. 'One of the oldest families in Hungary. She's had the most extraordinary life. You know that great rope of pearls she wears?'

Mr Satterthwaite nodded.

'That was given her by the King of Bosnia. She smuggled some secret papers out of the kingdom for him.'

'I heard,' said Mr Satterthwaite, 'that the pearls had been given her by the King of Bosnia.'

The fact was indeed a matter of common gossip, it being reported that the lady had been a *chère amie* of His Majesty's in days gone by.

'Now I'll tell you something more.'

Mr Satterthwaite listened, and the more he listened the more he admired the fertile imagination of the Countess Czarnova. No vulgar 'siren stuff' (as Elizabeth Martin had put it) for her. The young man was shrewd enough in that

106

way, clean living and idealistic. No, the Countess moved austerely through a labyrinth of diplomatic intrigues. She had enemies, detractors—naturally! It was a glimpse, so the young American was made to feel, into the life of the old régime with the Countess as the central figure, aloof, aristocratic, the friend of counsellors and princes, a figure to inspire romantic devotion.

'And she's had any amount to contend against,' ended the young man warmly. 'It's an extraordinary thing but she's never found a woman who would be a real friend to her. Women have been against her all her life.'

'Probably,' said Mr Satterthwaite.

'Don't you call it a scandalous thing?' demanded Rudge hotly.

'N—no,' said Mr Satterthwaite thoughtfully. 'I don't know that I do. Women have got their own standards, you know. It's no good our mixing ourselves up in their affairs. They must run their own show.'

'I don't agree with you,' said Rudge earnestly. 'It's one of the worst things in the world today, the unkindness of woman to woman. You know Elizabeth Martin? Now she agrees with me in theory absolutely. We've often discussed it together. She's only a kid, but her ideas are all right. But the moment it comes to a practical test—why, she's as bad as any of them. Got a real down on the Countess without knowing a darned thing about her, and won't listen when I try to tell her things. It's all *wrong*, Mr Satterthwaite. I believe in democracy—and—what's that but brotherhood between men and sisterhood between women?'

He paused earnestly. Mr Satterthwaite tried to think of any circumstances in which a sisterly feeling might arise between the Countess and Elizabeth Martin and failed.

'Now the Countess, on the other hand,' went on Rudge, 'admires Elizabeth immensely, and thinks her charming in every way. Now what does that show?'

'It shows,' said Mr Satterthwaite dryly, 'that the Countess has lived a considerable time longer than Miss Martin has.'

Franklin Rudge went off unexpectedly at a tangent.

'Do you know how old she is? She told me. Rather sporting of her. I should have guessed her to be twenty-nine, but she told me of her own accord that she was thirty-five. She doesn't look it, does she?'

Mr Satterthwaite, whose private estimate of the lady's age was between forty-five and forty-nine, merely raised his eyebrows.

'I should caution you against believing all you are told at Monte Carlo,' he murmured.

He had enough experience to know the futility of arguing with the lad. Franklin Rudge was at a pitch of white hot chivalry when he would have disbelieved any statement that was not backed with authoritative proof.

'Here is the Countess,' said the boy, rising.

She came up to them with the languid grace that so became her. Presently they all three sat down together. She was very charming to Mr Satterthwaite, but in rather an aloof manner. She deferred to him prettily, asking his opinion, and treating him as an authority on the Riviera.

The whole thing was cleverly managed. Very few minutes

had elapsed before Franklin Rudge found himself gracefully but unmistakably dismissed, and the Countess and Mr Satterthwaite were left *tête-à-tête*.

She put down her parasol and began drawing patterns with it in the dust.

'You are interested in the nice American boy, Mr Satterthwaite, are you not?'

Her voice was low with a caressing note in it.

'He's a nice young fellow,' said Mr Satterthwaite, noncommittally.

'I find him sympathetic, yes,' said the Countess reflectively. 'I have told him much of my life.'

'Indeed,' said Mr Satterthwaite.

'Details such as I have told to few others,' she continued dreamily. 'I have had an extraordinary life, Mr Satterthwaite. Few would credit the amazing things that have happened to me.'

Mr Satterthwaite was shrewd enough to penetrate her meaning. After all, the stories that she had told to Franklin Rudge *might* be the truth. It was extremely unlikely, and in the last degree improbable, but it was *possible* . . . No one could definitely say: 'That is not so—'

He did not reply, and the Countess continued to look out dreamily across the bay.

And suddenly Mr Satterthwaite had a strange and new impression of her. He saw her no longer as a harpy, but as a desperate creature at bay, fighting tooth and nail. He stole a sideways glance at her. The parasol was down, he could see the little haggard lines at the corners of her eyes. In one temple a pulse was beating.

It flowed through him again and again—that increasing certitude. She was a creature desperate and driven. She would be merciless to him or to anyone who stood between her and Franklin Rudge. But he still felt he hadn't got the hang of the situation. Clearly she had plenty of money. She was always beautifully dressed, and her jewels were marvellous. There could be no real urgency of that kind. Was it love? Women of her age did, he well knew, fall in love with boys. It might be that. There was, he felt sure, something out of the common about the situation.

Her *tête-à-tête* with him was, he recognized, a throwing down of the gauntlet. She had singled him out as her chief enemy. He felt sure that she hoped to goad him into speaking slightingly of her to Franklin Rudge. Mr Satterthwaite smiled to himself. He was too old a bird for that. He knew when it was wise to hold one's tongue.

He watched her that night in the Cercle Privé, as she tried her fortunes at roulette.

Again and again she staked, only to see her stake swept away. She bore her losses well, with the stoical *sang froid* of the old *habitué*. She staked *en plein* once or twice, put the maximum on red, won a little on the middle dozen and then lost it again, finally she backed *manque* six times and lost every time. Then with a little graceful shrug of the shoulders she turned away.

She was looking unusually striking in a dress of gold tissue with an underlying note of green. The famous Bosnian pearls were looped round her neck and long pearl ear-rings hung from her ears.

Mr Satterthwaite heard two men near him appraise her.

110

'The Czarnova,' said one, 'she wears well, does she not? The Crown jewels of Bosnia look fine on her.'

The other, a small Jewish-looking man, stared curiously after her.

'So those are the pearls of Bosnia, are they?' he asked. '*En vérité*. That is odd.'

He chuckled softly to himself.

Mr Satterthwaite missed hearing more, for at the moment he turned his head and was overjoyed to recognize an old friend.

'My dear Mr Quin.' He shook him warmly by the hand. 'The last place I should ever have dreamed of seeing you.'

Mr Quin smiled, his dark attractive face lighting up.

'It should not surprise you,' he said. 'It is Carnival time. I am often here in Carnival time.'

'Really? Well, this is a great pleasure. Are you anxious to remain in the rooms? I find them rather warm.'

'It will be pleasanter outside,' agreed the other. 'We will walk in the gardens.'

The air outside was sharp, but not chill. Both men drew deep breaths.

'That is better,' said Mr Satterthwaite.

'Much better,' agreed Mr Quin. 'And we can talk freely. I am sure that there is much that you want to tell me.'

'There is indeed.'

Speaking eagerly, Mr Satterthwaite unfolded his perplexities. As usual he took pride in his power of conveying atmosphere. The Countess, young Franklin, uncompromising Elizabeth—he sketched them all in with a deft touch.

'You have changed since I first knew you,' said Mr Quin, smiling, when the recital was over.

'In what way?'

'You were content then to look on at the drama that life offered. Now—you want to take part—to act.'

'It is true,' confessed Mr Satterthwaite. 'But in this case I do not know what to do. It is all very perplexing. Perhaps—' He hesitated. 'Perhaps you will help me?'

'With pleasure,' said Mr Quin. 'We will see what we can do.'

Mr Satterthwaite had an odd sense of comfort and reliance.

The following day he introduced Franklin Rudge and Elizabeth Martin to his friend Mr Harley Quin. He was pleased to see that they got on together. The Countess was not mentioned, but at lunch time he heard news that aroused his attention.

'Mirabelle is arriving in Monte this evening,' he confided excitedly to Mr Quin.

'The Parisian stage favourite?'

'Yes. I daresay you know—it's common property—she is the King of Bosnia's latest craze. He has showered jewels on her, I believe. They say she is the most exacting and extravagant woman in Paris.'

'It should be interesting to see her and the Countess Czarnova meet tonight.'

'Exactly what I thought.'

Mirabelle was a tall, thin creature with a wonderful head of dyed fair hair. Her complexion was a pale mauve with orange lips. She was amazingly chic. She was dressed in something that looked like a glorified bird of paradise, and she wore chains of jewels hanging down her bare back. A heavy bracelet set with immense diamonds clasped her left ankle.

She created a sensation when she appeared in the Casino.

'Your friend the Countess will have a difficulty in outdoing this,' murmured Mr Quin in Mr Satterthwaite's ear.

The latter nodded. He was curious to see how the Countess comported herself.

She came late, and a low murmur ran round as she walked unconcernedly to one of the centre roulette tables.

She was dressed in white—a mere straight slip of marocain such as a débutante might have worn and her gleaming white neck and arms were unadorned. She wore not a single jewel.

'It is clever, that,' said Mr Satterthwaite with instant approval. 'She disdains rivalry and turns the tables on her adversary.'

He himself walked over and stood by the table. From time to time he amused himself by placing a stake. Sometimes he won, more often he lost.

There was a terrific run on the last dozen. The numbers 31 and 34 turned up again and again. Stakes flocked to the bottom of the cloth.

With a smile Mr Satterthwaite made his last stake for the evening, and placed the maximum on Number 5.

The Countess in her turn leant forward and placed the maximum on Number 6.

'*Faites vos jeux*,' called the croupier hoarsely. '*Rien ne va plus. Plus rien.*'

The ball span, humming merrily. Mr Satterthwaite thought to himself: '*This means something different to each of us. Agonies of hope and despair, boredom, idle amusement, life and death.*'

Click!

The croupier bent forward to see.

'*Numéro cinque, rouge, impair et manque.*'

Mr Satterthwaite had won!

The croupier, having raked in the other stakes, pushed forward Mr Satterthwaite's winnings. He put out his hand to take them. The Countess did the same. The croupier looked from one to the other of them.

'*A madame,*' he said brusquely.

The Countess picked up the money. Mr Satterthwaite drew back. He remained a gentleman. The Countess looked him full in the face and he returned her glance. One or two of the people round pointed out to the croupier that he had made a mistake, but the man shook his head impatiently. He had decided. That was the end. He raised his raucous cry:

'*Faites vos jeux, Messieurs et Mesdames.*'

Mr Satterthwaite rejoined Mr Quin. Beneath his impeccable demeanour, he was feeling extremely indignant. Mr Quin listened sympathetically.

'Too bad,' he said, 'but these things happen.

'We are to meet your friend Franklin Rudge later. I am giving a little supper party.'

The three met at midnight, and Mr Quin explained his plan.

'It is what is called a "Hedges and Highways" party,' he

114

explained. 'We choose our meeting place, then each one goes out and is bound in honour to invite the first person he meets.'

Franklin Rudge was amused by the idea.

'Say, what happens if they won't accept?'

'You must use your utmost powers of persuasion.'

'Good. And where's the meeting place?'

'A somewhat Bohemian café—where one can take strange guests. It is called Le Caveau.'

He explained its whereabouts, and the three parted. Mr Satterthwaite was so fortunate as to run straight into Elizabeth Martin and he claimed her joyfully. They reached Le Caveau and descended into a kind of cellar where they found a table spread for supper and lit by old-fashioned candles in candlesticks.

'We are the first,' said Mr Satterthwaite. 'Ah! here comes Franklin—'

He stopped abruptly. With Franklin was the Countess. It was an awkward moment. Elizabeth displayed less graciousness than she might have done. The Countess, as a woman of the world, retained the honours.

Last of all came Mr Quin. With him was a small, dark man, neatly dressed, whose face seemed familiar to Mr Satterthwaite. A moment later he recognized him. It was the croupier who earlier in the evening had made such a lamentable mistake.

'Let me introduce you to the company, M. Pierre Vaucher,' said Mr Quin.

The little man seemed confused. Mr Quin performed the necessary introductions easily and lightly. Supper was brought—an excellent supper. Wine came—very excellent wine. Some of the frigidity went out of the atmosphere. The Countess was very silent, so was Elizabeth. Franklin Rudge became talkative. He told various stories—not humorous stories, but serious ones. And quietly and assiduously Mr Quin passed round the wine.

'I'll tell you—and this is a true story—about a man who made good,' said Franklin Rudge impressively.

For one coming from a Prohibition country he had shown no lack of appreciation of champagne.

He told his story—perhaps at somewhat unnecessary length. It was, like many true stories, greatly inferior to fiction.

As he uttered the last word, Pierre Vaucher, opposite him, seemed to wake up. He also had done justice to the champagne. He leaned forward across the table.

'I, too, will tell you a story,' he said thickly. 'But mine is the story of a man who did not make good. It is the story of a man who went, not up, but down the hill. And, like yours, it is a true story.'

'Pray tell it to us, monsieur,' said Mr Satterthwaite courteously.

Pierre Vaucher leant back in his chair and looked at the ceiling.

'It is in Paris that the story begins. There was a man there, a working jeweller. He was young and light-hearted and industrious in his profession. They said there was a future before him. A good marriage was already arranged for him, the bride not too bad-looking, the dowry most satisfactory. And then, what do you think? One morning he sees a girl. Such a miserable little wisp of a girl, messieurs. Beautiful? Yes, perhaps, if she were not half starved. But anyway, for this young man, she has a magic that he cannot resist. She has been struggling to find work, she is virtuous—or at least that is what she tells him. I do not know if it is true.'

The Countess's voice came suddenly out of the semi-darkness.

'Why should it not be true? There are many like that.'

'Well, as I say, the young man believed her. And he married her—an act of folly! His family would have no more to say to him. He had outraged their feelings. He married—I will call her Jeanne—it was a good action. He told her so. He felt that she should be very grateful to him. He had sacrificed much for her sake.'

'A charming beginning for the poor girl,' observed the Countess sarcastically.

'He loved her, yes, but from the beginning she maddened him. She had moods—tantrums—she would be cold to him one day, passionate the next. At last he saw the truth. She had never loved him. She had married him so as to keep body and soul together. That truth hurt him, it hurt him horribly, but he tried his utmost to let nothing appear on the surface. And he still felt he deserved gratitude and obedience to his wishes. They quarrelled. She reproached him—Mon Dieu, what did she not reproach him with?

'You can see the next step, can you not? The thing that was bound to come. She left him. For two years he was alone, working in his little shop with no news of

117

her. He had one friend—absinthe. The business did not prosper so well.

'And then one day he came into the shop to find her sitting there. She was beautifully dressed. She had rings on her hands. He stood considering her. His heart was beating—but beating! He was at a loss what to do. He would have liked to have beaten her, to have clasped her in his arms, to have thrown her down on the floor and trampled on her, to have thrown himself at her feet. He did none of those things. He took up his pincers and went on with his work. "Madame desires?" he asked formally.

'That upset her. She did not look for that, see you. "Pierre," she said, "I have come back." He laid aside his pincers and looked at her. "You wish to be forgiven?" he said. "You want me to take you back? You are sincerely repentant?" "Do you want me back?" she murmured. Oh! very softly she said it.

'He knew she was laying a trap for him. He longed to seize her in his arms, but he was too clever for that. He pretended indifference.

'"I am a Christian man," he said. "I try to do what the Church directs." "Ah!" he thought, "I will humble her, humble her to her knees."

'But Jeanne, that is what I will call her, flung back her head and laughed. Evil laughter it was. "I mock myself at you, little Pierre," she said. "Look at these rich clothes, these rings and bracelets. I came to show myself to you. I thought I would make you take me in your arms and when you did so, then—*then* I would spit in your face and tell you how I hated you!"

'And on that she went out of the shop. Can you believe, messieurs, that a woman could be as evil as all that—to come back only to torment me?'

'No,' said the Countess. 'I would not believe it, and any man who was not a fool would not believe it either. But all men are blind fools.'

Pierre Vaucher took no notice of her. He went on.

'And so that young man of whom I tell you sank lower and lower. He drank more absinthe. The little shop was sold over his head. He became of the dregs, of the gutter. Then came the war. Ah! it was good, the war. It took that man out of the gutter and taught him to be a brute beast no longer. It drilled him—and sobered him. He endured cold and pain and the fear of death—but he did not die and when the war ended, he was a man again.

'It was then, messieurs, that he came South. His lungs had been affected by the gas, they said he must find work in the South. I will not weary you with all the things he did. Suffice it to say that he ended up as a croupier, and there—there in the Casino one evening, he saw her again— the woman who had ruined his life. She did not recognize him, but he recognized her. She appeared to be rich and to lack for nothing—but messieurs, the eyes of a croupier are sharp. There came an evening when she placed her last stake in the world on the table. Ask me not how I know—I do know—one feels these things. Others might not believe. She still had rich clothes—why not pawn them, one would say? But to do that—pah! your credit is gone at once. Her jewels? Ah no! Was I not a jeweller in my time? Long ago the real jewels have gone. The pearls of a King are sold

119

one by one, are replaced with false. And meantime one must eat and pay one's hotel bill. Yes, and the rich men— well, they have seen one about for many years. Bah! they say—she is over fifty. A younger chicken for my money.'

A long shuddering sigh came out of the windows where the Countess leant back.

'Yes. It was a great moment, that. Two nights I have watched her. Lose, lose, and lose again. And now the end. She put all on one number. Beside her, an English milord stakes the maximum also—on the next number. The ball rolls . . . The moment has come, she has lost . . .

'Her eyes meet mine. What do I do? I jeopardize my place in the Casino. I rob the English milord. "*à Madame*" I say, and pay over the money.'

'Ah!' There was a crash, as the Countess sprang to her feet and leant across the table, sweeping her glass on to the floor.

'Why?' she cried. 'That's what I want to know, *why* did you do it?'

There was a long pause, a pause that seemed interminable, and still those two facing each other across the table looked and looked . . . It was like a duel.

A mean little smile crept across Pierre Vaucher's face. He raised his hands.

'Madame,' he said, 'there is such a thing as pity . . .'

'Ah!'

She sank down again.

'I see.'

She was calm, smiling, herself again.

'An interesting story, M. Vaucher, is it not? Permit me to give you a light for your cigarette.'

She deftly rolled up a spill, and lighted it at the candle and held it towards him. He leaned forward till the flame caught the tip of the cigarette he held between his lips.

Then she rose unexpectedly to her feet.

'And now I must leave you all. Please—I need no one to escort me.'

Before one could realize it she was gone. Mr Satterthwaite would have hurried out after her, but he was arrested by a startled oath from the Frenchman.

'*A thousand thunders!*'

He was staring at the half-burned spill which the Countess had dropped on the table. He unrolled it.

'*Mon Dieu!*' he muttered. 'A fifty thousand franc bank note. You understand? Her winnings tonight. All that she had in the world. And she lighted my cigarette with it! Because she was too proud to accept—pity. Ah! proud, she was always proud as the Devil. She is unique—wonderful.'

He sprang up from his seat and darted out. Mr Satterthwaite and Mr Quin had also risen. The waiter approached Franklin Rudge.

'*La note, monsieur,*' he observed unemotionally.

Mr Quin rescued it from him quickly.

'I feel kind of lonesome, Elizabeth,' remarked Franklin Rudge. 'These foreigners—they beat the band! I don't understand them. What's it all mean, anyhow?'

He looked across at her.

'Gee, it's good to look at anything so hundred per cent American as you.' His voice took on the plaintive note of a small child. 'These foreigners are so *odd*.'

They thanked Mr Quin and went out into the night together. Mr Quin picked up his change and smiled across at Mr Satterthwaite, who was preening himself like a contented bird.

'Well,' said the latter. 'That's all gone off splendidly. Our pair of love birds will be all right now.'

'Which ones?' asked Mr Quin.

'Oh!' said Mr Satterthwaite, taken aback. 'Oh! yes, well, I suppose you are right, allowing for the Latin point of view and all that—'

He looked dubious.

Mr Quin smiled, and a stained glass panel behind him invested him for just a moment in a motley garment of coloured light.

CHAPTER 6

The Man from the Sea

Mr Satterthwaite was feeling old. That might not have been surprising since in the estimation of many people he *was* old. Careless youths said to their partners: 'Old Satterthwaite? Oh! he must be a hundred—or at any rate about eighty.' And even the kindest of girls said indulgently, 'Oh! Satterthwaite. Yes, he's quite old. He *must* be sixty.' Which was almost worse, since he was sixty-nine.

In his own view, however, he was not old. Sixty-nine was an interesting age—an age of infinite possibilities—an age when at last the experience of a lifetime was beginning to tell. But to feel old—that was different, a tired discouraged state of mind when one was inclined to ask oneself depressing questions. What was he after all? A little dried-up elderly man, with neither chick nor child, with no human belongings, only a valuable art collection which seemed at the moment strangely unsatisfying. No one to care whether he lived or. died . . .

At this point in his meditations Mr Satterthwaite pulled

himself up short. What he was thinking was morbid and unprofitable. He knew well enough, who better, that the chances were that a wife would have hated him or alternatively that he would have hated her, that children would have been a constant source of worry and anxiety, and that demands upon his time and affection would have worried him considerably.

'To be safe and comfortable,' said Mr Satterthwaite firmly—that was the thing.

The last thought reminded him of a letter he had received that morning. He drew it from his pocket and re-read it, savouring its contents pleasurably. To begin with, it was from a Duchess, and Mr Satterthwaite liked hearing from Duchesses. It is true that the letter began by demanding a large subscription for charity and but for that would probably never have been written, but the terms in which it was couched were so agreeable that Mr Satterthwaite was able to gloss over the first fact.

So you've deserted the Riviera, wrote the Duchess. *What is this island of yours like? Cheap? Cannotti put up his prices shamefully this year, and I shan't go to the Riviera again. I might try your island next year if you report favourably, though I should hate five days on a boat. Still anywhere you recommend is sure to be pretty comfortable—too much so. You'll get to be one of those people who do nothing but coddle themselves and think of their comfort. There's only one thing that will save you, Satterthwaite, and that is your inordinate interest in other people's affairs . . .*

As Mr Satterthwaite folded the letter, a vision came up vividly before him of the Duchess. Her meanness, her unexpected and alarming kindness, her caustic tongue, her indomitable spirit.

Spirit! Everyone needed spirit. He drew out another letter with a German stamp upon it—written by a young singer in whom he had interested himself. It was a grateful affectionate letter.

> '*How can I thank you, dear Mr Satterthwaite? It seems too wonderful to think that in a few days I shall be singing Isolde . . .*'

A pity that she had to make her *début* as Isolde. A charming, hardworking child, Olga, with a beautiful voice but no temperament. He hummed to himself. '*Nay order him! Pray understand it! I command it. I, Isolde.*' No, the child hadn't got it in her—the spirit—the indomitable will—all expressed in that final 'Ich Isoldé!'

Well, at any rate he had done something for somebody. This island depressed him—why, oh! why had he deserted the Riviera which he knew so well and where he was so well known? Nobody here took any interest in him. Nobody seemed to realize that here was *the* Mr Satterthwaite—the friend of Duchesses and Countesses and singers and writers. No one in the island was of any social importance or of any artistic importance either. Most people had been there seven, fourteen, or twenty-one years running and valued themselves and were valued accordingly.

With a deep sigh Mr Satterthwaite proceeded down

from the hotel to the small straggling harbour below. His way lay between an avenue of bougainvillaea—a vivid mass of flaunting scarlet, that made him feel older and greyer than ever.

'I'm getting old,' he murmured. 'I'm getting old and tired.'

He was glad when he had passed the bougainvillaea and was walking down the white street with the blue sea at the end of it. A disreputable dog was standing in the middle of the road, yawning and stretching himself in the sun. Having prolonged his stretch to the utmost limits of ecstasy, he sat down and treated himself to a really good scratch. He then rose, shook himself, and looked round for any other good things that life might have to offer.

There was a dump of rubbish by the side of the road and to this he went sniffing in pleasurable anticipation. True enough, his nose had not deceived him! A smell of such rich putrescence that surpassed even his anticipations! He sniffed with growing appreciation, then suddenly abandoning himself, he lay on his back and rolled frenziedly on the delicious dump. Clearly the world this morning was a dog paradise!

Tiring at last, he regained his feet and strolled out once more into the middle of the road. And then, without the least warning, a ramshackle car careered wildly round the corner, caught him full and square and passed on unheeding.

The dog rose to his feet, stood a minute regarding Mr Satterthwaite, a vague dumb reproach in his eyes, then fell over. Mr Satterthwaite went up to him and bent down. The dog was dead. He went on his way, wondering at the sadness and cruelty of life. What a queer dumb look of reproach had been in the dog's eyes. 'Oh! World,' they seemed to say. 'Oh! Wonderful World in which I have trusted. Why have you done this to me?'

Mr Satterthwaite went on, past the palm trees and the straggling white houses, past the black lava beach where the surf thundered and where once, long ago, a well-known English swimmer had been carried out to sea and drowned, past the rock pools where children and elderly ladies bobbed up and down and called it bathing, along the steep road that winds upwards to the top of the cliff. For there on the edge of the cliff was a house, appropriately named La Paz. A white house with faded green shutters tightly closed, a tangled beautiful garden, and a walk between cypress trees that led to a plateau on the edge of the cliff where you looked down—down—down—to the deep blue sea below.

It was to this spot that Mr Satterthwaite was bound. He had developed a great love for the garden of La Paz. He had never entered the villa. It seemed always to be empty. Manuel, the Spanish gardener, wished one good-morning with a flourish and gallantly presented ladies with a bouquet and gentlemen with a single flower as a buttonhole, his dark face wreathed in smiles.

Sometimes Mr Satterthwaite made up stories in his own mind about the owner of the villa. His favourite was a Spanish dancer, once world-famed for her beauty, who hid herself here so that the world should never know that she was no longer beautiful.

He pictured her coming out of the house at dusk and walking through the garden. Sometimes he was tempted to ask Manuel for the truth, but he resisted the temptation. He preferred his fancies.

After exchanging a few words with Manuel and graciously accepting an orange rosebud, Mr Satterthwaite passed on down the cypress walk to the sea. It was rather wonderful sitting there—on the edge of nothing—with that sheer drop below one. It made him think of Tristan and Isolde, of the beginning of the third act with Tristan and Kurwenal—that lonely waiting and of Isolde rushing up from the sea and Tristan dying in her arms. (No, little Olga would never make an Isolde. Isolde of Cornwall, that Royal hater and Royal lover . . .) He shivered. He felt old, chilly, alone . . . What had he had out of life? Nothing—nothing. Not as much as that dog in the street . . .

It was an unexpected sound that roused him from his reverie. Footsteps coming along the cypress walk were inaudible, the first he knew of somebody's presence was the English monosyllable 'Damn.'

He looked round to find a young man staring at him in obvious surprise and disappointment. Mr Satterthwaite recognized him at once as an arrival of the day before who had more or less intrigued him. Mr Satterthwaite called him a young man—because in comparison to most of the die-hards in the Hotel he *was* a young man, but he would certainly never see forty again and was probably drawing appreciably near to his half century. Yet in spite of that, the term young man fitted him—Mr Satterthwaite was usually right about such things—there was an impression of immaturity about him. As there is a touch of puppyhood about many a full grown dog so it was with the stranger.

Mr Satterthwaite thought: 'This chap has really never grown up—not properly, that is.'

And yet there was nothing Peter Pannish about him. He was sleek—almost plump, he had the air of one who has always done himself exceedingly well in the material sense and denied himself no pleasure or satisfaction. He had brown eyes—rather round—fair hair turning grey—a little moustache and rather florid face.

The thing that puzzled Mr Satterthwaite was what had brought him to the island. He could imagine him shooting things, hunting things, playing polo or golf or tennis, making love to pretty women. But in the island there was nothing to hunt or shoot, no games except golf-croquet, and the nearest approach to a pretty woman was represented by elderly Miss Baba Kindersley. There were, of course, artists, to whom the beauty of the scenery made appeal, but Mr Satterthwaite was quite certain that the young man was not an artist. He was clearly marked with the stamp of the Philistine.

While he was resolving these things in his mind, the other spoke, realizing somewhat belatedly that his single ejaculation so far might be open to criticism.

'I beg your pardon,' he said with some embarrassment. 'As a matter of fact, I was—well, startled. I didn't expect anyone to be here.'

He smiled disarmingly. He had a charming smile—friendly—appealing.

'It is rather a lonely spot,' agreed Mr Satterthwaite, as he moved politely a little further up the bench. The other accepted the mute invitation and sat down.

'I don't know about lonely,' he said. 'There always seems to be *someone* here.'

There was a tinge of latent resentment in his voice. Mr Satterthwaite wondered why. He read the other as a friendly soul. Why this insistence on solitude? A rendezvous, perhaps? No—not that. He looked again with carefully veiled scrutiny at his companion. Where had he seen that particular expression before quite lately? That look of dumb bewildered resentment.

'You've been up here before then?' said Mr Satterthwaite, more for the sake of saying something than for anything else.

'I was up here last night—after dinner.'

'Really? I thought the gates were always locked.'

There was a moment's pause and then, almost sullenly, the young man said:

'I climbed over the wall.'

Mr Satterthwaite looked at him with real attention now. He had a sleuth-like habit of mind and he was aware that his companion had only arrived on the preceding afternoon. He had had little time to discover the beauty of the villa by daylight and he had so far spoken to nobody. Yet after dark he had made straight for La Paz. Why? Almost involuntarily Mr Satterthwaite turned his head to look at the green-shuttered villa, but it was as ever serenely lifeless, close shuttered. No, the solution of the mystery was not there.

'And you actually found someone here then?'

The other nodded.

'Yes. Must have been from the other hotel. He had on fancy dress.'

130

'Fancy dress?'

'Yes. A kind of Harlequin rig.'

'What?'

The query fairly burst from Mr Satterthwaite's lips. His companion turned to stare at him in surprise.

'They often do have fancy dress shows at the hotels, I suppose?'

'Oh! quite,' said Mr Satterthwaite. 'Quite, quite, quite.'

He paused breathlessly, then added:

'You must excuse my excitement. Do you happen to know anything about catalysis?'

The young man stared at him.

'Never heard of it. What is it?'

Mr Satterthwaite quoted gravely: '*A chemical reaction depending for its success on the presence of a certain substance which itself remains unchanged.*'

'Oh,' said the young man uncertainly.

'I have a certain friend—his name is Mr Quin, and he can best be described in the terms of catalysis. His presence is a sign that things are going to happen, because when he is there strange revelations come to light, discoveries are made. And yet—he himself takes no part in the proceedings. I have a feeling that it was my friend you met here last night.'

'He's a very sudden sort of chap then. He gave me quite a shock. One minute he wasn't there and the next minute he was! Almost as though he came up out of the sea.'

Mr Satterthwaite looked along the little plateau and down the sheer drop below.

'That's nonsense, of course,' said the other. 'But it's the

feeling he gave me. Of course, really, there isn't the foothold for a fly.' He looked over the edge. 'A straight clear drop. If you went over—well, that would be the end right enough.'

'An ideal spot for a murder, in fact,' said Mr Satterthwaite pleasantly.

The other stared at him, almost as though for the moment he did not follow. Then he said vaguely: 'Oh! yes—of course . . .'

He sat there, making little dabs at the ground with his stick and frowning. Suddenly Mr Satterthwaite got the resemblance he had been seeking. That dumb bewildered questioning. *So had the dog looked who was run over*. His eyes and this young man's eyes asked the same pathetic question with the same reproach. '*Oh! world that I have trusted—what have you done to me?*'

He saw other points of resemblance between the two, the same pleasure-loving easy-going existence, the same joyous abandon to the delights of life, the same absence of intellectual questioning. Enough for both to live in the moment—the world was a good place, a place of carnal delights—sun, sea, sky—a discreet garbage heap. And then—what? A car had hit the dog. What had hit the man?

The subject of these cogitations broke in at this point, speaking, however, more to himself than to Mr Satterthwaite.

'One wonders,' he said, 'what it's All For?'

Familiar words—words that usually brought a smile to Mr Satterthwaite's lips, with their unconscious betrayal of the innate egoism of humanity which insists on regarding every manifestation of life as directly designed for its delight or its torment. He did not answer and presently the stranger said with a slight, rather apologetic laugh:

'I've heard it said that every man should build a house, plant a tree and have a son.' He paused and then added: 'I believe I planted an acorn once . . .'

Mr Satterthwaite stirred slightly. His curiosity was aroused—that ever-present interest in the affairs of other people of which the Duchess had accused him was roused. It was not difficult. Mr Satterthwaite had a very feminine side to his nature, he was as good a listener as any woman, and he knew the right moment to put in a prompting word. Presently he was hearing the whole story.

Anthony Cosden, that was the stranger's name, and his life had been much as Mr Satterthwaite had imagined it. He was a bad hand at telling a story but his listener supplied the gaps easily enough. A very ordinary life— an average income, a little soldiering, a good deal of sport whenever sport offered, plenty of friends, plenty of pleasant things to do, a sufficiency of women. The kind of life that practically inhibits thought of any description and substitutes sensation. To speak frankly, an animal's life. 'But there are worse things than that,' thought Mr Satterthwaite from the depths of his experience. 'Oh! many worse things than that . . .' This world had seemed a very good place to Anthony Cosden. He had grumbled because everyone always grumbled but it had never been a serious grumble. And then—*this*.

He came to it at last—rather vaguely and incoherently. Hadn't felt quite the thing—nothing much. Saw his doctor, and the doctor had persuaded him to go to a Harley Street man. And then—the incredible truth. They'd tried to hedge about it—spoke of great care—a quiet life, but they hadn't been able to disguise that that was all eyewash—letting him down lightly. It boiled down to this—six months. That's what they gave him. Six months.

He turned those bewildered brown eyes on Mr Satterthwaite. It was, of course, rather a shock to a fellow. One didn't—one didn't somehow, know what do *do*.

Mr Satterthwaite nodded gravely and understandingly.

It was a bit difficult to take in all at once, Anthony Cosden went on. How to put in the time. Rather a rotten business waiting about to get pipped. He didn't feel really ill—not yet. Though that might come later, so the specialist had said—in fact, it was bound to. It seemed such nonsense to be going to die when one didn't in the least want to. The best thing, he had thought, would be to carry on as usual. But somehow that hadn't worked.

Here Mr Satterthwaite interrupted him. Wasn't there, he hinted delicately, any woman?

But apparently there wasn't. There were women, of course, but not that kind. His crowd was a very cheery crowd. They didn't, so he implied, like corpses. He didn't wish to make a kind of walking funeral of himself. It would have been embarrassing for everybody. So he had come abroad.

'You came to see these islands? But why?' Mr Satterthwaite was hunting for something, something intangible but delicate that eluded him and yet which he was sure was there. 'You've been here before, perhaps?'

'Yes.' He admitted it almost unwillingly. 'Years ago when I was a youngster.'

And suddenly, almost unconsciously so it seemed, he shot a quick glance backward over his shoulder in the direction of the villa.

'I remembered this place,' he said, nodding at the sea. '*One step to eternity!*'

'And that is why you came up here last night,' finished Mr Satterthwaite calmly.

Anthony Cosden shot him a dismayed glance.

'Oh! I say—really—' he protested.

'Last night you found someone here. This afternoon you have found me. Your life has been saved—twice.'

'You may put it that way if you like—but damn it all, it's *my* life. I've a right to do what I like with it.'

'That is a cliché,' said Mr Satterthwaite wearily.

'Of course I see your point,' said Anthony Cosden generously. 'Naturally you've got to say what you can. I'd try to dissuade a fellow myself, even though I knew deep down that he was right. And you know that I'm right. A clean quick end is better than a lingering one—causing trouble and expense and bother to all. In any case it's not as though I had anyone in the world belonging to me . . .'

'If you had—?' said Mr Satterthwaite sharply.

Cosden drew a deep breath.

'I don't know. Even then, I think, this way would be best. But anyway—I haven't . . .'

He stopped abruptly. Mr Satterthwaite eyed him curiously. Incurably romantic, he suggested again that there was, somewhere, some woman. But Cosden negatived it. He oughtn't, he said, to complain. He had had, on the whole, a very good life. It was a pity it was going to be over so soon, that was all. But at any rate he had had, he supposed, everything worth having. Except a son. He would have liked a son. He would like to know now that he had a son living after him. Still, he reiterated the fact, he had had a very good life—

It was at this point that Mr Satterthwaite lost patience. Nobody, he pointed out, who was still in the larval stage, could claim to know anything of life at all. Since the words *larval stage* clearly meant nothing at all to Cosden, he proceeded to make his meaning clearer.

'You have not begun to live yet. You are still at the beginning of life.'

Cosden laughed.

'Why, my hair's grey. I'm forty—'

Mr Satterthwaite interrupted him.

'That has nothing to do with it. Life is a compound of physical and mental experiences. I, for instance, am sixty-nine, and I am really sixty-nine. I have known, either at first or second hand, nearly all the experiences life has to offer. You are like a man who talks of a full year and has seen nothing but snow and ice! The flowers of Spring, the languorous days of Summer, the falling leaves of Autumn— he knows nothing of them—not even that there are such things. And you are going to turn your back on even this opportunity of knowing them.'

'You seem to forget,' said Anthony Cosden dryly, 'that, in any case, I have only six months.'

'Time, like everything else, is relative,' said Mr Satterthwaite. 'That six months might be the longest and most varied experience of your whole life.'

Cosden looked unconvinced.

'In my place,' he said, 'you would do the same.'

Mr Satterthwaite shook his head.

'No,' he said simply. 'In the first place, I doubt if I should have the courage. It needs courage and I am not at all a brave individual. And in the second place—'

'Well?'

'I always want to know what is going to happen tomorrow.'

Cosden rose suddenly with a laugh.

'Well, sir, you've been very good in letting me talk to you. I hardly know why—anyway, there it is. I've said a lot too much. Forget it.'

'And tomorrow, when an accident is reported, I am to leave it at that? To make no suggestion of suicide?'

'That's as you like. I'm glad you realize one thing—that you can't prevent me.'

'My dear young man,' said Mr Satterthwaite placidly, 'I can hardly attach myself to you like the proverbial limpet. Sooner or later you would give me the slip and accomplish your purpose. But you are frustrated at any rate for this afternoon. You would hardly like to go to your death leaving me under the possible imputation of having pushed you over.'

'That is true,' said Cosden. 'If you insist on remaining here—'

'I do,' said Mr Satterthwaite firmly.

Cosden laughed good-humouredly.

'Then the plan must be deferred for the moment. In which case I will go back to the hotel. See you later perhaps.'

Mr Satterthwaite was left looking at the sea.

'And now,' he said to himself softly, 'what next? There must be a next. I wonder . . .'

He got up. For a while he stood at the edge of the plateau looking down on the dancing water beneath. But he found no inspiration there, and turning slowly he walked back along the path between the cypresses and into the quiet garden. He looked at the shuttered, peaceful house and he wondered, as he had often wondered before, who had lived there and what had taken place within those placid walls. On a sudden impulse he walked up some crumbling stone steps and laid a hand on one of the faded green shutters.

To his surprise it swung back at his touch. He hesitated a moment, then pushed it boldly open. The next minute he stepped back with a little exclamation of dismay. A woman stood in the window facing him. She wore black and had a black lace mantilla draped over her head.

Mr Satterthwaite floundered wildly in Italian interspersed with German—the nearest he could get in the hurry of the moment to Spanish. He was desolated and ashamed, he explained haltingly. The Signora must forgive. He thereupon retreated hastily, the woman not having spoken one word.

He was halfway across the courtyard when she spoke—two sharp words like a pistol crack.

'Come back!'

It was a barked-out command such as might have been addressed to a dog, yet so absolute was the authority it conveyed, that Mr Satterthwaite had swung round hurriedly and trotted back to the window almost automatically before it occurred to him to feel any resentment. He obeyed like a dog. The woman was still standing motionless at the window. She looked him up and down appraising him with perfect calmness.

'You are English,' she said. 'I thought so.'

Mr Satterthwaite started off on a second apology.

'If I had known you were English,' he said, 'I could have expressed myself better just now. I offer my most sincere apologies for my rudeness in trying the shutter. I am afraid I can plead no excuse save curiosity. I had a great wish to see what the inside of this charming house was like.'

She laughed suddenly, a deep, rich laugh.

'If you really want to see it,' she said, 'you had better come in.'

She stood aside, and Mr Satterthwaite, feeling pleasurably excited, stepped into the room. It was dark, since the shutters of the other windows were closed, but he could see that it was scantily and rather shabbily furnished and that the dust lay thick everywhere.

'Not here,' she said. 'I do not use this room.'

She led the way and he followed her, out of the room across a passage and into a room the other side. Here the windows gave on the sea and the sun streamed in. The furniture, like that of the other room, was poor in quality, but there were some worn rugs that had been good in their time, a large screen of Spanish leather and bowls of fresh flowers.

'You will have tea with me,' said Mr Satterthwaite's hostess. She added reassuringly: 'It is perfectly good tea and will be made with boiling water.'

She went out of the door and called out something in Spanish, then she returned and sat down on a sofa opposite her guest. For the first time, Mr Satterthwaite was able to study her appearance.

The first effect she had upon him was to make him feel even more grey and shrivelled and elderly than usual by contrast with her own forceful personality. She was a tall woman, very sunburnt, dark and handsome though no longer young. When she was in the room the sun seemed to be shining twice as brightly as when she was out of it, and presently a curious feeling of warmth and aliveness began to steal over Mr Satterthwaite. It was as though he stretched out thin, shrivelled hands to a reassuring flame. He thought, 'She's so much vitality herself that she's got a lot left over for other people.'

He recalled the command in her voice when she had stopped him, and wished that his protégée, Olga, could be imbued with a little of that force. He thought: 'What an Isolde she'd make! And yet she probably hasn't got the ghost of a singing voice. Life is badly arranged.' He was, all the same, a little afraid of her. He did not like domineering women.

She had clearly been considering him as she sat with her chin in her hands, making no pretence about it. At last she nodded as though she had made up her mind.

'I am glad you came,' she said at last. 'I needed someone very badly to talk to this afternoon. And you are used to that, aren't you?'

'I don't quite understand.'

'I meant people tell you things. You knew what I meant! Why pretend?'

'Well—perhaps—'

She swept on, regardless of anything he had been going to say.

'One could say anything to you. That is because you are half a woman. You know what we feel—what we think— the queer, queer things we do.'

Her voice died away. Tea was brought by a large, smiling Spanish girl. It was good tea—China—Mr Satterthwaite sipped it appreciatively.

'You live here?' he inquired conversationally.

'Yes.'

'But not altogether. The house is usually shut up, is it not? At least so I have been told.'

'I am here a good deal, more than anyone knows. I only use these rooms.'

'You have had the house long?'

'It has belonged to me for twenty-two years—and I lived here for a year before that.'

Mr Satterthwaite said rather inanely (or so he felt): 'That is a very long time.'

'The year? Or the twenty-two years?'

His interest stirred, Mr Satterthwaite said gravely: 'That depends.'

She nodded.

'Yes, it depends. They are two separate periods. They have nothing to do with each other. Which is long? Which is short? Even now I cannot say.'

She was silent for a minute, brooding. Then she said with a little smile:

'It is such a long time since I have talked with anyone—such a long time! I do not apologize. You came to my shutter. You wished to look through my window. And that is what you are always doing, is it not? Pushing aside the shutter and looking through the window into the truth of people's lives. If they will let you. And often if they will not let you! It would be difficult to hide anything from you. You would guess—and guess right.'

Mr Satterthwaite had an odd impulse to be perfectly sincere.

'I am sixty-nine,' he said. 'Everything I know of life I know at second hand. Sometimes that is very bitter to me. And yet, because of it, I know a good deal.'

She nodded thoughtfully.

'I know. Life is very strange. I cannot imagine what it must be like to be that—always a looker-on.'

Her tone was wondering. Mr Satterthwaite smiled.

'No, you would not know. Your place is in the centre of the stage. You will always be the Prima Donna.'

'What a curious thing to say.'

'But I am right. Things have happened to you—will always happen to you. Sometimes, I think, there have been tragic things. Is that so?'

Her eyes narrowed. She looked across at him.

'If you are here long, somebody will tell you of the English swimmer who was drowned at the foot of this cliff. They will tell you how young and strong he was, how handsome, and they will tell you that his young wife looked down from the top of the cliff and saw him drowning.'

'Yes, I have already heard that story.'

'That man was my husband. This was his villa. He brought me out here with him when I was eighteen, and a year later he died—driven by the surf on the black rocks, cut and bruised and mutilated, battered to death.'

Mr Satterthwaite gave a shocked exclamation. She leant forward, her burning eyes focused on his face.

'You spoke of tragedy. Can you imagine a greater tragedy than that? For a young wife, only a year married, to stand helpless while the man she loved fought for his life—and lost it—horribly.'

'Terrible,' said Mr Satterthwaite. He spoke with real emotion. 'Terrible. I agree with you. Nothing in life could be so dreadful.'

Suddenly she laughed. Her head went back.

'You are wrong,' she said. 'There is something more terrible. And that is for a young wife to stand there and hope and long for her husband to drown . . .'

'But good God,' cried Mr Satterthwaite, 'you don't mean—?'

'Yes, I do. That's what it was really. I knelt there—knelt down on the cliff and prayed. The Spanish servants thought I was praying for his life to be saved. I wasn't. I was praying that I might wish him to be spared. I was saying one thing over and over again, "God, help me not to wish him dead. God, help me not to wish him dead." But it wasn't any good. All the time I hoped—hoped—and my hope came true.'

She was silent for a minute or two and then she said very gently in quite a different voice:

'That is a terrible thing, isn't it? It's the sort of thing one can't forget. I was terribly happy when I knew he was really dead and couldn't come back to torture me any more.'

'My child,' said Mr Satterthwaite, shocked.

'I know. I was too young to have that happen to me. Those things should happen to one when one is older—when one is more prepared for—for beastliness. Nobody knew, you know, what he was really like. I thought he was wonderful when I first met him and was so happy and proud when he asked me to marry him. But things went wrong almost at once. He was angry with me—nothing I could do pleased him—and yet I tried so hard. And then he began to like hurting me. And above all to terrify me. That's what he enjoyed most. He thought out all sorts of things . . . dreadful things. I won't tell you. I suppose, really, he must have been a little mad. I was alone here, in his power, and cruelty began to be his hobby.' Her eyes widened and darkened. 'The worst was my baby. I was going to have a baby. Because of some of the things he did to me—it was born dead. My little baby. I nearly died, too—but I didn't. I wish I had.'

Mr Satterthwaite made an inarticulate sound.

'And then I was delivered—in the way I've told you. Some girls who were staying at the hotel dared him. That's how it happened. All the Spaniards told him it was madness to risk the sea just there. But he was very vain—he wanted to show off. And I—I saw him drown—and was glad. God oughtn't to let such things happen.'

144

Mr Satterthwaite stretched out his little dry hand and took hers. She squeezed it hard as a child might have done. The maturity had fallen away from her face. He saw her without difficulty as she had been at nineteen.

'At first it seemed too good to be true. The house was mine and I could live in it. And no one could hurt me any more! I was an orphan, you know, I had no near relations, no one to care what became of me. That simplified things. I lived on here—in this villa—and it seemed like Heaven. Yes, like Heaven. I've never been so happy since, and never shall again. Just to wake up and know that everything was all right—no pain, no terror, no wondering what he was going to do to me next. Yes, it was Heaven.'

She paused a long time, and Mr Satterthwaite said at last: 'And then?'

'I suppose human beings aren't ever satisfied. At first, just being free was enough. But after a while I began to get—well, lonely, I suppose. I began to think about my baby that died. If only I had had my baby! I wanted it as a baby, and also as a plaything. I wanted dreadfully something or someone to play with. It sounds silly and childish, but there it was.'

'I understand,' said Mr Satterthwaite gravely.

'It's difficult to explain the next bit. It just—well, happened, you see. There was a young Englishman staying at the hotel. He strayed in the garden by mistake. I was wearing Spanish dress and he took me for a Spanish girl. I thought it would be rather fun to pretend I was one, so I played up. His Spanish was very bad but he could just manage a little. I told him the villa belonged to an English lady who was away. I said she had taught me a little English and I pretended to speak broken English. It was such fun—such fun—even now I can remember what fun it was. He began to make love to me. We agreed to pretend that the villa was our home, that we were just married and coming to live there. I suggested that we should try one of the shutters—the one you tried this evening. It was open and inside the room was dusty and uncared for. We crept in. It was exciting and wonderful. We pretended it was our own house.'

She broke off suddenly, looked appealingly at Mr Satterthwaite.

'It all seemed lovely—like a fairy tale. And the lovely thing about it, to me, was that it wasn't true. It wasn't real.'

Mr Satterthwaite nodded. He saw her, perhaps more clearly than she saw herself—that frightened, lonely child entranced with her make-believe that was so safe because it wasn't real.

'He was, I suppose, a very ordinary young man. Out for adventure, but quite sweet about it. We went on pretending.'

She stopped, looked at Mr Satterthwaite and said again: 'You understand? We went on pretending . . .'

She went on again in a minute.

'He came up again the next morning to the villa. I saw him from my bedroom through the shutter. Of course he didn't dream I was inside. He still thought I was a little Spanish peasant girl. He stood there looking about him. He'd asked me to meet him. I'd said I would but I never meant to.

'He just stood there looking worried. I think he was worried about me. It was nice of him to be worried about me. He *was* nice . . .'

She paused again.

'The next day he left. I've never seen him again.

'My baby was born nine months later. I was wonderfully happy all the time. To be able to have a baby so peacefully, with no one to hurt you or make you miserable. I wished I'd remembered to ask my English boy his Christian name. I would have called the baby after him. It seemed unkind not to. It seemed rather unfair. He'd given me the thing I wanted most in the world, and he would never even know about it! But of course I told myself that he wouldn't look at it that way—that to know would probably only worry and annoy him. I had been just a passing amusement for him, that was all.'

'And the baby?' asked Mr Satterthwaite.

'He was splendid. I called him John. Splendid. I wish you could see him now. He's twenty. He's going to be a mining engineer. He's been the best and dearest son in the world to me. I told him his father had died before he was born.'

Mr Satterthwaite stared at her. A curious story. And somehow, a story that was not completely told. There was, he felt sure, something else.

'Twenty years is a long time,' he said thoughtfully. 'You've never contemplated marrying again?'

She shook her head. A slow, burning blush spread over her tanned cheeks.

'The child was enough for you—always?'

She looked at him. Her eyes were softer than he had yet seen them.

'Such queer things happen!' she murmured. 'Such queer things . . . You wouldn't believe them—no, I'm wrong, *you* might, perhaps. I didn't love John's father, not at the time. I don't think I even knew what love was. I assumed, as a matter of course, that the child would be like me. But he wasn't. He mightn't have been my child at all. He was like his father—he was like no one but his father. I learnt to know that man—through his child. Through the child, I learnt to love him. I love him now. I always shall love him. You may say that it's imagination, that I've built up an ideal, but it isn't so. I love the man, the real, human man. I'd know him if I saw him tomorrow—even though it's over twenty years since we met. Loving him has made me into a woman. I love him as a woman loves a man. For twenty years I've lived loving him. I shall die loving him.'

She stopped abruptly—then challenged her listener.

'Do you think I'm mad—to say these strange things?'

'Oh! my dear,' said Mr Satterthwaite. He took her hand again.

'You do understand?'

'I think I do. But there's something more, isn't there? Something that you haven't yet told me?'

Her brow clouded over.

'Yes, there's something. It was clever of you to guess. I knew at once you weren't the sort one can hide things from. But I don't want to tell you—and the reason I don't want to tell you is because it's best for you not to know.'

He looked at her. Her eyes met his bravely and defiantly.

He said to himself: 'This is the test. All the clues are in my hand. I ought to be able to know. If I reason rightly I shall know.'

There was a pause, then he said slowly:

'Something's gone wrong.' He saw her eyelids give the faintest quiver and knew himself to be on the right track.

'Something's gone wrong—suddenly—after all these years.' He felt himself groping—groping—in the dark recesses of her mind where she was trying to hide her secret from him.

'The boy—it's got to do with him. You wouldn't mind about anything else.'

He heard the very faint gasp she gave and knew he had probed correctly. A cruel business but necessary. It was her will against his. She had got a dominant, ruthless will, but he too had a will hidden beneath his meek manners. And he had behind him the Heaven-sent assurance of a man who is doing his proper job. He felt a passing contemptuous pity for men whose business it was to track down such crudities as crime. This detective business of the mind, this assembling of clues, this delving for the truth, this wild joy as one drew nearer to the goal . . . Her very passion to keep the truth from him helped her. He felt her stiffen defiantly as he drew nearer and nearer.

'It is better for me not to know, you say. Better for *me*? But you are not a very considerate woman. You would not shrink from putting a stranger to a little temporary inconvenience. It is more than that, then? If you tell me you make me an accomplice before the fact. That sounds like crime. Fantastic! I could not associate crime with you. Or only one sort of crime. A crime against yourself.'

Her lids drooped in spite of herself, veiled her eyes. He leaned forward and caught her wrist.

'It *is* that, then! You are thinking of taking your life.'

She gave a low cry.

'How did you know? How did you know?'

'But why? You are not tired of life. I never saw a woman less tired of it—more radiantly alive.'

She got up, went to the window, pushing back a strand of her dark hair as she did so.

'Since you have guessed so much I might as well tell you the truth. I should not have let you in this evening. I might have known that you would see too much. You are that kind of man. You were right about the cause. It's the boy. He knows nothing. But last time he was home, he spoke tragically of a friend of his, and I discovered something. If he finds out that he is illegitimate it will break his heart. He is proud—horribly proud! There is a girl. Oh! I won't go into details. But he is coming very soon—and he wants to know all about his father—he wants details. The girl's parents, naturally, want to know. When he discovers the truth, he will break with her, exile himself, ruin his life. Oh! I know the things you would say. He is young, foolish, wrong-headed to take it like that! All true, perhaps. But does it matter what people ought to be? They are what they are. *It will break his heart* . . . But if, before he comes, there has been an accident, everything will be swallowed up in grief for me. He will look through my papers, find nothing, and be annoyed that I told him so little. But he will not suspect the truth. It is the best way. One must pay for happiness, and I have had so much—oh! so much happiness. And in reality the price will be easy, too. A little courage—to take the leap—perhaps a moment or so of anguish.'

'But, my dear child—'

'Don't argue with me.' She flared round on him. 'I won't listen to conventional arguments. My life is my own. Up to now, it has been needed—for John. But he needs it no longer. He wants a mate—a companion—he will turn to her all the more willingly because I am no longer there. My life is useless, but my death will be of use. And I have the right to do what I like with my own life.'

'Are you sure?'

The sternness of his tone surprised her. She stammered slightly.

'If it is no good to anyone—and I am the best judge of that—'

He interrupted her again.

'Not necessarily.'

'What do you mean?'

'Listen. I will put a case to you. A man comes to a certain place—to commit suicide, shall we say? But by chance he finds another man there, so he fails in his purpose and goes away—to live. The second man has saved the first man's life, not by being necessary to him or prominent in his life, but just by the mere physical fact of having been in a certain place at a certain moment. You take your life today and perhaps, some five, six, seven years hence, someone will go to death or disaster simply for lack of your presence in a given spot or place. It may be a runaway horse coming down a street that swerved aside at sight of you and so fails to trample a child that is playing in the gutter. That child may live to grow up and be a great musician, or discover a cure for cancer. Or it may be less melodramatic than that. He may just grow up to ordinary everyday happiness . . .'

She stared at him.

'You are a strange man. These things you say—I have never thought of them . . .'

'You say your life is your own,' went on Mr Satterthwaite. 'But can you dare to ignore the chance that you are taking part in a gigantic drama under the orders of a divine Producer? Your cue may not come till the end of the play—it may be totally unimportant, a mere walking-on part, but upon it may hang the issues of the play if you do not give the cue to another player. The whole edifice may crumple. You as you, may not matter to anyone in the world, but you as a person in a particular place may matter unimaginably.'

She sat down, still staring.

'What do you want me to do?' she said simply.

It was Mr Satterthwaite's moment of triumph. He issued orders.

'I want you at least to promise me one thing—to do nothing rash for twenty-four hours.'

She was silent for a moment or two and then she said: 'I promise.'

'There is one other thing—a favour.'

'Yes?'

'Leave the shutter of the room I came in by unfastened, and keep vigil there tonight.'

She looked at him curiously, but nodded assent.

'And now,' said Mr Satterthwaite, slightly conscious of anticlimax, 'I really must be going. God bless you, my dear.'

He made a rather embarrassed exit. The stalwart Spanish girl met him in the passage and opened a side door for him, staring curiously at him the while.

It was just growing dark as he reached the hotel. There was a solitary figure sitting on the terrace. Mr Satterthwaite made straight for it. He was excited and his heart was beating quite fast. He felt that tremendous issues lay in his hands. One false move—

But he tried to conceal his agitation and to speak naturally and casually to Anthony Cosden.

'A warm evening,' he observed. 'I quite lost count of time sitting up there on the cliff.'

'Have you been up there all this time?'

Mr Satterthwaite nodded. The swing door into the hotel opened to let someone through, and a beam of light fell suddenly on the other's face, illuminating its look of dull suffering, of uncomprehending dumb endurance.

Mr Satterthwaite thought to himself: 'It's worse for him than it would be for me. Imagination, conjecture, speculation—they can do a lot for you. You can, as it were, ring the changes upon pain. The uncomprehending blind suffering of an animal—that's terrible . . .'

Cosden spoke suddenly in a harsh voice.

'I'm going for a stroll after dinner. You—you understand? The third time's lucky. For God's sake don't interfere. I know your interference will be well-meaning and all that—but take it from me, it's useless.'

Mr Satterthwaite drew himself up.

'I never interfere,' he said, thereby giving the lie to the whole purpose and object of his existence.

'I know what you think—' went on Cosden, but he was interrupted.

'You must excuse me, but there I beg to differ from you,' said Mr Satterthwaite. 'Nobody knows what another person is thinking. They may imagine they do, but they are nearly always wrong.'

'Well, perhaps that's so.' Cosden was doubtful, slightly taken aback.

'Thought is yours only,' said his companion. 'Nobody can alter or influence the use you mean to make of it. Let us talk of a less painful subject. That old villa, for instance. It has a curious charm, withdrawn, sheltered from the world, shielding heaven knows what mystery. It tempted me to do a doubtful action. I tried one of the shutters.'

'You did?' Cosden turned his head sharply. 'But it was fastened, of course?'

'No,' said Mr Satterthwaite. 'It was open.' He added gently: 'The third shutter from the end.'

'Why,' Cosden burst out, 'that was the one—'

He broke off suddenly, but Mr Satterthwaite had seen the light that had sprung up in his eyes. He rose—satisfied.

Some slight tinge of anxiety still remained with him. Using his favourite metaphor of a drama, he hoped that he had spoken his few lines correctly. For they were very important lines.

But thinking it over, his artistic judgment was satisfied. On his way up to the cliff, Cosden would try that shutter. It was not in human nature to resist. A memory of twenty odd years ago had brought him to this spot, the same memory would take him to the shutter. And afterwards?

'I shall know in the morning,' said Mr Satterthwaite, and proceeded to change methodically for his evening meal.

It was somewhere round ten o'clock that Mr Satterthwaite set foot once more in the garden of La Paz. Manuel bade him a smiling 'Good morning,' and handed him a single rosebud which Mr Satterthwaite put carefully into his buttonhole. Then he went on to the house. He stood there for some minutes looking up at the peaceful white walls, the trailing orange creeper, and the faded green shutters. So silent, so peaceful. Had the whole thing been a dream?

But at that moment one of the windows opened and the lady who occupied Mr Satterthwaite's thoughts came out. She came straight to him with a buoyant swaying walk, like someone carried on a great wave of exultation. Her eyes were shining, her colour high. She looked like a figure of joy on a frieze. There was no hesitation about her, no doubts or tremors. Straight to Mr Satterthwaite she came, put her hands on his shoulders and kissed him—not once but many times. Large, dark, red roses, very velvety—that is how he thought of it afterwards. Sunshine, summer, birds singing—that was the atmosphere into which he felt himself caught up. Warmth, joy and tremendous vigour.

'I'm so happy,' she said. 'You darling! How did you

know? How *could* you know? You're like the good magician in the fairy tales.'

She paused, a sort of breathlessness of happiness upon her.

'We're going over today—to the Consul—to get married. When John comes, his father will be there. We'll tell him there was some misunderstanding in the past. Oh! he won't ask questions. Oh! I'm so happy—so happy—so happy.'

Happiness did indeed surge from her like a tide. It lapped round Mr Satterthwaite in a warm exhilarating flood.

'It's so wonderful to Anthony to find he has a son. I never dreamt he'd mind or care.' She looked confidently into Mr Satterthwaite's eyes. 'Isn't it strange how things come right and end all beautifully?'

He had his clearest vision of her yet. A child—still a child—with her love of make-believe—her fairy tales that ended beautifully with two people 'living happily ever afterwards'.

He said gently:

'If you bring this man of yours happiness in these last months, you will indeed have done a very beautiful thing.'

Her eyes opened wide—surprised.

'Oh!' she said. 'You don't think I'd let him die, do you? After all these years—when he's come to me. I've known lots of people whom doctors have given up and who are alive today. Die? Of course he's not going to die!'

He looked at her—her strength, her beauty, her vitality—her indomitable courage and will. He, too, had known doctors to be mistaken . . . The personal factor—you never knew how much and how little it counted.

She said again, with scorn and amusement in her voice: 'You don't think I'd let him die, do you?'

'No,' said Mr Satterthwaite at last very gently. 'Somehow, my dear, I don't think you will . . .'

Then at last he walked down the cypress path to the bench overlooking the sea and found there the person he was expecting to see. Mr Quin rose and greeted him—the same as ever, dark, saturnine, smiling and sad.

'You expected me?' he asked.

And Mr Satterthwaite answered: 'Yes, I expected you.'

They sat together on the bench.

'I have an idea that you have been playing Providence once more, to judge by your expression,' said Mr Quin presently.

Mr Satterthwaite looked at him reproachfully.

'As if you didn't know all about it.'

'You always accuse me of omniscience,' said Mr Quin, smiling.

'If you know nothing, why were you here the night before last—waiting?' countered Mr Satterthwaite.

'Oh, that—?'

'Yes, that.'

'I had a—commission to perform.'

'For whom?'

'You have sometimes fancifully named me an advocate for the dead.'

'The dead?' said Mr Satterthwaite, a little puzzled. 'I don't understand.'

Mr Quin pointed a long, lean finger down at the blue depths below.

'A man was drowned down there twenty-two years ago.'

'I know—but I don't see—'

'Supposing that, after all, that man loved his young wife. Love can make devils of men as well as angels. She had a girlish adoration for him, but he could never touch the womanhood in her—and that drove him mad. He tortured her because he loved her. Such things happen. You know that as well as I do.'

'Yes,' admitted Mr Satterthwaite, 'I have seen such things—but rarely—very rarely . . .'

'And you have also seen, more commonly, that there is such a thing as remorse—the desire to make amends—at all costs to make amends.'

'Yes, but death came too soon . . .'

'Death!' There was contempt in Mr Quin's voice. 'You believe in a life after death, do you not? And who are you to say that the same wishes, the same desires, may not operate in that other life? If the desire is strong enough—a messenger may be found.'

His voice tailed away.

Mr Satterthwaite got up, trembling a little.

'I must get back to the hotel,' he said. 'If you are going that way.'

But Mr Quin shook his head.

'No,' he said. 'I shall go back the way I came.'

When Mr Satterthwaite looked back over his shoulder, he saw his friend walking towards the edge of the cliff.

CHAPTER 7

The Voice in the Dark

'I am a little worried about Margery,' said Lady Stranleigh.

'My girl, you know,' she added.

She sighed pensively.

'It makes one feel terribly old to have a grown-up daughter.'

Mr Satterthwaite, who was the recipient of these confidences, rose to the occasion gallantly.

'No one could believe it possible,' he declared with a little bow.

'Flatterer,' said Lady Stranleigh, but she said it vaguely and it was clear that her mind was elsewhere.

Mr Satterthwaite looked at the slender white-clad figure in some admiration. The Cannes sunshine was searching, but Lady Stranleigh came through the test very well. At a distance the youthful effect was really extraordinary. One almost wondered if she were grown-up or not. Mr Satterthwaite, who knew everything, knew that it was perfectly possible for Lady Stranleigh to have grown-up grandchildren. She represented the extreme triumph of art

159

over nature. Her figure was marvellous, her complexion was marvellous. She had enriched many beauty parlours and certainly the results were astounding.

Lady Stranleigh lit a cigarette, crossed her beautiful legs encased in the finest of nude silk stockings and murmured:

'Yes, I really am rather worried about Margery.'

'Dear me,' said Mr Satterthwaite, 'what is the trouble?'

Lady Stranleigh turned her beautiful blue eyes upon him

'You have never met her, have you? She is Charles' daughter,' she added helpfully.

If entries in *Who's Who* were strictly truthful, the entries concerning Lady Stranleigh might have ended as follows: *hobbies: getting married*. She had floated through life shedding husbands as she went. She had lost three by divorce and one by death.

'If she had been Rudolph's child I could have understood it,' mused Lady Stranleigh. 'You remember Rudolf? He was always temperamental. Six months after we married I had to apply for those queer things—what do they call them? Conjugal what nots, you know what I mean. Thank goodness it is all much simpler nowadays. I remember I had to write him the silliest kind of letter—my lawyer practically dictated it to me. Asking him to come back, you know, and that I would do all I could, etc., etc., but you never could count on Rudolf, he was so temperamental. He came rushing home at once, which was quite the wrong thing to do, and not at all what the lawyers meant.'

She sighed.

'About Margery?' suggested Mr Satterthwaite, tactfully leading her back to the subject under discussion.

'Of course. I was just going to tell you, wasn't I? Margery has been seeing things, or hearing them. Ghosts, you know, and all that. I should never have thought that Margery could be so imaginative. She is a dear good girl, always has been, but just a shade—dull.'

'Impossible,' murmured Mr Satterthwaite with a confused idea of being complimentary.

'In fact, very dull,' said Lady Stranleigh. 'Doesn't care for dancing, or cocktails or any of the things a young girl ought to care about. She much prefers staying at home to hunt instead of coming out here with me.'

'Dear, dear,' said Mr Satterthwaite, 'she wouldn't come out with you, you say?'

'Well, I didn't exactly press her. Daughters have a depressing effect upon one, I find.'

Mr Satterthwaite tried to think of Lady Stranleigh accompanied by a serious-minded daughter and failed.

'I can't help wondering if Margery is going off her head,' continued Margery's mother in a cheerful voice. 'Hearing voices is a very bad sign, so they tell me. It is not as though Abbot's Mede were haunted. The old building was burnt to the ground in 1836, and they put up a kind of early Victorian château which simply cannot be haunted. It is much too ugly and commonplace.'

Mr Satterthwaite coughed. He was wondering why he was being told all this.

'I thought perhaps,' said Lady Stranleigh, smiling brilliantly upon him, 'that *you* might be able to help me.'

'I?'

'Yes. You are going back to England tomorrow, aren't you?'

'I am. Yes, that is so,' admitted Mr Satterthwaite cautiously.

'And you know all these psychical research people. Of course you do, you know everybody.'

Mr Satterthwaite smiled a little. It was one of his weaknesses to know everybody.

'So what can be simpler?' continued Lady Stranleigh. 'I never get on with that sort of person. You know—earnest men with beards and usually spectacles. They bore me terribly and I am quite at my worst with them.'

Mr Satterthwaite was rather taken aback. Lady Stranleigh continued to smile at him brilliantly.

'So that is all settled, isn't it?' she said brightly. 'You will go down to Abbot's Mede and see Margery, and make all the arrangements. I shall be terribly grateful to you. Of course if Margery is *really* going off her head, I will come home. Ah! here is Bimbo.'

Her smile from being brilliant became dazzling.

A young man in white tennis flannels was approaching them. He was about twenty-five years of age and extremely good-looking.

The young man said simply:

'I have been looking for you everywhere, Babs.'

'What has the tennis been like?'

'Septic.'

Lady Stranleigh rose. She turned her head over her shoulder and murmured in dulcet tones to Mr Satterthwaite: 'It is simply marvellous of you to help me. I shall never forget it.'

Mr Satterthwaite looked after the retreating couple.

'I wonder,' he mused to himself, 'If Bimbo is going to be No 5.'

The conductor of the Train de Luxe was pointing out to Mr Satterthwaite where an accident on the line had occurred a few years previously. As he finished his spirited narrative, the other looked up and saw a well-known face smiling at him over the conductor's shoulder.

'My dear Mr Quin,' said Mr Satterthwaite.

His little withered face broke into smiles.

'What a coincidence! That we should both be returning to England on the same train. You are going there, I suppose.'

'Yes,' said Mr Quin. 'I have business there of rather an important nature. Are you taking the first service of dinner?'

'I always do so. Of course, it is an absurd time—half-past six, but one runs less risk with the cooking.'

Mr Quin nodded comprehendingly.

'I also,' he said. 'We might perhaps arrange to sit together.'

Half-past six found Mr Quin and Mr Satterthwaite established opposite each other at a small table in the dining-car. Mr Satterthwaite gave due attention to the wine list and then turned to his companion.

'I have not seen you since—ah, yes not since Corsica. You left very suddenly that day.'

Mr Quin shrugged his shoulders.

'Not more so than usual. I come and go, you know. I come and go.'

The words seemed to awake some echo of remembrance

in Mr Satterthwaite's mind. A little shiver passed down his spine—not a disagreeable sensation, quite the contrary. He was conscious of a pleasurable sense of anticipation.

Mr Quin was holding up a bottle of red wine, examining the label on it. The bottle was between him and the light but for a minute or two a red glow enveloped his person.

Mr Satterthwaite felt again that sudden stir of excitement.

'I too have a kind of mission in England,' he remarked, smiling broadly at the remembrance. 'You know Lady Stranleigh perhaps?'

Mr Quin shook his head.

'It is an old title,' said Mr Satterthwaite, 'a very old title. One of the few that can descend in the female line. She is a Baroness in her own right. Rather a romantic history really.'

Mr Quin settled himself more comfortably in his chair. A waiter, flying down the swinging car, deposited cups of soup before them as if by a miracle. Mr Quin sipped it cautiously.

'You are about to give me one of those wonderful descriptive portraits of yours,' he murmured, 'that is so, is it not?'

Mr Satterthwaite beamed on him.

'She is really a marvellous woman,' he said. 'Sixty, you know—yes, I should say at least sixty. I knew them as girls, she and her sister. Beatrice, that was the name of the elder one. Beatrice and Barbara. I remember them as the Barron girls. Both good-looking and in those days very hard up. But that was a great many years ago—why, dear

164

me, I was a young man myself then.' Mr Satterthwaite sighed. 'There were several lives then between them and the title. Old Lord Stranleigh was a first cousin once removed, I think. Lady Stranleigh's life has been quite a romantic affair. Three unexpected deaths—two of the old man's brothers and a nephew. Then there was the "Uralia". You remember the wreck of the "Uralia"? She went down off the coast of New Zealand. The Barron girls were on board. Beatrice was drowned. This one, Barbara, was amongst the few survivors. Six months later, old Stranleigh died and she succeeded to the title and came into a considerable fortune. Since then she has lived for one thing only—herself! She has always been the same, beautiful, unscrupulous, completely callous, interested solely in herself. She has had four husbands, and I have no doubt could get a fifth in a minute.'

He went on to describe the mission with which he had been entrusted by Lady Stranleigh.

'I thought of running down to Abbot's Mede to see the young lady,' he explained. 'I—I feel that something ought to be done about the matter. It is impossible to think of Lady Stranleigh as an ordinary mother.' He stopped, looking across the table at Mr Quin.

'I wish you would come with me,' he said wistfully. 'Would it not be possible?'

'I'm afraid not,' said Mr Quin. 'But let me see, Abbot's Mede is in Wiltshire, is it not?'

Mr Satterthwaite nodded.

'I thought as much. As it happens, I shall be staying not far from Abbot's Mede, at a place you and I both know.' He smiled. 'You remember that little inn, the "Bells and Motley"?'

'Of course,' cried Mr Satterthwaite; 'you will be there?'

Mr Quin nodded. 'For a week or ten days. Possibly longer. If you will come and look me up one day, I shall be delighted to see you.'

And somehow or other Mr Satterthwaite felt strangely comforted by the assurance.

'My dear Miss—er—Margery,' said Mr Satterthwaite, 'I assure you that I should not dream of laughing at you.'

Margery Gale frowned a little. They were sitting in the large comfortable hall of Abbot's Mede. Margery Gale was a big squarely built girl. She bore no resemblance to her mother, but took entirely after her father's side of the family, a line of hard-riding country squires. She looked fresh and wholesome and the picture of sanity. Nevertheless, Mr Satterthwaite was reflecting to himself that the Barrons as a family were all inclined to mental instability. Margery might have inherited her physical appearance from her father and at the same time have inherited some mental kink from her mother's side of the family.

'I wish,' said Margery, 'that I could get rid of that Casson woman. I don't believe in spiritualism, and I don't like it. She is one of these silly women that run a craze to death. She is always bothering me to have a medium down here.'

Mr Satterthwaite coughed, fidgeted a little in his chair and then said in a judicial manner:

166

'Let me be quite sure that I have all the facts. The first of the—er—phenomena occurred two months ago, I understand?'

'About that,' agreed the girl. 'Sometimes it was a whisper and sometimes it was quite a clear voice but it always said much the same thing.'

'Which was?'

'*Give back what is not yours. Give back what you have stolen.* On each occasion I switched on the light, but the room was quite empty and there was no one there. In the end I got so nervous that I got Clayton, mother's maid, to sleep on the sofa in my room.'

'And the voice came just the same?'

'Yes—and this is what frightens me—Clayton did not hear it.'

Mr Satterthwaite reflected for a minute or two.

'Did it come loudly or softly that evening?'

'It was almost a whisper,' admitted Margery. 'If Clayton was sound asleep I suppose she would not really have heard it. She wanted me to see a doctor.' The girl laughed bitterly.

'But since last night even Clayton believes,' she continued.

'What happened last night?'

'I am just going to tell you. I have told no one as yet. I had been out hunting yesterday and we had had a long run. I was dead tired, and slept very heavily. I dreamt—a horrible dream—that I had fallen over some iron railings and that one of the spikes was entering slowly into my throat. I woke to find that it was true—there was some sharp point pressing into the side of my neck, and at the same time a voice was murmuring softly: "*You have stolen what is mine. This is death.*"

'I screamed,' continued Margery, 'and clutched at the air, but there was nothing there. Clayton heard me scream from the room next door where she was sleeping. She came rushing in, and she distinctly felt something brushing past her in the darkness, but she says that whatever that something was, it was not anything human.'

Mr Satterthwaite stared at her. The girl was obviously very shaken and upset. He noticed on the left side of her throat a small square of sticking plaster. She caught the direction of his gaze and nodded.

'Yes,' she said, 'it was not imagination, you see.'

Mr Satterthwaite put a question almost apologetically, it sounded so melodramatic.

'You don't know of anyone—er—who has a grudge against you?' he asked.

'Of course not,' said Margery, 'what an idea!'

Mr Satterthwaite started on another line of attack.

'What visitors have you had during the last two months?'

'You don't mean just people for week-ends, I suppose? Marcia Keane has been with me all along. She is my best friend, and just as keen on horses as I am. Then my cousin Roley Vavasour has been here a good deal.'

Mr Satterthwaite nodded. He suggested that he should see Clayton, the maid.

'She has been with you a long time, I suppose?' he asked.

'Donkey's years,' said Margery. 'She was Mother's and Aunt Beatrice's maid when they were girls. That is why

Mother has kept her on, I suppose, although she has got a French maid for herself. Clayton does sewing and pottering little odd jobs.'

She took him upstairs and presently Clayton came to them. She was a tall, thin, old woman, with grey hair neatly parted, and she looked the acme of respectability.

'No, sir,' she said in answer to Mr Satterthwaite's inquiries. 'I have never heard anything of the house being haunted. To tell you the truth, sir, I thought it was all Miss Margery's imagination until last night. But I actually felt something—brushing by me in the darkness. And I can tell you this, sir, *it was not anything human*. And then there is that wound in Miss Margery's neck. She didn't do that herself, poor lamb.'

But her words were suggestive to Mr Satterthwaite. Was it possible that Margery could have inflicted that wound herself? He had heard of strange cases where girls apparently just as sane and well-balanced as Margery had done the most amazing things.

'It will soon heal up,' said Clayton. 'It's not like this scar of mine.'

She pointed to a mark on her own forehead.

'That was done forty years ago, sir; I still bear the mark of it.'

'It was the time the "Uralia" went down,' put in Margery. 'Clayton was hit on the head by a spar, weren't you, Clayton?'

'Yes, Miss.'

'What do you think yourself, Clayton,' asked Mr Satterthwaite, 'what do you think was the meaning of this attack on Miss Margery?'

'I really should not like to say, sir.'

Mr Satterthwaite read this correctly as the reserve of the well-trained servant.

'What do you really think, Clayton?' he said persuasively.

'I think, sir, that something very wicked must have been done in this house, and that until that is wiped out there won't be any peace.'

The woman spoke gravely, and her faded blue eyes met his steadily.

Mr Satterthwaite went downstairs rather disappointed. Clayton evidently held the orthodox view, a deliberate 'haunting' as a consequence of some evil deed in the past. Mr Satterthwaite himself was not so easily satisfied. The phenomena had only taken place in the last two months. Had only taken place since Marcia Keane and Roley Vavasour had been there. He must find out something about these two. It was possible that the whole thing was a practical joke. But he shook his head, dissatisfied with that solution. The thing was more sinister than that. The post had just come in and Margery was opening and reading her letters. Suddenly she gave an exclamation.

'Mother is too absurd,' she said. 'Do read this.' She handed the letter to Mr Satterthwaite.

It was an epistle typical of Lady Stranleigh.

Darling Margery (she wrote),

I am so glad you have that nice little Mr Satterthwaite there. He is awfully clever and knows all the big-wig spook people. You must have them all down and investigate things thoroughly. I am sure you will have a

170

*perfectly marvellous time, and I only wish I could be
there, but I have really been quite ill the last few days.
The hotels are so careless about the food they give one.
The doctor says it is some kind of food poisoning. I was
really very ill.*

*Sweet of you to send me the chocolates, darling, but
surely just a wee bit silly, wasn't it? I mean, there's such
wonderful confectionery out here.*

*Bye-bye, darling, and have a lovely time laying the
family ghosts. Bimbo says my tennis is coming on
marvellously. Oceans of love.*

Yours,
Barbara.

'Mother always wants me to call her Barbara,' said
Margery, 'simply silly, I think.'

Mr Satterthwaite smiled a little. He realized that the stolid
conservatism of her daughter must on occasions be very
trying to Lady Stranleigh. The contents of her letter struck
him in a way in which obviously they did not strike Margery.

'Did you send your mother a box of chocolates?' he
asked.

Margery shook her head. 'No, I didn't, it must have been
someone else.'

Mr Satterthwaite looked grave. Two things struck him
as of significance. Lady Stranleigh had received a gift of a
box of chocolates and she was suffering from a severe
attack of poisoning. Apparently she had not connected
these two things. Was there a connection? He himself was
inclined to think there was.

171

A tall dark girl lounged out of the morning-room and joined them.

She was introduced to Mr Satterthwaite as Marcia Keane. She smiled on the little man in an easy good-humoured fashion.

'Have you come down to hunt Margery's pet ghost?' she asked in a drawling voice. 'We all rot her about that ghost. Hello, here's Roley.'

A car had just drawn up at the front door. Out of it tumbled a tall young man with fair hair and an eager boyish manner.

'Hello, Margery,' he cried. 'Hello, Marcia! I have brought down reinforcements.' He turned to the two women who were just entering the hall. Mr Satterthwaite recognized in the first one of the two the Mrs Casson of whom Margery had spoken just now.

'You must forgive me, Margery, dear,' she drawled, smiling broadly. 'Mr Vavasour told us that it would be quite all right. It was really his idea that I should bring down Mrs Lloyd with me.'

She indicated her companion with a slight gesture of the hand.

'This is Mrs Lloyd,' she said in a tone of triumph. 'Simply the most wonderful medium that ever existed.'

Mrs Lloyd uttered no modest protest, she bowed and remained with her hands crossed in front of her. She was a highly-coloured young woman of commonplace appearance. Her clothes were unfashionable but rather ornate. She wore a chain of moonstones and several rings.

Margery Gale, as Mr Satterthwaite could see, was not too pleased at this intrusion. She threw an angry look at

Roley Vavasour, who seemed quite unconscious of the offence he had caused.

'Lunch is ready, I think,' said Margery.

'Good,' said Mrs Casson. 'We will hold a *séance* immediately afterwards. Have you got some fruit for Mrs Lloyd? She never eats a solid meal before a *séance*.'

They all went into the dining-room. The medium ate two bananas and an apple, and replied cautiously and briefly to the various polite remarks which Margery addressed to her from time to time. Just before they rose from the table, she flung back her head suddenly and sniffed the air.

'There is something very wrong in this house. I feel it.'

'Isn't she wonderful?' said Mrs Casson in a low delighted voice.

'Oh! undoubtedly,' said Mr Satterthwaite dryly.

The *séance* was held in the library. The hostess was, as Mr Satterthwaite could see, very unwilling, only the obvious delight of her guests in the proceedings reconciled her to the ordeal.

The arrangements were made with a good deal of care by Mrs Casson, who was evidently well up in those matters, the chairs were set round in a circle, the curtains were drawn, and presently the medium announced herself ready to begin.

'Six people,' she said, looking round the room. 'That is bad. We must have an uneven number, Seven is ideal. I get my best results out of a circle of seven.'

'One of the servants,' suggested Roley. He rose. 'I will rout out the butler.'

'Let's have Clayton,' said Margery.

Mr Satterthwaite saw a look of annoyance pass over Roley Vavasour's good-looking face.

'But why Clayton?' he demanded.

'You don't like Clayton,' said Margery slowly.

Roley shrugged his shoulders. 'Clayton doesn't like me,' he said whimsically. 'In fact she hates me like poison.' He waited a minute or two, but Margery did not give way. 'All right,' he said, 'have her down.'

The circle was formed.

There was a period of silence broken by the usual coughs and fidgetings. Presently a succession of raps were heard and then the voice of the medium's control, a Red Indian called Cherokee.

'Indian Brave says you Good evening ladies and gentlemen. Someone here very anxious speak. Someone here very anxious give message to young lady. I go now. The spirit say what she come to say.'

A pause and then a new voice, that of a woman, said softly:

'Is Margery here?'

Roley Vavasour took it upon himself to answer.

'Yes,' he said, 'she is. Who is that speaking?'

'I am Beatrice.'

'Beatrice? Who is Beatrice?'

To everyone's annoyance the voice of the Red Indian Cherokee was heard once more.

'I have message for all of you people. Life here very bright and beautiful. We all work very hard. Help those who have not yet passed over.'

Again a silence and then the woman's voice was heard once more.

'This is Beatrice speaking.'

'Beatrice who?'

'Beatrice Barron.'

Mr Sattherwaite leaned forward. He was very excited.

'Beatrice Barron who was drowned in the "Uralia"?'

'Yes, that is right. I remember the "Uralia". I have a message—for this house—*Give back what is not yours.*'

'I don't understand,' said Margery helplessly. 'I—oh, are you really Aunt Beatrice?'

'Yes, I am your aunt.'

'Of course she is,' said Mrs Casson reproachfully. 'How can you be so suspicious? The spirits don't like it.'

And suddenly Mr Satterthwaite thought of a very simple test. His voice quivered as he spoke.

'Do you remember Mr Bottacetti?' he asked.

Immediately there came a ripple of laughter.

'Poor old Boatsupsetty. Of course.'

Mr Sattherwaite was dumbfounded. The test had succeeded. It was an incident of over forty years ago which had happened when he and the Barron girls had found themselves at the same seaside resort. A young Italian acquaintance of theirs had gone out in a boat and capsized, and Beatrice Barron had jestingly named him Boatsupsetty. It seemed impossible that anyone in the room could know of this incident except himself.

The medium stirred and groaned.

175

'She is coming out,' said Mrs Casson. 'That is all we will get out of her today, I am afraid.'

The daylight shone once more on the room full of people, two of whom at least were badly scared.

Mr Satterthwaite saw by Margery's white face that she was deeply perturbed. When they had got rid of Mrs Casson and the medium, he sought a private interview with his hostess.

'I want to ask you one or two questions, Miss Margery. If you and your mother were to die who succeeds to the title and estates?'

'Roley Vavasour, I suppose. His mother was Mother's first cousin.'

Mr Satterthwaite nodded.

'He seems to have been here a lot this winter,' he said gently. 'You will forgive me asking—but is he—fond of you?'

'He asked me to marry him three weeks ago,' said Margery quietly. 'I said No.'

'Please forgive me, but are you engaged to anyone else?'

He saw the colour sweep over her face.

'I am,' she said emphatically. 'I am going to marry Noel Barton. Mother laughs and says it is absurd. She seems to think it is ridiculous to be engaged to a curate. Why, I should like to know! There are curates and curates! You should see Noel on a horse.'

'Oh, quite so,' said Mr Satterthwaite. 'Oh, undoubtedly.'

A footman entered with a telegram on a salver. Margery tore it open. 'Mother is arriving home tomorrow,' she said. 'Bother. I wish to goodness she would stay away.'

Mr Satterthwaite made no comment on this filial sentiment. Perhaps he thought it justified. 'In that case,' he murmured, 'I think I am returning to London.'

*

Mr Satterthwaite was not quite pleased with himself. He felt that he had left this particular problem in an unfinished state. True that, on Lady Stranleigh's return, his responsibility was ended, yet he felt assured that he had not heard the last of the Abbot's Mede mystery.

But the next development when it came was so serious in its character that it found him totally unprepared. He learnt of it in the pages of his morning paper. 'Baroness Dies in her Bath,' as the *Daily Megaphone* had it. The other papers were more restrained and delicate in their language, but the fact was the same. Lady Stranleigh had been found dead in her bath and her death was due to drowning. She had, it was assumed, lost consciousness, and whilst in that state her head had slipped below the water.

But Mr Satterthwaite was not satisfied with that explanation. Calling for his valet he made his toilet with less than his usual care, and ten minutes later his big Rolls-Royce was carrying him out of London as fast as it could travel.

But strangely enough it was not for Abbot's Mede he was bound, but for a small inn some fifteen miles distant which bore the rather unusual name of the 'Bells and Motley'. It was with great relief that he heard that Mr Harley Quin was still staying there. In another minute he was face to face with his friend.

Mr Satterthwaite clasped him by the hand and began to speak at once in an agitated manner.

'I am terribly upset. You must help me. Already I have a dreadful feeling that it may be too late—that that nice girl may be the next to go, for she is a nice girl, nice through and through.'

'If you will tell me,' said Mr Quin, smiling, 'what it is all about?'

Mr Satterthwaite looked at him reproachfully.

'You know. I am perfectly certain that you know. But I will tell you.'

He poured out the story of his stay at Abbot's Mede and, as always with Mr Quin, he found himself taking pleasure in his narrative. He was eloquent and subtle and meticulous as to detail.

'So you see,' he ended, 'there must be an explanation.'

He looked hopefully at Mr Quin as a dog looks at his master.

'But it is you who must solve the problem, not I,' said Mr Quin. 'I do not know these people. You do.'

'I knew the Barron girls forty years ago,' said Mr Satterthwaite with pride.

Mr Quin nodded and looked sympathetic, so much so that the other went on dreamily.

'That time at Brighton now, Bottacetti-Boatsupsetty, quite a silly joke but how we laughed. Dear, dear, I was young then. Did a lot of foolish things. I remember the maid they had with them. Alice, her name was, a little bit of a thing—very ingenuous. I kissed her in the passage of the hotel, I remember, and one of the girls nearly caught me doing it. Dear, dear, how long ago that all was.'

He shook his head again and sighed. Then he looked at Mr Quin.

'So you can't help me?' he said wistfully. 'On other occasions—'

'On other occasions you have proved successful owing entirely to your own efforts,' said Mr Quin gravely. 'I think it will be the same this time. If I were you, I should go to Abbot's Mede now.'

'Quite so, quite so,' said Mr Satterthwaite, 'as a matter of fact that is what I thought of doing. I can't persuade you to come with me?'

Mr Quin shook his head.

'No,' he said, 'my work here is done. I am leaving almost immediately.'

At Abbot's Mede, Mr Satterthwaite was taken at once to Margery Gale. She was sitting dry-eyed at a desk in the morning-room on which were strewn various papers. Something in her greeting touched him. She seemed so very pleased to see him.

'Roley and Maria have just left. Mr Satterthwaite, it is not as the doctors think. I am convinced, absolutely convinced, that Mother was pushed under the water and held there. She was murdered, and whoever murdered her wants to murder me too. I am sure of that. That is why—' she indicated the document in front of her.

'I have been making my will,' she explained. 'A lot of the money and some of the property does not go with the title, and there is my father's money as well. I am leaving everything I can to Noel. I know he will make a good use of it and I do not trust Roley, he has always been out for what he can get. Will you sign it as a witness?'

'My dear young lady,' said Mr Satterthwaite, 'you should sign a will in the presence of two witnesses and they should then sign themselves at the same time.'

Margery brushed aside this legal pronouncement.

'I don't see that it matters in the least,' she declared. 'Clayton saw me sign and then she signed her name. I was going to ring for the butler, but you will do instead.'

Mr Satterthwaite uttered no fresh protest, he unscrewed his fountain pen and then, as he was about to append his signature, he paused suddenly. The name, written just above his own, recalled a flow of memories. Alice Clayton.

Something seemed to be struggling very hard to get through to him. Alice Clayton, there was some significance about that. Something to do with Mr Quin was mixed up with it. Something he had said to Mr Quin only a very short time ago.

Ah, he had it now. Alice Clayton, that was her name. *The little bit of a thing.* People changed—yes, *but not like that.* And the Alice Clayton he knew had had brown eyes. The room seemed whirling round him. He felt for a chair and presently, as though from a great distance, he heard Margery's voice speaking to him anxiously. 'Are you ill? Oh, what is it? I am sure you are ill.'

He was himself again. He took her hand.

'My dear, I see it all now. You must prepare yourself for a great shock. The woman upstairs whom you call Clayton is not Clayton at all. The real Alice Clayton was drowned on the "Uralia".'

Margery was staring at him. 'Who—who is she then?'

'I am not mistaken, I cannot be mistaken. The woman you call Clayton is your mother's sister, Beatrice Barron. You remember telling me that she was struck on the head by a spar? I should imagine that that blow destroyed her memory, and that being the case, your mother saw the chance—'

'Of pinching the title, you mean?' asked Margery bitterly. 'Yes, she would do that. It seems dreadful to say that now she is dead, but she was like that.'

'Beatrice was the elder sister,' said Mr Satterthwaite. 'By your uncle's death she would inherit everything and your mother would get nothing. Your mother claimed the wounded girl as her *maid*, not as her *sister*. The girl recovered from the blow and believed, of course, what was told her, that she was Alice Clayton, your mother's maid. I should imagine that just lately her memory had begun to return, but that the blow on the head, given all these years ago, has at last caused mischief on the brain.'

Margery was looking at him with eyes of horror.

'She killed Mother and she wanted to kill me,' she breathed.

'It seems so,' said Mr Satterthwaite. 'In her brain there was just one muddled idea—that her inheritance had been stolen and was being kept from her by you and your mother.'

'But—but Clayton is so old.'

Mr Satterthwaite was silent for a minute as a vision rose up before him—the faded old woman with grey hair, and the radiant golden-haired creature sitting in the sunshine at Cannes. Sisters! Could it really be so? He remembered

181

the Barron girls and their likeness to each other. Just because two lives had developed on different tracks—

He shook his head sharply, obsessed by the wonder and pity of life . . .

He turned to Margery and said gently: 'We had better go upstairs and see her.'

They found Clayton sitting in the little workroom where she sewed. She did not turn her head as they came in for a reason that Mr Satterthwaite soon found out.

'Heart failure,' he murmured, as he touched the cold rigid shoulder. 'Perhaps it is best that way.'

CHAPTER 8

The Face of Helen

Mr Satterthwaite was at the Opera and sat alone in his big box on the first tier. Outside the door was a printed card bearing his name. An appreciator and a connoisseur of all the arts, Mr Satterthwaite was especially fond of good music, and was a regular subscriber to Covent Garden every year, reserving a box for Tuesdays and Fridays throughout the season.

But it was not often that he sat in it alone. He was a gregarious little gentleman, and he liked filling his box with the élite of the great world to which he belonged, and also with the aristocracy of the artistic world in which he was equally at home. He was alone tonight because a Countess had disappointed him. The Countess, besides being a beautiful and celebrated woman, was also a good mother. Her children had been attacked by that common and distressing disease, the mumps, and the Countess remained at home in tearful confabulation with exquisitely starched nurses. Her husband, who had supplied her with the aforementioned children and a title, but who was otherwise a complete nonentity, had seized at the chance to escape. Nothing bored him more than music.

So Mr Satterthwaite sat alone. *Cavalleria Rusticana* and *Pagliacci* were being given that night, and since the first had never appealed to him, he arrived just after the curtain went down, on Santuzza's death agony, in time to glance round the house with practised eyes, before everyone streamed out, bent on paying visits or fighting for coffee or lemonade. Mr Satterthwaite adjusted his opera glasses, looked round the house, marked down his prey and sallied forth with a well mapped out plan of campaign ahead of him. A plan, however, which he did not put into execution, for just outside his box he cannoned into a tall dark man, and recognized him with a pleasurable thrill of excitement.

'Mr Quin,' cried Mr Satterthwaite.

He seized his friend warmly by the hand, clutching him as though he feared any minute to see him vanish into thin air.

'You must share my box,' said Mr Satterthwaite determinedly. 'You are not with a party?'

'No, I am sitting by myself in the stalls,' responded Mr Quin with a smile.

'Then, that is settled,' said Mr Satterthwaite with a sigh of relief.

His manner was almost comic, had there been anyone to observe it.

'You are very kind,' said Mr Quin.

'Not at all. It is a pleasure. I didn't know you were fond of music?'

'There are reasons why I am attracted to—*Pagliacci*.'

'Ah! of course,' said Mr Satterthwaite, nodding sapiently, though, if put to it, he would have found it hard to explain just why he had used that expression. 'Of course, you would be.'

They went back to the box at the first summons of the bell, and leaning over the front of it, they watched the people returning to the stalls.

'That's a beautiful head,' observed Mr Satterthwaite suddenly.

He indicated with his glasses a spot immediately beneath them in the stalls circle. A girl sat there whose face they could not see—only the pure gold of her hair that fitted with the closeness of a cap till it merged into the white neck.

'A Greek head,' said Mr Satterthwaite reverently. 'Pure Greek.' He sighed happily. 'It's a remarkable thing when you come to think of it—how very few people have hair that *fits* them. It's more noticeable now that everyone is shingled.'

'You are so observant,' said Mr Quin.

'I see things,' admitted Mr Satterthwaite. 'I do see things. For instance, I picked out that head at once. We must have a look at her face sooner or later. But it won't match, I'm sure. That would be a chance in a thousand.'

Almost as the words left his lips, the lights flickered and went down, the sharp rap of the conductor's baton was heard, and the opera began. A new tenor, said to be a second Caruso, was singing that night. He had been referred to by the newspapers as a Jugo Slav, a Czech, an Albanian, a Magyar, and a Bulgarian, with a beautiful

185

impartiality. He had given an extraordinary concert at the Albert Hall, a programme of the folk songs of his native hills, with a specially tuned orchestra. They were in strange half-tones and the would-be musical had pronounced them 'too marvellous'. Real musicians had reserved judgment, realizing that the ear had to be specially trained and attuned before any criticism was possible. It was quite a relief to some people to find this evening that Yoaschbim could sing in ordinary Italian with all the traditional sobs and quivers.

The curtain went down on the first act and applause burst out vociferously. Mr Satterthwaite turned to Mr Quin. He realized that the latter was waiting for him to pronounce judgment, and plumed himself a little. After all, he *knew*. As a critic he was well-nigh infallible.

Very slowly he nodded his head.

'It is the real thing,' he said.

'You think so?'

'As fine a voice as Caruso's. People will not recognize that it is so at first, for his technique is not yet perfect. There are ragged edges, a lack of certainty in the attack. But the voice is there—magnificent.'

'I went to his concert at the Albert Hall,' said Mr Quin.

'Did you? I could not go.'

'He made a wonderful hit with a Shepherd's Song.'

'I read about it,' said Mr Satterthwaite. 'The refrain ends each time with a high note—a kind of cry. A note midway between A and B flat. Very curious.'

Yoaschbim had taken three calls, bowing and smiling. The lights went up and the people began to file out. Mr

Satterthwaite leant over to watch the girl with the golden head. She rose, adjusted her scarf, and turned.

Mr Satterthwaite caught his breath. There were, he knew, such faces in the world—faces that made history.

The girl moved to the gangway, her companion, a young man, beside her. And Mr Satterthwaite noticed how every man in the vicinity looked—and continued to look covertly.

'Beauty!' said Mr Satterthwaite to himself. 'There is such a thing. Not charm, nor attraction, nor magnetism, nor any of the things we talk about so glibly—just sheer beauty. The shape of a face, the line of an eyebrow, the curve of a jaw. He quoted softly under his breath: '*The face that launched a thousand ships.*' And for the first time he realized the meaning of those words.

He glanced across at Mr Quin, who was watching him in what seemed such perfect comprehension that Mr Satterthwaite felt there was no need for words.

'I've always wondered,' he said simply, 'what such women were really like.'

'You mean?'

'The Helens, the Cleopatras, the Mary Stuarts.'

Mr Quin nodded thoughtfully.

'If we go out,' he suggested, 'we may—see.'

They went out together, and their quest was successful. The pair they were in search of were seated on a lounge half-way up the staircase. For the first time, Mr Satterthwaite noted the girl's companion, a dark young man, not handsome, but with a suggestion of restless fire about him. A face full of strange angles; jutting cheek-bones, a forceful, slightly crooked jaw, deep-set eyes that were curiously light under the dark, overhanging brows.

'An interesting face,' said Mr Satterthwaite to himself. 'A real face. It means something.'

The young man was leaning forward talking earnestly. The girl was listening. Neither of them belonged to Mr Satterthwaite's world. He took them to be of the 'Arty' class. The girl wore a rather shapeless garment of cheap green silk. Her shoes were of soiled, white satin. The young man wore his evening clothes with an air of being uncomfortable in them.

The two men passed and re-passed several times. The fourth time they did so, the couple had been joined by a third—a fair young man with a suggestion of the clerk about him. With his coming a certain tension had set in. The newcomer was fidgetting with his tie and seemed ill at ease, the girl's beautiful face was turned gravely up towards him, and her companion was scowling furiously.

'The usual story,' said Mr Quin very softly, as they passed.

'Yes,' said Mr Satterthwaite with a sigh. 'It's inevitable, I suppose. The snarling of two dogs over a bone. It always has been, it always will be. And yet, one could wish for something different. Beauty—' he stopped. Beauty, to Mr Satterthwaite, meant something very wonderful. He found it difficult to speak of it. He looked at Mr Quin, who nodded his head gravely in understanding.

They went back to their seats for the second act.

At the close of the performance, Mr Satterthwaite turned eagerly to his friend.

'It is a wet night. My car is here. You must allow me to drive you—er—somewhere.'

The last word was Mr Satterthwaite's delicacy coming into play. 'To drive you home' would, he felt, have savoured of curiosity. Mr Quin had always been singularly reticent. It was extraordinary how little Mr Satterthwaite knew about him.

'But perhaps,' continued the little man, 'you have your own car waiting?'

'No,' said Mr Quin, 'I have no car waiting.'

'Then—'

But Mr Quin shook his head.

'You are most kind,' he said, 'but I prefer to go my own way. Besides,' he said with a rather curious smile, 'if anything should—happen, it will be for you to act. Goodnight, and thank you. Once again we have seen the drama together.'

He had gone so quickly that Mr Satterthwaite had no time to protest, but he was left with a faint uneasiness stirring in his mind. To what drama did Mr Quin refer? *Pagliacci* or another?

Masters, Mr Satterthwaite's chauffeur, was in the habit of waiting in a side street. His master disliked the long delay while the cars drew up in turn before the Opera house. Now, as on previous occasions, he walked rapidly round the corner and along the street towards where he knew he should find Masters awaiting him. Just in front of him were a girl and a man, and even as he recognized them, another man joined them.

It all broke out in a minute. A man's voice, angrily

189

uplifted. Another man's voice in injured protest. And then the scuffle. Blows, angry breathing, more blows, the form of a policeman appearing majestically from nowhere—and in another minute Mr Satterthwaite was beside the girl where she shrank back against the wall.

'Allow me,' he said. 'You must not stay here.'

He took her by the arm and marshalled her swiftly down the street. Once she looked back.

'Oughtn't I—?' she began uncertainly.

Mr Satterthwaite shook his head.

'It would be very unpleasant for you to be mixed up in it. You would probably be asked to go along to the police station with them. I am sure neither of your—friends would wish that.'

He stopped.

'This is my car. If you will allow me to do so, I shall have much pleasure in driving you home.'

The girl looked at him searchingly. The staid respectability of Mr Satterthwaite impressed her favourably. She bent her head.

'Thank you,' she said, and got into the car, the door of which Masters was holding open.

In reply to a question from Mr Satterthwaite, she gave an address in Chelsea, and he got in beside her.

The girl was upset and not in the mood for talking, and Mr Satterthwaite was too tactful to intrude upon her thoughts. Presently, however, she turned to him and spoke of her own accord.

'I wish,' she said pettishly, 'people wouldn't be so silly.'

'It is a nuisance,' agreed Mr Satterthwaite.

His matter-of-fact manner put her at her ease, and she went on as though feeling the need of confiding in someone.

'It wasn't as though—I mean, well, it was like this. Mr Eastney and I have been friends for a long time—ever since I came to London. He's taken no end of trouble about my voice, and got me some very good introductions, and he's been more kind to me than I can say. He's absolutely music mad. It was very good of him to take me tonight. I'm sure he can't really afford it. And then Mr Burns came up and spoke to us—quite nicely, I'm sure, and Phil (Mr Eastney) got sulky about it. I don't know why he should. It's a free country, I'm sure. And Mr Burns is always pleasant, and good-tempered. Then just as we were walking to the Tube, he came up and joined us, and he hadn't so much as said two words before Philip flew out at him like a madman. And—Oh! I don't like it.'

'Don't you?' asked Mr Satterthwaite very softly.

She blushed, but very little. There was none of the conscious siren about her. A certain measure of pleasurable excitement in being fought for there must be—that was only nature, but Mr Satterthwaite decided that a worried perplexity lay uppermost, and he had the clue to it in another moment when she observed inconsequently:

'I do hope he hasn't hurt him.'

'Now which is "him"?' thought Mr Satterthwaite, smiling to himself in the darkness.

He backed his own judgment and said:

'You hope Mr—er—Eastney hasn't hurt Mr Burns?'

She nodded.

'Yes, that's what I said. It seems so dreadful. I wish I knew.'

The car was drawing up.

'Are you on the telephone?' he asked.

'Yes.'

'If you like, I will find out exactly what has happened, and then telephone to you.'

The girl's face brightened.

'Oh, that would be very kind of you. Are you sure it's not too much bother?'

'Not in the least.'

She thanked him again and gave him her telephone number, adding with a touch of shyness: 'My name is Gillian West.'

As he was driven through the night, bound on his errand, a curious smile came to Mr Satterthwaite's lips.

He thought: 'So that is all it is . . . "*The shape of a face, the curve of a jaw!*"'

But he fulfilled his promise.

The following Sunday afternoon Mr Satterthwaite went to Kew Gardens to admire the rhododendrons. Very long ago (incredibly long ago, it seemed to Mr Satterthwaite) he had driven down to Kew Gardens with a certain young lady to see the bluebells. Mr Satterthwaite had arranged very carefully beforehand in his own mind exactly what he was going to say, and the precise words he would use in asking the young lady for her hand in marriage. He was just conning them over in his mind, and responding to her raptures about the bluebells a little absent-mindedly, when the shock came. The young lady stopped exclaiming at the bluebells and suddenly confided in Mr Satterthwaite (as a true friend) her love for another. Mr Satterthwaite put away the little set speech he had prepared, and hastily rummaged for sympathy and friendship in the bottom drawer of his mind.

Such was Mr Satterthwaite's romance—a rather tepid early Victorian one, but it had left him with a romantic attachment to Kew Gardens, and he would often go there to see the bluebells, or, if he had been abroad later than usual, the rhododendrons, and would sigh to himself, and feel rather sentimental, and really enjoy himself very much indeed in an old-fashioned, romantic way.

This particular afternoon he was strolling back past the tea houses when he recognized a couple sitting at one of the small tables on the grass. They were Gillian West and the fair young man, and at that same moment they recognized him. He saw the girl flush and speak eagerly to her companion. In another minute he was shaking hands with them both in his correct, rather prim fashion, and had accepted the shy invitation proffered him to have tea with them.

'I can't tell you, sir,' said Mr Burns, 'how grateful I am to you for looking after Gillian the other night. She told me all about it.'

'Yes, indeed,' said the girl. 'It was ever so kind of you.'

Mr Satterthwaite felt pleased and interested in the pair. Their naïveté and sincerity touched him. Also, it was to him a peep into a world with which he was not well acquainted. These people were of a class unknown to him.

In his little dried-up way, Mr Satterthwaite could be very sympathetic. Very soon he was hearing all about his new friends. He noted that Mr Burns had become Charlie, and he was not unprepared for the statement that the two were engaged.

'As a matter of fact,' said Mr Burns with refreshing candour, 'it just happened this afternoon, didn't it, Gil?'

Burns was a clerk in a shipping firm. He was making a fair salary, had a little money of his own, and the two proposed to be married quite soon.

Mr Satterthwaite listened, and nodded, and congratulated.

'An ordinary young man,' he thought to himself, 'a very ordinary young man. Nice, straightforward young chap, plenty to say for himself, good opinion of himself without being conceited, nice-looking without being unduly handsome. Nothing remarkable about him and will never set the Thames on fire. And the girl loves him . . .'

Aloud he said: 'And Mr Eastney—'

He purposely broke off, but he had said enough to produce an effect for which he was not unprepared. Charlie Burns's face darkened, and Gillian looked troubled. More than troubled, he thought. She looked afraid.

'I don't like it,' she said in a low voice. Her words were addressed to Mr Satterthwaite, as though she knew by instinct that he would understand a feeling incomprehensible to her lover. 'You see—he's done a lot for me. He's encouraged me to take up singing, and—and helped me with it. But I've known all the time that my voice wasn't really good—not first-class. Of course, I've had engagements—'

She stopped.

'You've had a bit of trouble too,' said Burns. 'A girl wants someone to look after her. Gillian's had a lot of unpleasantness, Mr Satterthwaite. Altogether she's had a lot of unpleasantness. She's a good-looker, as you can see, and—well, that often leads to trouble for a girl.'

Between them, Mr Satterthwaite became enlightened as to various happenings which were vaguely classed by Burns under the heading of 'unpleasantness'. A young man who had shot himself, the extraordinary conduct of a Bank Manager (who was a married man!), a violent stranger (who must have been balmy!), the wild behaviour of an elderly artist. A trail of violence and tragedy that Gillian West had left in her wake, recited in the commonplace tones of Charles Burns. 'And it's my opinion,' he ended, 'that this fellow Eastney is a bit cracked. Gillian would have had trouble with him if I hadn't turned up to look after her.'

His laugh sounded a little fatuous to Mr Satterthwaite, and no responsive smile came to the girl's face. She was looking earnestly at Mr Satterthwaite.

'Phil's all right,' she said slowly. 'He cares for me, I know, and I care for him like a friend—but—but not anything more. I don't know how he'll take the news about Charlie, I'm sure. He—I'm so afraid he'll be—'

She stopped, inarticulate in face of the dangers she vaguely sensed.

'If I can help you in any way,' said Mr Satterthwaite warmly, 'pray command me.'

He fancied Charlie Burns looked vaguely resentful, but Gillian said at once: 'Thank you.'

Mr Satterthwaite left his new friends after having promised to take tea with Gillian on the following Thursday.

When Thursday came, Mr Satterthwaite felt a little thrill of pleasurable anticipation. He thought: 'I'm an old man—but not too old to be thrilled by a face. A face . . .' Then he shook his head with a sense of foreboding.

Gillian was alone. Charlie Burns was to come in later. She looked much happier, Mr Satterthwaite thought, as though a load had been lifted from her mind. Indeed, she frankly admitted as much.

'I dreaded telling Phil about Charles. It was silly of me. I ought to have known Phil better. He was upset, of course, but no one could have been sweeter. Really sweet he was. Look what he sent me this morning—a wedding present. Isn't it magnificent?'

It was indeed rather magnificent for a young man in Philip Eastney's circumstances. A four-valve wireless set, of the latest type.

'We both love music so much, you see,' explained the girl. 'Phil said that when I was listening to a concert on this, I should always think of him a little. And I'm sure I shall. Because we have been such friends.'

'You must be proud of your friend,' said Mr Satterthwaite gently. 'He seems to have taken the blow like a true sportsman.'

Gillian nodded. He saw the quick tears come into her eyes.

'He asked me to do one thing for him. Tonight is the anniversary of the day we first met. He asked me if I would stay at home quietly this evening and listen to the wireless programme—not to go out with Charlie anywhere. I said, of course I would, and that I was very touched, and that I would think of him with a lot of gratitude and affection.'

Mr Satterthwaite nodded, but he was puzzled. He was seldom at fault in his delineation of character, and he would have judged Philip Eastney quite incapable of such a sentimental request. The young man must be of a more banal order than he supposed. Gillian evidently thought the idea quite in keeping with her rejected lover's character. Mr Satterthwaite was a little—just a little—disappointed. He was sentimental himself, and knew it, but he expected better things of the rest of the world. Besides sentiment belonged to his age. It had no part to play in the modern world.

He asked Gillian to sing and she complied. He told her her voice was charming, but he knew quite well in his own mind that it was distinctly second-class. Any success that could have come to her in the profession she had adopted would have been won by her face, not her voice.

He was not particularly anxious to see young Burns again, so presently he rose to go. It was at that moment that his attention was attracted by an ornament on the mantelpiece which stood out among the other rather gimcrack objects like a jewel on a dust heap.

It was a curving beaker of thin green glass, long-stemmed and graceful, and poised on the edge of it was what looked like a gigantic soap-bubble, a ball of iridescent glass. Gillian noticed his absorption.

'That's an extra wedding present from Phil. It's rather pretty, I think. He works in a sort of glass factory.'

'It is a beautiful thing,' said Mr Satterthwaite reverently. 'The glass blowers of Murano might have been proud of that.'

He went away with his interest in Philip Eastney strangely stimulated. An extraordinarily interesting young man. And yet the girl with the wonderful face preferred Charlie Burns. What a strange and inscrutable universe!

It had just occurred to Mr Satterthwaite that, owing to the remarkable beauty of Gillian West, his evening with Mr Quin had somehow missed fire. As a rule, every meeting with that mysterious individual had resulted in some strange and unforeseen happening. It was with the hope of perhaps running against the man of mystery that Mr Satterthwaite bent his steps towards the *Arlecchino* Restaurant where once, in the days gone by, he had met Mr Quin, and which Mr Quin had said he often frequented.

Mr Satterthwaite went from room to room at the *Arlecchino*, looking hopefully about him, but there was no sign of Mr Quin's dark, smiling face. There was, however, somebody else. Sitting at a small table alone was Philip Eastney.

The place was crowded and Mr Satterthwaite took his seat opposite the young man. He felt a sudden strange sense of exultation, as though he were caught up and made part of a shimmering pattern of events. He was in this thing—whatever it was. He knew now what Mr Quin had meant that evening at the Opera. There was a drama going on, and in it was a part, an important part, for Mr

Satterthwaite. He must not fail to take his cue and speak his lines.

He sat down opposite Philip Eastney with the sense of accomplishing the inevitable. It was easy enough to get into conversation. Eastney seemed anxious to talk. Mr Satterthwaite was, as always, an encouraging and sympathetic listener. They talked of the war, of explosives, of poison gases. Eastney had a lot to say about these last, for during the greater part of the war he had been engaged in their manufacture. Mr Satterthwaite found him really interesting.

There was one gas, Eastney said, that had never been tried. The Armistice had come too soon. Great things had been hoped for it. One whiff of it was deadly. He warmed to animation as he spoke.

Having broken the ice, Mr Satterthwaite gently turned the conversation to music. Eastney's thin face lit up. He spoke with the passion and abandon of the real music lover. They discussed Yoaschbim, and the young man was enthusiastic. Both he and Mr Satterthwaite agreed that nothing on earth could surpass a really fine tenor voice. Eastney as a boy had heard Caruso and he had never forgotten it.

'Do you know that he could sing to a wine-glass and shatter it?' he demanded.

'I always thought that was a fable,' said Mr Satterthwaite smiling.

'No, it's gospel truth, I believe. The thing's quite possible. It's a question of resonance.'

He went off into technical details. His face was flushed and his eyes shone. The subject seemed to fascinate him, and Mr Satterthwaite noted that he seemed to have a thorough grasp of what he was talking about. The elder man realized that he was talking to an exceptional brain, a brain that might almost be described as that of a genius. Brilliant, erratic, undecided as yet as to the true channel to give it outlet, but undoubtedly genius.

And he thought of Charlie Burns and wondered at Gillian West.

It was with quite a start that he realized how late it was getting, and he called for his bill. Eastney looked slightly apologetic.

'I'm ashamed of myself—running on so,' he said. 'But it was a lucky chance sent you along here tonight. I—I needed someone to talk to this evening.'

He ended his speech with a curious little laugh. His eyes were still blazing with some subdued excitement. Yet there was something tragic about him.

'It has been quite a pleasure,' said Mr Satterthwaite. 'Our conversation has been most interesting and instructive to me.'

He then made his funny, courteous little bow and passed out of the restaurant. The night was a warm one and as he walked slowly down the street a very odd fancy came to him. He had the feeling that he was not alone—that someone was walking by his side. In vain he told himself that the idea was a delusion—it persisted. Someone was walking beside him down that dark, quiet street, someone whom he could not see. He wondered what it was that brought the figure of Mr Quin so clearly before his mind. He felt exactly as though Mr Quin were there walking beside him, and yet he had only to use his eyes to assure himself that it was not so, that he was alone.

But the thought of Mr Quin persisted, and with it came something else: a need, an urgency of some kind, an oppressive foreboding of calamity. There was something he must do—and do quickly. There was something very wrong, and it lay in his hands to put it right.

So strong was the feeling that Mr Satterthwaite forebore to fight against it. Instead, he shut his eyes and tried to bring that mental image of Mr Quin nearer. If he could only have asked Mr Quin—but even as the thought flashed through his mind he knew it was wrong. It was never any use asking Mr Quin anything. 'The threads are all in your hands'—that was the kind of thing Mr Quin would say.

The threads. Threads of what? He analysed his own feeling and impressions carefully. That presentiment of danger, now. Whom did it threaten?

At once a picture rose up before his eyes, the picture of Gillian West sitting alone listening to the wireless.

Mr Satterthwaite flung a penny to a passing newspaper boy, and snatched at a paper. He turned at once to the London Radio programme. Yoaschbim was broadcasting tonight, he noted with interest. He was singing 'Salve Dimora', from *Faust* and, afterwards, a selection of his folk songs. 'The Shepherd's Song', 'The Fish', 'The Little Deer', etc.

Mr Satterthwaite crumpled the paper together. The knowledge of what Gillian was listening to seemed to make the picture of her clearer. Sitting there alone . . .

An odd request, that, of Philip Eastney's. Not like the man, not like him at all. There was no sentimentality in Eastney. He was a man of violent feeling, a dangerous man, perhaps—

Again his thought brought up with a jerk. *A dangerous man*—that meant something. '*The threads are all in your hands.*' That meeting with Philip Eastney tonight—rather odd. A lucky chance, Eastney had said. Was it chance? Or was it part of that interwoven design of which Mr Satterthwaite had once or twice been conscious this evening?

He cast his mind back. There must be *something* in Eastney's conversation, some clue there. There must, or else why this strange feeling of urgency? What had he talked about? Singing, war work, Caruso.

Caruso—Mr Satterthwaite's thoughts went off at a tangent. Yoaschbim's voice was very nearly equal to that of Caruso. Gillian would be sitting listening to it now as it rang out true and powerful, echoing round the room, setting glasses ringing—

He caught his breath. Glasses ringing! Caruso, singing to a wine-glass and the wine-glass breaking. Yoachbim singing in the London studio and in a room over a mile away the crash and tinkle of glass—not a wine-glass, a thin, green, glass beaker. A crystal soap bubble falling, a soap bubble that perhaps was not empty . . .

It was at that moment that Mr Satterthwaite, as judged by passers-by, suddenly went mad. He tore open the newspaper once more, took a brief glance at the wireless announcements and then began to run for his life down the quiet street. At the end of it he found a crawling taxi, and jumping into it, he yelled an address to the driver and the information that it was life or death to get there quickly. The driver, judging him mentally afflicted but rich, did his utmost.

Mr Satterthwaite lay back, his head a jumble of fragmentary thoughts, forgotten bits of science learned at school, phrases used by Eastney that night. Resonance—natural periods—if the period of the force coincides with the natural period—there was something about a suspension bridge, soldiers marching over it and the swing of their stride being the same as the period of the bridge. Eastney had studied the subject. Eastney knew. And Eastney was a genius.

At 10.45 Yoaschbim was to broadcast. It was that now. Yes, but the *Faust* had to come first. It was the 'Shepherd's Song', with the great shout after the refrain that would—that would—do what?

His mind went whirling round again. Tones, overtones, half-tones. He didn't know much about these things—but Eastney knew. Pray heaven he would be in time!

The taxi stopped. Mr Satterthwaite flung himself out and raced up the stone stairs to a second floor like a young athlete. The door of the flat was ajar. He pushed it open and the great tenor voice welcomed him. The words of the 'Shepherd's Song' were familiar to him in a less unconventional setting.

'Shepherd, see they horse's flowing main—'

He was in time then. He burst open the sitting-room door. Gillian was sitting there in a tall chair by the fireplace.

'*Bayra Mischa's daughter is to wed today:
To the wedding I must haste away.*'

She must have thought him mad. He clutched at her, crying out something incomprehensible, and half pulled, half dragged her out till they stood upon the stairway.

'*To the wedding I must haste away—
Ya-ha!*'

A wonderful high note, full-throated, powerful, hit full in the middle, a note any singer might be proud of. And with it another sound, the faint tinkle of broken glass.

A stray cat darted past them and in through the flat door. Gillian made a movement, but Mr Satterthwaite held her back, speaking incoherently.

'No, no—it's deadly: no smell, nothing to warn you. A mere whiff, and it's all over. Nobody knows quite how deadly it would be. It's unlike anything that's ever been tried before.'

He was repeating the things that Philip Eastney had told him over the table at dinner.

Gillian stared at him uncomprehendingly.

Philip Eastney drew out his watch and looked at it. It was just half-past eleven. For the past three-quarters of an hour he had been pacing up and down the Embankment.

He looked out over the Thames and then turned—to look into the face of his dinner companion.

'That's odd,' he said, and laughed. 'We seem fated to run into each other tonight.'

'If you call it Fate,' said Mr Satterthwaite.

Philip Eastney looked at him more attentively and his own expression changed.

'Yes?' he said quietly.

Mr Satterthwaite went straight to the point.

'I have just come from Miss West's flat.'

'Yes?'

The same voice, with the same deadly quiet.

'We have—taken a dead cat out of it.'

There was silence, then Eastney said:

'Who are you?'

Mr Satterthwaite spoke for some time. He recited the whole history of events.

'So you see, I was in time,' he ended up. He paused and added quite gently:

'Have you anything—to say?'

He expected something, some outburst, some wild justification. But nothing came.

'No,' said Philip Eastney quietly, and turned on his heel and walked away.

Mr Satterthwaite looked after him till his figure was swallowed up in the gloom. In spite of himself, he had a strange fellow-feeling for Eastney, the feeling of an artist for another artist, of a sentimentalist for a real lover, of a plain man for a genius.

At last he roused himself with a start and began to walk

in the same direction as Eastney. A fog was beginning to come up. Presently he met a policeman who looked at him suspiciously.

'Did you hear a kind of splash just now?' asked the policeman.

'No,' said Mr Satterthwaite.

The policeman was peering out over the river.

'Another of these suicides, I expect,' he grunted disconsolately. 'They will do it.'

'I suppose,' said Mr Satterthwaite, 'that they have their reasons.'

'Money, mostly,' said the policeman. 'Sometimes it's a woman,' he said, as he prepared to move away. 'It's not always their fault, but some women cause a lot of trouble.'

'Some women,' agreed Mr Satterthwaite softly.

When the policeman had gone on, he sat down on a seat with the fog coming up all around him, and thought about Helen of Troy, and wondered if she were a nice, ordinary woman, blessed or cursed with a wonderful face.

CHAPTER 9

The Dead Harlequin

Mr Satterthwaite walked slowly up Bond Street enjoying the sunshine. He was, as usual, carefully and beautifully dressed, and was bound for the Harchester Galleries where there was an exhibition of the paintings of one Frank Bristow, a new and hitherto unknown artist who showed signs of suddenly becoming the rage. Mr Satterthwaite was a patron of the arts.

As Mr Satterthwaite entered the Harchester Galleries, he was greeted at once with a smile of pleased recognition.

'Good morning, Mr Satterthwaite, I thought we should see you before long. You know Bristow's work? Fine—very fine indeed. Quite unique of its kind.'

Mr Satterthwaite purchased a catalogue and stepped through the open archway into the long room where the artist's works were displayed. They were water colours, executed with such extraordinary technique and finish that they resembled coloured etchings. Mr Satterthwaite walked slowly round the walls scrutinizing and, on the whole, approving. He thought that this young man deserved to arrive. Here was originality, vision, and a most severe and exacting technique. There were crudities, of course. That was only to be expected—but there was also something closely allied to genius. Mr Satterthwaite paused before a little masterpiece representing Westminster Bridge with its crowd of buses, trams and hurrying pedestrians. A tiny thing and wonderfully perfect. It was called, he noted, The Ant Heap. He passed on and quite suddenly drew in his breath with a gasp, his imagination held and riveted.

The picture was called The Dead Harlequin. The forefront of it represented a floor of inlaid squares of black and white marble. In the middle of the floor lay Harlequin on his back with his arms outstretched, in his motley of black and red. Behind him was a window and outside that window, gazing in at the figure on the floor, was what appeared to be the same man silhouetted against the red glow of the setting sun.

The picture excited Mr Satterthwaite for two reasons, the first was that he recognized, or thought that he recognized, the face of the man in the picture. It bore a distinct resemblance to a certain Mr Quin, an acquaintance whom Mr Satterthwaite had encountered once or twice under somewhat mystifying circumstances.

'Surely I can't be mistaken,' he murmured. 'If it *is* so— what does it mean?'

For it had been Mr Satterthwaite's experience that every appearance of Mr Quin had some distinct significance attaching to it.

There was, as already mentioned, a second reason for Mr Satterthwaite's interest. He recognized the scene of the picture.

'The Terrace Room at Charnley,' said Mr Satterthwaite, 'curious—and very interesting.'

He looked with more attention at the picture, wondering what exactly had been in the artist's mind. One Harlequin dead on the floor, another Harlequin looking through the window—or was it the same Harlequin? He moved slowly along the walls gazing at other pictures with unseeing eyes, with his mind always busy on the same subject. He was excited. Life, which had seemed a little drab this morning, was drab no longer. He knew quite certainly that he was on the threshold of exciting and interesting events. He crossed to the table where sat Mr Cobb, a dignitary of the Harchester Galleries, whom he had known for many years.

'I have a fancy for buying No 39,' he said, 'if it is not already sold.'

Mr Cobb consulted a ledger.

'The pick of the bunch,' he murmured, 'quite a little gem, isn't it? No, it is not sold.' He quoted a price. 'It is a good investment, Mr Satterthwaite. You will have to pay three times as much for it this time next year.'

'That is always said on these occasions,' said Mr Satterthwaite, smiling.

'Well, and haven't I been right?' demanded Mr Cobb. 'I don't believe if you were to sell your collection, Mr Satterthwaite, that a single picture would fetch less than you gave for it.'

'I will buy this picture,' said Mr Satterthwaite. 'I will give you a cheque now.'

'You won't regret it. We believe in Bristow.'

'He is a young man?'

'Twenty-seven or -eight, I should say.'

'I should like to meet him,' said Mr Satterthwaite. 'Perhaps he will come and dine with me one night?'

'I can give you his address. I am sure he would leap at the chance. Your name stands for a good deal in the artistic world.'

'You flatter me,' said Mr Satterthwaite, and was going on when Mr Cobb interrupted:

'Here he is now. I will introduce you to him right away.'

He rose from behind his table. Mr Satterthwaite accompanied him to where a big, clumsy young man was leaning against the wall surveying the world at large from behind the barricade of a ferocious scowl.

Mr Cobb made the necessary introductions and Mr Satterthwaite made a formal and gracious little speech.

'I have just had the pleasure of acquiring one of your pictures—The Dead Harlequin.'

'Oh! Well, you won't lose by it,' said Mr Bristow ungraciously. 'It's a bit of damned good work, although I say it.'

'I can see that,' said Mr Satterthwaite. 'Your work interests me very much, Mr Bristow. It is extraordinarily mature for so young a man. I wonder if you would give me the pleasure of dining with me one night? Are you engaged this evening?'

'As a matter of fact, I am not,' said Mr Bristow, still with no overdone appearance of graciousness.

'Then shall we say eight o'clock?' said Mr Satterthwaite. 'Here is my card with the address on it.'

'Oh, all right,' said Mr Bristow. 'Thanks,' he added as a somewhat obvious afterthought.

'A young man who has a poor opinion of himself and is afraid that the world should share it.'

Such was Mr Satterthwaite's summing up as he stepped out into the sunshine of Bond Street, and Mr Satterthwaite's judgment of his fellow men was seldom far astray.

Frank Bristow arrived about five minutes past eight to find his host and a third guest awaiting him. The other guest was introduced as a Colonel Monckton. They went in to dinner almost immediately. There was a fourth place laid at the oval mahogany table and Mr Satterthwaite uttered a word of explanation.

'I half expected my friend, Mr Quin, might drop in,' he said. 'I wonder if you have ever met him. Mr Harley Quin?'

'I never meet people,' growled Bristow.

Colonel Monckton stared at the artist with the detached interest he might have accorded to a new species of jelly fish. Mr Satterthwaite exerted himself to keep the ball of conversation rolling amicably.

'I took a special interest in that picture of yours because I thought I recognized the scene of it as being the Terrace Room at Charnley. Was I right?' As the artist nodded, he went on. 'That is very interesting. I have stayed at Charnley several times myself in the past. Perhaps you know some of the family?'

'No, I don't!' said Bristow. 'That sort of family wouldn't care to know me. I went there in a charabanc.'

'Dear me,' said Colonel Monckton for the sake of saying something. 'In a charabanc! Dear me.'

Frank Bristow scowled at him.

'Why not?' he demanded ferociously.

Poor Colonel Monckton was taken aback. He looked reproachfully at Mr Satterthwaite as though to say:

'These primitive forms of life may be interesting to you as a naturalist, but why drag *me* in?'

'Oh, beastly things, charabancs!' he said. 'They jolt you so going over the bumps.'

'If you can't afford a Rolls Royce you have got to go in charabancs,' said Bristow fiercely.

Colonel Monckton stared at him. Mr Satterthwaite thought:

'Unless I can manage to put this young man at his ease we are going to have a very distressing evening.'

'Charnley aways fascinated me,' he said. 'I have been there only once since the tragedy. A grim house—and a ghostly one.'

'That's true,' said Bristow.

'There are actually two authentic ghosts,' said Monckton. 'They say that Charles I walks up and down the terrace with his head under his arm—I have forgotten why, I'm sure. Then there is the Weeping Lady with the Silver Ewer, who is always seen after one of the Charnleys dies.'

'Tosh,' said Bristow scornfully.

'They have certainly been a very ill-fated family,' said Mr Satterthwaite hurriedly. 'Four holders of the title have died a violent death and the late Lord Charnley committed suicide.'

'A ghastly business,' said Monckton gravely. 'I was there when it happened.'

'Let me see, that must be fourteen years ago,' said Mr Satterthwaite, 'the house has been shut up ever since.'

'I don't wonder at that,' said Monckton. 'It must have been a terrible shock for a young girl. They had been married a month, just home from their honeymoon. Big fancy dress ball to celebrate their home-coming. Just as the guests were starting to arrive Charnley locked himself into the Oak Parlour and shot himself. That sort of thing isn't done. I beg your pardon?'

He turned his head sharply to the left and looked across at Mr Satterthwaite with an apologetic laugh.

'I am beginning to get the jimjams, Satterthwaite. I thought for a moment there was someone sitting in that empty chair and that he said something to me.

'Yes,' he went on after a minute or two, 'it was a pretty ghastly shock to Alix Charnley. She was one of the prettiest girls you could see anywhere and cram full of what people call the joy of living, and now they say she is like a ghost herself. Not that I have seen her for years. I believe she lives abroad most of the time.'

'And the boy?'

'The boy is at Eton. What he will do when he comes of age I don't know. I don't think, somehow, that he will reopen the old place.'

'It would make a good People's Pleasure Park,' said Bristow.

Colonel Monckton looked at him with cold abhorrence.

'No, no, you don't really mean that,' said Mr Satterthwaite. 'You wouldn't have painted that picture if you did. Tradition and atmosphere are intangible things. They take centuries

213

to build up and if you destroyed them you couldn't rebuild them again in twenty-four hours.'

He rose. 'Let us go into the smoking-room. I have some photographs there of Charnley which I should like to show you.'

One of Mr Satterthwaite's hobbies was amateur photography. He was also the proud author of a book, *Homes of My Friends*. The friends in question were all rather exalted and the book itself showed Mr Satterthwaite forth in rather a more snobbish light than was really fair to him.

'That is a photograph I took of the Terrace Room last year,' he said. He handed it to Bristow. 'You see it is taken at almost the same angle as is shown in your picture. That is rather a wonderful rug—it is a pity that photographs can't show colouring.'

'I remember it,' said Bristow, 'a marvellous bit of colour. It glowed like a flame. All the same it looked a bit incongruous there. The wrong size for that big room with its black and white squares. There is no rug anywhere else in the room. It spoils the whole effect—it was like a gigantic blood stain.'

'Perhaps that gave you your idea for your picture?' said Mr Satterthwaite.

'Perhaps it did,' said Bristow thoughtfully. 'On the face of it, one would naturally stage a tragedy in the little panelled room leading out of it.'

'The Oak Parlour,' said Monckton. 'Yes, that is the haunted room right enough. There is a Priests' hiding hole there—a movable panel by the fireplace. Tradition has it that Charles

I was concealed there once. There were two deaths from duelling in that room. And it was there, as I say, that Reggie Charnley shot himself.'

He took the photograph from Bristow's hand.

'Why, that is the Bokhara rug,' he said, 'worth a couple of thousand pounds, I believe. When I was there it was in the Oak Parlour—the right place for it. It looks silly on that great expanse of marble flags.'

Mr Satterthwaite was looking at the empty chair which he had drawn up beside his. Then he said thoughtfully: 'I wonder when it was moved?'

'It must have been recently. Why, I remember having a conversation about it on the very day of the tragedy. Charnley was saying it really ought to be kept under glass.'

Mr Satterthwaite shook his head. 'The house was shut up immediately after the tragedy and everything was left exactly as it was.'

Bristow broke in with a question. He had laid aside his aggressive manner.

'Why did Lord Charnley shoot himself?' he asked.

Colonel Monckton shifted uncomfortably in his chair.

'No one ever knew,' he said vaguely.

'I suppose,' said Mr Satterthwaite slowly, 'that it *was* suicide.'

The Colonel looked at him in blank astonishment.

'Suicide,' he said, 'why, of course it was suicide. My dear fellow, I was there in the house myself.'

Mr Satterthwaite looked towards the empty chair at his side and, smiling to himself as though at some hidden joke the others could not see, he said quietly:

'Sometimes one sees things more clearly years afterwards than one could possibly at the time.'

'Nonsense,' spluttered Monckton, 'arrant nonsense! How can you possibly see things better when they are vague in your memory instead of clear and sharp?'

But Mr Satterthwaite was reinforced from an unexpected quarter.

'I know what you mean,' said the artist. 'I should say that possibly you were right. It is a question of proportion, isn't it? And more than proportion probably. Relativity and all that sort of thing.'

'If you ask me,' said the Colonel, 'all this Einstein business is a lot of dashed nonsense. So are spiritualists and the spook of one's grandmother!' He glared round fiercely.

'Of course it was suicide,' he went on. 'Didn't I practically see the thing happen with my own eyes?'

'Tell us about it,' said Mr Satterthwaite, 'so that we shall see it with our eyes also.'

With a somewhat mollified grunt the Colonel settled himself more comfortably in his chair.

'The whole thing was extraordinarily unexpected,' he began. 'Charnley had been his usual normal self. There was a big party staying in the house for this ball. No one could ever have guessed he would go and shoot himself just as the guests began arriving.'

'It would have been better taste if he had waited until they had gone,' said Mr Satterthwaite.

'Of course it would. Damned bad taste—to do a thing like that.'

'Uncharacteristic,' said Mr Satterthwaite.

'Yes,' admitted Monckton, 'it wasn't like Charnley.'

'And yet it *was* suicide?'

'Of course it was suicide. Why, there were three or four of us there at the top of the stairs. Myself, the Ostrander girl, Algie Darcy—oh, and one or two others. Charnley passed along the hall below and went into the Oak Parlour. The Ostrander girl said there was a ghastly look on his face and his eyes were staring—but, of course, that is nonsense—she couldn't even see his face from where we were—but he did walk in a hunched way, as if he had the weight of the world on his shoulders. One of the girls called to him—she was somebody's governess, I think, whom Lady Charnley had included in the party out of kindness. She was looking for him with a message. She called out "Lord Charnley, Lady Charnley wants to know—" He paid no attention and went into the Oak Parlour and slammed the door and we heard the key turn in the lock. Then, one minute after, *we heard the shot.*

'We rushed down to the hall. There is another door from the Oak Parlour leading into the Terrace Room. We tried that but it was locked, too. In the end we had to break the door down. Charnley was lying on the floor—dead—with a pistol close beside his right hand. Now, what could that have been but suicide? Accident? Don't tell me. There is only one other possibility—murder—and you can't have murder without a murderer. You admit that, I suppose.'

'The murderer might have escaped,' suggested Mr Satterthwaite.

'That is impossible. If you have a bit of paper and a pencil I will draw you a plan of the place. There are two doors into the Oak Parlour, one into the hall and one into the Terrace Room. Both these doors were locked in the inside *and the keys were in the locks.*'

'The window?'

'Shut, and the shutters fastened across it.'

There was a pause.

'So that is that,' said Colonel Monckton triumphantly.

'It certainly seems to be,' said Mr Satterthwaite sadly.

'Mind you,' said the Colonel, 'although I was laughing just now at the spiritualists, I don't mind admitting that there was a deuced rummy atmosphere about the place— about that room in particular. There are several bullet holes in the panels of the walls, the results of the duels that took place in that room, and there is a queer stain on the floor, that always comes back though they have replaced the wood several times. I suppose there will be another blood stain on the floor now—poor Charnley's blood.'

'Was there much blood?' asked Mr Satterthwaite.

'Very little—curiously little—so the doctor said.'

'Where did he shoot himself, through the head?'

'No, through the heart.'

'That is not the easy way to do it,' said Bristow. 'Frightfully difficult to know where one's heart is. I should never do it that way myself.'

Mr Satterthwaite shook his head. He was vaguely dissatisfied. He had hoped to get at something—he hardly knew what. Colonel Monckton went on.

'It is a spooky place, Charnley. Of course, *I* didn't see anything.'

'You didn't see the Weeping Lady with the Silver Ewer?'

'No, I did not, sir,' said the Colonel emphatically. 'But I expect every servant in the place swore they did.'

'Superstition was the curse of the Middle Ages,' said Bristow. 'There are still traces of it here and there, but thank goodness, we are getting free from it.'

'Superstition,' mused Mr Satterthwaite, his eyes turned again to the empty chair. 'Sometimes, don't you think—it might be useful?'

Bristow stared at him.

'Useful, that's a queer word.'

'Well, I hope you are convinced now, Satterthwaite,' said the Colonel.

'Oh, quite,' said Mr Satterthwaite. 'On the face of it, it seems odd—so purposeless for a newly-married man, young, rich, happy, celebrating his home-coming—curious—but I agree there is no getting away from the facts.' He repeated softly, 'The facts,' and frowned.

'I suppose the interesting thing is a thing we none of us will ever know,' said Monckton, 'the story behind it all. Of course there were rumours—all sorts of rumours. You know the kind of things people say.'

'But no one *knew* anything,' said Mr Satterthwaite thoughtfully.

'It's not a best seller mystery, is it?' remarked Bristow. 'No one gained by the man's death.'

'No one except an unborn child,' said Mr Satterthwaite.

Monckton gave a sharp chuckle. 'Rather a blow to poor

Hugo Charnley,' he observed. 'As soon as it was known that there was going to be a child he had the graceful task of sitting tight and waiting to see if it would be a girl or boy. Rather an anxious wait for his creditors, too. In the end a boy it was and a disappointment for the lot of them.'

'Was the widow very disconsolate?' asked Bristow.

'Poor child,' said Monckton, 'I shall never forget her. She didn't cry or break down or anything. She was like something—frozen. As I say, she shut up the house shortly afterwards and, as far as I know, it has never been reopened since.'

'So we are left in the dark as to motive,' said Bristow with a slight laugh. 'Another man or another woman, it must have been one or the other, eh?'

'It seems like it,' said Mr Satterthwaite.

'And the betting is strongly on another woman,' continued Bristow, 'since the fair widow has not married again. I hate women,' he added dispassionately.

Mr Satterthwaite smiled a little and Frank Bristow saw the smile and pounced upon it.

'You may smile,' he said, 'but I do. They upset everything. They interfere. They get between you and your work. They—I only once met a woman who was—well, interesting.'

'I thought there would be one,' said Mr Satterthwaite.

'Not in the way you mean. I—I just met her casually. As a matter of fact—it was in a train. After all,' he added defiantly, 'why shouldn't one meet people in trains?'

'Certainly, certainly,' said Mr Satterthwaite soothingly, 'a train is as good a place as anywhere else.'

'It was coming down from the North. We had the carriage to ourselves. I don't know why, but we began to talk. I don't know her name and I don't suppose I shall ever meet her again. I don't know that I want to. It might be—a pity.' He paused, struggling to express himself. 'She wasn't quite real, you know. Shadowy. Like one of the people who come out of the hills in Gaelic fairy tales.'

Mr Satterthwaite nodded gently. His imagination pictured the scene easily enough. The very positive and realistic Bristow and a figure that was silvery and ghostly— shadowy, as Bristow had said.

'I suppose if something very terrible had happened, so terrible as to be almost unbearable, one might get like that. One might run away from reality into a half world of one's own and then, of course, after a time, one wouldn't be able to get back.'

'Was that what had happened to her?' asked Mr Satterthwaite curiously.

'I don't know,' said Bristow. 'She didn't tell me anything, I am only guessing. One has to guess if one is going to get anywhere.'

'Yes,' said Mr Satterthwaite slowly. 'One has to guess.'

He looked up as the door opened. He looked up quickly and expectantly but the butler's words disappointed him.

'A lady, sir, has called to see you on very urgent business. Miss Aspasia Glen.'

Mr Satterthwaite rose in some astonishment. He knew the name of Aspasia Glen. Who in London did not? First advertised as the Woman with the Scarf, she had given a series of matinées single-handed that had taken London by storm. With the aid of her scarf she had impersonated rapidly various characters. In turn the scarf had been the coif of a nun, the shawl of a mill-worker, the head-dress of a peasant and a hundred other things, and in each impersonation Aspasia Glen had been totally and utterly different. As an artist, Mr Satterthwaite paid full reverence to her. As it happened, he had never made her acquaintance. A call upon him at this unusual hour intrigued him greatly. With a few words of apology to the others he left the room and crossed the hall to the drawing-room.

Miss Glen was sitting in the very centre of a large settee upholstered in gold brocade. So poised she dominated the room. Mr Satterthwaite perceived at once that she meant to dominate the situation. Curiously enough, his first feeling was one of repulsion. He had been a sincere admirer of Aspasia Glen's art. Her personality, as conveyed to him over the footlights, had been appealing and sympathetic. Her effects there had been wistful and suggestive rather than commanding. But now, face to face with the woman herself, he received a totally different impression. There was something hard—bold—forceful about her. She was tall and dark, possibly about thirty-five years of age. She was undoubtedly very good-looking and she clearly relied upon the fact.

'You must forgive this unconventional call, Mr Satterthwaite,' she said. Her voice was full and rich and seductive.

'I won't say that I have wanted to know you for a long time, but I *am* glad of the excuse. As for coming

222

tonight'—she laughed—'well, when I want a thing, I simply can't wait. When I want a thing, I simply *must* have it.'

'Any excuse that has brought me such a charming lady guest must be welcomed by me,' said Mr Satterthwaite in an old-fashioned gallant manner.

'How nice you are to me,' said Aspasia Glen.

'My dear lady,' said Mr Satterthwaite, 'may I thank you here and now for the pleasure you have so often given me—in my seat in the stalls.'

She smiled delightfully at him.

'I am coming straight to the point. I was at the Harchester Galleries today. I saw a picture there I simply couldn't live without. I wanted to buy it and I couldn't because you had already bought it. So'—she paused—'I do want it so,' she went on. 'Dear Mr Satterthwaite, I simply *must* have it. I brought my cheque book.' She looked at him hopefully. 'Everyone tells me you are so frightfully kind. People *are* kind to me, you know. It is very bad for me—but there it is.'

So these were Aspasia Glen's methods. Mr Satterthwaite was inwardly coldly critical of this ultra-femininity and of this spoilt child pose. It ought to appeal to him, he supposed, but it didn't. Aspasia Glen had made a mistake. She had judged him as an elderly dilettante, easily flattered by a pretty woman. But Mr Satterthwaite behind his gallant manner had a shrewd and critical mind. He saw people pretty well as they were, not as they wished to appear to him. He saw before him, not a charming woman pleading for a whim, but a ruthless egoist determined to get her own way for some reason which was obscure to him. And he knew quite certainly that Aspasia Glen was not going to get her own way. He was not going to give up the picture of the Dead Harlequin to her. He sought rapidly in his mind for the best way of circumventing her without overt rudeness.

'I am sure,' he said, 'that everyone gives you your own way as often as they can and is only too delighted to do so.'

'Then you are really going to let me have the picture?'

Mr Satterthwaite shook his head slowly and regretfully.

'I am afraid that is impossible. You see'—he paused—'I bought that picture for a lady. It is a present.'

'Oh! but surely—'

The telephone on the table rang sharply. With a murmured word of excuse Mr Satterthwaite took up the receiver. A voice spoke to him, a small, cold voice that sounded very far away.

'Can I speak to Mr Satterthwaite, please?'

'It is Mr Satterthwaite speaking.'

'I am Lady Charnley, Alix Charnley. I daresay you don't remember me, Mr Satterthwaite, it is a great many years since we met.'

'My dear Alix. Of course, I remember you.'

'There is something I wanted to ask you. I was at the Harchester Galleries at an exhibition of pictures today, there was one called The Dead Harlequin, perhaps you recognized it—it was the Terrace Room at Charnley. I—I want to have that picture. It was sold to you.' She paused. 'Mr Satterthwaite, for reasons of my own I want that picture. Will you resell it to me?'

Mr Satterthwaite thought to himself: 'Why, this is a

miracle.' As he spoke into the receiver he was thankful that Aspasia Glen could only hear one side of the conversation. 'If you will accept my gift, dear lady, it will make me very happy.' He heard a sharp exclamation behind him and hurried on. 'I bought it for you. I did indeed. But listen, my dear Alix, I want to ask you to do me a great favour, if you will.'

'Of course. Mr Satterthwaite, I am so *very* grateful.'

He went on. 'I want you to come round now to my house, at once.'

There was a slight pause and then she answered quietly: 'I will come at once.'

Mr Satterthwaite put down the receiver and turned to Miss Glen.

She said quickly and angrily:

'That was the picture you were talking about?'

'Yes,' said Mr Satterthwaite, 'the lady to whom I am presenting it is coming round to this house in a few minutes.'

Suddenly Aspasia Glen's face broke once more into smiles. 'You will give me a chance of persuading her to turn the picture over to me?'

'I will give you a chance of persuading her.'

Inwardly he was strangely excited. He was in the midst of a drama that was shaping itself to some foredoomed end. He, the looker-on, was playing a star part. He turned to Miss Glen.

'Will you come into the other room with me? I should like you to meet some friends of mine.'

He held the door open for her and, crossing the hall, opened the door of the smoking-room.

'Miss Glen,' he said, 'let me introduce you to an old friend of mine, Colonel Monckton. Mr Bristow, the painter of the picture you admire so much.' Then he started as a third figure rose from the chair which he had left empty beside his own.

'I think you expected me this evening,' said Mr Quin. 'During your absence I introduced myself to your friends. I am so glad I was able to drop in.'

'My dear friend,' said Mr Satterthwaite, 'I—I have been carrying on as well as I am able, but—' He stopped before the slightly sardonic glance of Mr Quin's dark eyes. 'Let me introduce you. Mr Harley Quin, Miss Aspasia Glen.'

Was it fancy—or did she shrink back slightly? A curious expression flitted over her face. Suddenly Bristow broke in boisterously. 'I have got it.'

'Got what?'

'Got hold of what was puzzling me. There is a likeness, there is a distinct likeness.' He was staring curiously at Mr Quin. 'You see it?'—he turned to Mr Satterthwaite—'don't you see a distinct likeness to the Harlequin of my picture—the man looking in through the window?'

It was no fancy this time. He distinctly heard Miss Glen draw in her breath sharply and even saw that she stepped back one pace.

'I told you that I was expecting someone,' said Mr Satterthwaite. He spoke with an air of triumph. 'I must tell you that my friend, Mr Quin, is a most extraordinary person. He can unravel mysteries. He can make you see things.'

'Are you a medium, sir?' demanded Colonel Monckton, eyeing Mr Quin doubtfully.

The latter smiled and slowly shook his head.

'Mr Satterthwaite exaggerates,' he said quietly. 'Once or twice when I have been with him he has done some extraordinarily good deductive work. Why he puts the credit down to me I can't say. His modesty, I suppose.'

'No, no,' said Mr Satterthwaite excitedly. 'It isn't. You make me see things—things that I ought to have seen all along—that I actually have seen—but without knowing that I saw them.'

'It sounds to me deuced complicated,' said Colonel Monckton.

'Not really,' said Mr Quin. 'The trouble is that we are not content just to see things—we will tack the wrong interpretation on to the things we see.'

Aspasia Glen turned to Frank Bristow.

'I want to know,' she said nervously, 'what put the idea of painting that picture into your head?'

Bristow shrugged his shoulders. 'I don't quite know,' he confessed. 'Something about the place—about Charnley, I mean, took hold of my imagination. The big empty room. The terrace outside, the idea of ghosts and things, I suppose. I have just been hearing the tale of the last Lord Charnley, who shot himself. Supposing you are dead, and your spirit lives on? It must be odd, you know. You might stand outside on the terrace looking in at the window at your own dead body, and you would see everything.'

'What do you mean?' said Aspasia Glen. '*See* everything?'

'Well, you would see what happened. You would see—'

The door opened and the butler announced Lady Charnley.

Mr Satterthwaite went to meet her. He had not seen her for nearly thirteen years. He remembered her as she once was, an eager, glowing girl. And now he saw—a Frozen Lady. Very fair, very pale, with an air of drifting rather than walking, a snowflake driven at random by an icy breeze. Something unreal about her. So cold, so far away.

'It was very good of you to come,' said Mr Satterthwaite.

He led her forward. She made a half gesture of recognition towards Miss Glen and then paused as the other made no response.

'I am so sorry,' she murmured, 'but surely I have met you somewhere, haven't I?'

'Over the footlights, perhaps,' said Mr Satterthwaite. 'This is Miss Aspasia Glen, Lady Charnley.'

'I am very pleased to meet you, Lady Charnley,' said Aspasia Glen.

Her voice had suddenly a slight transatlantic tinge to it. Mr Satterthwaite was reminded of one of her various stage impersonations.

'Colonel Monckton you know,' continued Mr Satterthwaite, 'and this is Mr Bristow.'

He saw a sudden faint tinge of colour in her cheeks.

'Mr Bristow and I have met too,' she said, and smiled a little. 'In a train.'

'And Mr Harley Quin.'

He watched her closely, but this time there was no flicker of recognition. He set a chair for her, and then, seating himself, he cleared his throat and spoke a little nervously. 'I—this is rather an unusual little gathering. It centres round

228

this picture. I—I think that if we liked we could—clear things up.'

'You are not going to hold a *séance*, Satterthwaite?' asked Colonel Monckton. 'You are very odd this evening.'

'No,' said Mr Satterthwaite, 'not exactly a *séance*. But my friend, Mr Quin, believes, and I agree, that one can, by looking back over the past, see things as they were and not as they appeared to be.'

'The past?' said Lady Charnley.

'I am speaking of your husband's suicide, Alix. I know it hurts you—'

'No,' said Alix Charnley, 'it doesn't hurt me. Nothing hurts me now.'

Mr Satterthwaite thought of Frank Bristow's words. *'She was not quite real, you know. Shadowy. Like one of the people who come out of the hills in Gaelic fairy tales.'*

'Shadowy,' he had called her. That described her exactly. A shadow, a reflection of something else. Where then was the real Alix, and his mind answered quickly: *'In the past. Divided from us by fourteen years of time.'*

'My dear,' he said, 'you frighten me. You are like the Weeping Lady with the Silver Ewer.'

Crash! The coffee cup on the table by Aspasia's elbow fell shattered to the floor. Mr Satterthwaite waved aside her apologies. He thought: 'We are getting nearer, we are getting nearer every minute—but nearer to what?'

'Let us take our minds back to that night fourteen years ago,' he said. 'Lord Charnley killed himself. For what reason? No one knows.'

Lady Charnley stirred slightly in her chair.

'Lady Charnley knows,' said Frank Bristow abruptly.

'Nonsense,' said Colonel Monckton, then stopped, frowning at her curiously.

She was looking across at the artist. It was as though he drew the words out of her. She spoke, nodding her head slowly, and her voice was like a snowflake, cold and soft.

'Yes, you are quite right. I *know*. That is why as long as I live I can never go back to Charnley. That is why when my boy Dick wants me to open the place up and live there again I tell him it can't be done.'

'Will you tell us the reason, Lady Charnley?' said Mr Quin.

She looked at him. Then, as though hypnotised, she spoke as quietly and naturally as a child.

'I will tell you if you like. Nothing seems to matter very much now. I found a letter among his papers and I destroyed it.'

'What letter?' said Mr Quin.

'The letter from the girl—from that poor child. She was the Merriams' nursery governess. He had—he had made love to her—yes, while he was engaged to me just before we were married. And she—she was going to have a child too. She wrote saying so, and that she was going to tell me about it. So, you see, he shot himself.'

She looked round at them wearily and dreamily like a child who has repeated a lesson it knows too well.

Colonel Monckton blew his nose.

'My God,' he said, 'so that was it. Well, that explains things with a vengeance.'

'Does it?' said Mr Satterthwaite, 'it doesn't explain one

thing. *It doesn't explain why Mr Bristow painted that picture.'*

'What do you mean?'

Mr Satterthwaite looked across at Mr Quin as though for encouragement, and apparently got it, for he proceeded:

'Yes, I know I sound mad to all of you, but that picture is the focus of the whole thing. We are all here tonight because of that picture. That picture *had* to be painted—that is what I mean.'

'You mean the uncanny influence of the Oak Parlour?' began Colonel Monckton.

'No,' said Mr Satterthwaite. '*Not* the Oak Parlour. The Terrace Room. That is it! The spirit of the dead man standing outside the window and looking in and seeing his own dead body on the floor.'

'Which he couldn't have done,' said the Colonel, 'because the body was in the Oak Parlour.'

'Supposing it wasn't,' said Mr Satterthwaite, 'supposing it was exactly where Mr Bristow saw it, saw it imaginatively, I mean on the black and white flags in front of the window.'

'You are talking nonsense,' said Colonel Monckton, 'if it was there we shouldn't have found it in the Oak Parlour.'

'Not unless someone carried it there,' said Mr Satterthwaite.

'And in that case how could we have seen Charnley going in at the door of the Oak Parlour?' inquired Colonel Monckton.

'Well, you didn't see his face, did you?' asked Mr Satterthwaite. 'What I mean is, you saw a man going into the Oak Parlour in fancy dress, I suppose.'

'Brocade things and a wig,' said Monckton.

'Just so, and you thought it was Lord Charnley because the girl called out to him as Lord Charnley.'

'And because when we broke in a few minutes later there was only Lord Charnley there dead. You can't get away from that, Satterthwaite.'

'No,' said Mr Satterthwaite, discouraged. 'No—unless there was a hiding-place of some kind.'

'Weren't you saying something about there being a Priests' hole in that room?' put in Frank Bristow.

'Oh!' cried Mr Satterthwaite. 'Supposing—?' He waved a hand for silence and sheltered his forehead with his other hand and then spoke slowly and hesitatingly.

'I have got an idea—it may be just an idea, but I think it hangs together. Supposing someone shot Lord Charnley. Shot him in the Terrace Room. Then he—and another person—dragged the body into the Oak Parlour. They laid it down there with the pistol by its right hand. Now we go on to the next step. It must seem absolutely certain that Lord Charnley has committed suicide. I think that could be done very easily. The man in his brocade and wig passes along the hall by the Oak Parlour door and someone, to make sure of things, calls out to him as Lord Charnley from the top of the stairs. He goes in and locks both doors and fires a shot into the woodwork. There were bullet holes already in that room if you remember, one more wouldn't be noticed. He then hides quietly in the secret chamber. The doors are broken open and people rush in. It seems certain that Lord Charnley has committed suicide. No other hypothesis is even entertained.'

'Well, I think that is balderdash,' said Colonel Monckton. 'You forget that Charnley had a motive right enough for suicide.'

'A letter found afterwards,' said Mr Satterthwaite. 'A lying cruel letter written by a very clever and unscrupulous little actress who meant one day to be Lady Charnley herself.'

'You mean?'

'I mean the girl in league with Hugo Charnley,' said Mr Satterthwaite. 'You know, Monckton, everyone knows, that that man was a blackguard. He thought that he was certain to come into the title.' He turned sharply to Lady Charnley. 'What was the name of the girl who wrote that letter?'

'Monica Ford,' said Lady Charnley.

'Was it Monica Ford, Monckton, who called out to Lord Charnley from the top of the stairs?'

'Yes, now you come to speak of it, I believe it was.'

'Oh, that's impossible,' said Lady Charnley. 'I—I went to her about it. She told me it was all true. I only saw her once afterwards, but surely she couldn't have been acting the whole time.'

Mr Satterthwaite looked across the room at Aspasia Glen.

'I think she could,' he said quietly. 'I think she had in her the makings of a very accomplished actress.'

'There is one thing you haven't got over,' said Frank Bristow, 'there would be blood on the floor of the Terrace Room. Bound to be. They couldn't clear that up in a hurry.'

'No,' admitted Mr Satterthwaite, 'but there is one thing they could do—a thing that would only take a second or two—they could throw over the blood-stains the Bokhara rug. Nobody ever saw the Bokhara rug in the Terrace Room before that night.'

'I believe you are right,' said Monckton, 'but all the same those blood-stains would have to be cleared up some time?'

'Yes,' said Mr Satterthwaite, 'in the middle of the night. A woman with a jug and basin could go down the stairs and clear up the blood-stains quite easily.'

'But supposing someone saw her?'

'It wouldn't matter,' said Mr Satterthwaite. 'I am speaking now of things as they *are*. I said a woman with a jug and basin. But if I had said a Weeping Lady with a Silver Ewer that is what they would have *appeared* to be.' He got up and went across to Aspasia Glen. 'That is what you did, wasn't it?' he said. 'They call you the "Woman with the Scarf" now, but it was that night you played your first part, the "Weeping Lady with the Silver Ewer". That is why you knocked the coffee cup off that table just now. You were afraid when you saw that picture. You thought someone knew.'

Lady Charnley stretched out a white accusing hand.

'Monica Ford,' she breathed. 'I recognize you now.'

Aspasia Glen sprang to her feet with a cry. She pushed little Mr Satterthwaite aside with a shove of the hand and stood shaking in front of Mr Quin.

'So I was right. Someone *did* know! Oh, I haven't been deceived by this tomfoolery. This pretence of working things out.' She pointed at Mr Quin. '*You* were there. *You* were

234

there outside the window looking in. You saw what we did, Hugo and I. I *knew* there was someone looking in, I felt it all the time. And yet when I looked up, there was nobody there. I knew someone was watching us. I thought once I caught a glimpse of a face at the window. It has frightened me all these years. Why did you break silence now? That is what I want to know?'

'Perhaps so that the dead may rest in peace,' said Mr Quin.

Suddenly Aspasia Glen made a rush for the door and stood there flinging a few defiant words over her shoulder.

'Do what you like. God knows there are witnesses enough to what I have been saying. I don't care, I don't care. I loved Hugo and I helped him with the ghastly business and he chucked me afterwards. He died last year. You can set the police on my tracks if you like, but as that little dried-up fellow there said, I am a pretty good actress. They will find it hard to find me.' She crashed the door behind her, and a moment later they heard the slam of the front door, also.

'Reggie,' cried Lady Charnley, 'Reggie.' The tears were streaming down her face. 'Oh, my dear, my dear, I can go back to Charnley now. I can live there with Dickie. I can tell him what his father was, the finest, the most splendid man in all the world.'

'We must consult very seriously as to what must be done in the matter,' said Colonel Monckton. 'Alix, my dear, if you will let me take you home I shall be glad to have a few words with you on the subject.'

Lady Charnley rose. She came across to Mr Satterthwaite,

and laying both hands on his shoulders, she kissed him very gently.

'It is so wonderful to be alive again after being so long dead,' she said. 'It was like being dead, you know. Thank you, dear Mr Satterthwaite.' She went out of the room with Colonel Monckton. Mr Satterthwaite gazed after them. A grunt from Frank Bristow whom he had forgotten made him turn sharply round.

'She is a lovely creature,' said Bristow moodily. 'But she's not nearly so interesting as she was,' he said gloomily.

'There speaks the artist,' said Mr Satterthwaite.

'Well, she isn't,' said Mr Bristow. 'I suppose I should only get the cold shoulder if I ever went butting in at Charnley. I don't want to go where I am not wanted.'

'My dear young man,' said Mr Satterthwaite, 'if you will think a little less of the impression you are making on other people, you will, I think, be wiser and happier. You would also do well to disabuse your mind of some very old-fashioned notions, one of which is that birth has any significance at all in our modern conditions. You are one of those large proportioned young men whom women always consider good-looking, and you have possibly, if not certainly, genius. Just say that over to yourself ten times before you go to bed every night and in three months' time go and call on Lady Charnley at Charnley. That is my advice to you, and I am an old man with considerable experience of the world.'

A very charming smile suddenly spread over the artist's face.

'You have been thunderingly good to me,' he said suddenly. He seized Mr Sattherthwaite's hand and wrung it in a powerful grip. 'I am no end grateful. I must be off now. Thanks very much for one of the most extraordinary evenings I have ever spent.'

He looked round as though to say goodbye to someone else and then started.

'I say, sir, your friend has gone. I never saw him go. He is rather a queer bird, isn't he?'

'He goes and comes very suddenly,' said Mr Satterthwaite. 'That is one of his characteristics. One doesn't always see him come and go.'

'Like Harlequin,' said Frank Bristow, 'he is invisible,' and laughed heartily at his own joke.

CHAPTER 10

The Bird with the Broken Wing

Mr Satterthwaite looked out of the window. It was raining steadily. He shivered. Very few country houses, he reflected, were really properly heated. It cheered him to think that in a few hours' time he would be speeding towards London. Once one had passed sixty years of age, London was really much the best place.

He was feeling a little old and pathetic. Most of the members of the house party were so young. Four of them had just gone off into the library to do table turning. They had invited him to accompany them, but he had declined. He failed to derive any amusement from the monotonous counting of the letters of the alphabet and the usual meaningless jumble of letters that resulted.

Yes, London was the best place for him. He was glad that he had declined Madge Keeley's invitation when she had rung up to invite him over to Laidell half an hour ago. An adorable young person, certainly, but London was best.

Mr Satterthwaite shivered again and remembered

that the fire in the library was usually a good one. He opened the door and adventured cautiously into the darkened room.

'If I'm not in the way—'

'Was that N or M? We shall have to count again. No, of course not, Mr Satterthwaite. Do you know, the most exciting things have been happening. The spirit says her name is Ada Spiers, and John here is going to marry someone called Gladys Bun almost immediately.'

Mr Satterthwaite sat down in a big easy chair in front of the fire. His eyelids drooped over his eyes and he dozed. From time to time he returned to consciousness, hearing fragments of speech.

'It can't be P A B Z L—not unless he's a Russian. John, you're shoving. I *saw* you. I believe it's a new spirit come.'

Another interval of dozing. Then a name jerked him wide awake.

'Q-U-I-N. Is that right?' 'Yes, it's rapped once for "Yes." Quin. Have you a message for someone here? Yes. For me? For John? For Sarah? For Evelyn? No—but there's no one else. Oh! it's for Mr Satterthwaite, perhaps? It says "Yes." Mr Satterthwaite, it's a message for you.'

'What does it say?'

Mr Satterthwaite was broad awake now, sitting taut and erect in his chair, his eyes shining.

The table rocked and one of the girls counted.

'LAI—it can't be—that doesn't make sense. No word begins LAI.'

'Go on,' said Mr Satterthwaite, and the command in his voice was so sharp that he was obeyed without question.

'LAIDEL? and another L—Oh! that seems to be all.'

'Go on.'

'Tell us some more, please.'

A pause.

'There doesn't seem to be any more. The table's gone quite dead. How silly.'

'No,' said Mr Satterthwaite thoughtfully. 'I don't think it's silly.'

He rose and left the room. He went straight to the telephone. Presently he was through.

'Can I speak to Miss Keeley? Is that you, Madge, my dear? I want to change my mind, if I may, and accept your kind invitation. It is not so urgent as I thought that I should get back to town. Yes—yes—I will arrive in time for dinner.'

He hung up the receiver, a strange flush on his withered cheeks. Mr Quin—the mysterious Mr Harley Quin. Mr Satterthwaite counted over on his fingers the times he had been brought into contact with that man of mystery. Where Mr Quin was concerned—things happened! What had happened or was going to happen—at Laidell?

Whatever it was, there was work for him, Mr Satterthwaite, to do. In some way or other, he would have an active part to play. He was sure of that.

Laidell was a large house. Its owner, David Keeley, was one of those quiet men with indeterminate personalities who seem to count as part of the furniture. Their inconspicuousness has nothing to do with brain power—David Keeley was a most brilliant mathematician, and had written a book totally incomprehensible to ninety-nine hundreds of humanity. But like so many men of brilliant intellect, he radiated no bodily vigour or magnetism. It was a standing joke that David Keeley was a real 'invisible man'. Footmen passed him by with the vegetables, and guests forgot to say how do you do or goodbye.

His daughter Madge was very different. A fine upstanding young woman, bursting with energy and life. Thorough, healthy and normal, and extremely pretty.

It was she who received Mr Satterthwaite when he arrived.

'How nice of you to come—after all.'

'Very delightful of you to let me change my mind. Madge, my dear, you're looking very well.'

'Oh! I'm always well.'

'Yes, I know. But it's more than that. You look—well, blooming is the word I have in mind. Has anything happened, my dear? Anything—well—special?'

She laughed—blushed a little.

'It's too bad, Mr Satterthwaite. You always guess things.'

He took her hand.

'So it's that, is it? Mr Right has come along?'

It was an old-fashioned term, but Madge did not object to it. She rather liked Mr Satterthwaite's old-fashioned ways.

'I suppose so—yes. But nobody's supposed to know. It's a secret. But I don't really mind your knowing, Mr Satterthwaite. You're always so nice and sympathetic.'

Mr Satterthwaite thoroughly enjoyed romance at second hand. He was sentimental and Victorian.

'I mustn't ask who the lucky man is? Well, then all I can say is that I hope he is worthy of the honour you are conferring on him.'

Rather a duck, old Mr Satterthwaite, thought Madge.

'Oh! we shall get on awfully well together, I think,' she said. 'You see, we like doing the same things, and that's so awfully important, isn't it? We've really got a lot in common—and we know all about each other and all that. It's really been coming on for a long time. That gives one such a nice safe feeling, doesn't it?'

'Undoubtedly,' said Mr Satterthwaite. 'But in my experience one can never really know all about anyone else. That is part of the interest and charm of life.'

'Oh! I'll risk it,' said Madge, laughing, and they went up to dress for dinner.

Mr Satterthwaite was late. He had not brought a valet, and having his things unpacked for him by a stranger always flurried him a little. He came down to find everyone assembled, and in the modern style Madge merely said: 'Oh! here's Mr Satterthwaite. I'm starving. Let's go in.'

She led the way with a tall grey-haired woman—a woman of striking personality. She had a very clear, rather incisive voice, and her face was clear cut and rather beautiful.

'How d'you do, Satterthwaite,' said Mr Keeley.

Mr Satterthwaite jumped.

'How do you do,' he said. 'I'm afraid I didn't see you.'

'Nobody does,' said Mr Keeley sadly.

They went in. The table was a low oval of mahogany. Mr Satterthwaite was placed between his young hostess and a short dark girl—a very hearty girl with a loud voice and a ringing determined laugh that expressed more the determination to be cheerful at all costs than any real mirth. Her name seemed to be Doris, and she was the type of young woman Mr Satterthwaite most disliked. She had, he considered, no artistic justification for existence.

On Madge's other side was a man of about thirty, whose likeness to the grey-haired woman proclaimed them mother and son.

Next to him—

Mr Satterthwaite caught his breath.

He didn't know what it was exactly. It was not beauty. It was something else—something much more elusive and intangible than beauty.

She was listening to Mr Keeley's rather ponderous dinner-table conversation, her head bent a little sideways. She was there, it seemed to Mr Satterthwaite—and yet she was not there! She was somehow a great deal less substantial than anyone else seated round the oval table. Something in the droop of her body sideways was beautiful—was more than beautiful. She looked up—her eyes met Mr Satterthwaite's for a moment across the table—and the word he wanted leapt to his mind.

Enchantment—that was it. She had the quality of enchantment. She might have been one of those creatures who are only half-human—one of the Hidden People from the Hollow Hills. She made everyone else look rather too real . . .

But at the same time, in a queer way, she stirred his pity. It was as though semi-humanity handicapped her. He sought for a phrase and found it.

'A bird with a broken wing,' said Mr Satterthwaite.

Satisfied, he turned his mind back to the subject of Girl Guides and hoped that the girl Doris had not noticed his abstraction. When she turned to the man on the other side of her—a man Mr Satterthwaite had hardly noticed, he himself turned to Madge.

'Who is the lady sitting next to your father?' he asked in a low voice.

'Mrs Graham? Oh, no! you mean Mabelle. Don't you know her? Mabelle Annesley. She was a Clydesley—one of the ill-fated Clydesleys.'

He started. The ill-fated Clydesleys. He remembered. A brother had shot himself, a sister had been drowned, another had perished in an earthquake. A queer doomed family. This girl must be the youngest of them.

His thoughts were recalled suddenly. Madge's hand touched his under the table. Everyone else was talking. She gave a faint inclination of her head to her left.

'That's him,' she murmured ungrammatically.

Mr Satterthwaite nodded quickly in comprehension. So this young Graham was the man of Madge's choice. Well, she could hardly have done better as far as appearances went—and Mr Satterthwaite was a shrewd observer. A pleasant, likeable, rather matter-of-fact young fellow. They'd make a nice pair—no nonsense about either of them—good healthy sociable young folk.

Laidell was run on old-fashioned lines. The ladies left the dining-room first. Mr Satterthwaite moved up to Graham and began to talk to him. His estimate of the young man was confirmed, yet there was something that struck him as being not quite true to type. Roger Graham was distrait, his mind seemed far away, his hand shook as he replaced the glass on the table.

'He's got something on his mind,' thought Mr Satterthwaite acutely. 'Not nearly as important as he thinks it is, I dare say. All the same, I wonder what it is.'

Mr Satterthwaite was in the habit of swallowing a couple of digestive pastilles after meals. Having neglected to bring them down with him, he went up to his room to fetch them.

On his way down to the drawing-room, he passed along the long corridor on the ground floor. About half-way along it was a room known as the terrace room. As Mr Satterthwaite looked through the open doorway in passing, he stopped short.

Moonlight was streaming into the room. The latticed panes gave it a queer rhythmic pattern. A figure was sitting on the low window sill, drooping a little sideways and softly twanging the string of a ukelele—not in a jazz rhythm, but in a far older rhythm, the beat of fairy horses riding on fairy hills.

Mr Satterthwaite stood fascinated. She wore a dress of dull dark blue chiffon, ruched and pleated so that it looked like the feathers of a bird. She bent over the instrument crooning to it.

He came into the room—slowly, step by step. He was close to her when she looked up and saw him. She didn't start, he noticed, or seem surprised.

'I hope I'm not intruding,' he began.

'Please—sit down.'

He sat near her on a polished oak chair. She hummed softly under her breath.

'There's a lot of magic about tonight,' she said. 'Don't you think so?'

'Yes, there was a lot of magic about.'

'They wanted me to fetch my uke,' she explained. 'And as I passed here, I thought it would be so lovely to be alone here—in the dark and the moon.'

'Then I—' Mr Satterthwaite half rose, but she stopped him.

'Don't go. You—you fit in, somehow. It's queer, but you do.'

He sat down again.

'It's been a queer sort of evening,' she said. 'I was out in the woods late this afternoon, and I met a man—such a strange sort of man—tall and dark, like a lost soul. The sun was setting, and the light of it through the trees made him look like a kind of Harlequin.'

'Ah!' Mr Satterthwaite leant forward—his interest quickened.

'I wanted to speak to him—he—he looked so like somebody I know. But I lost him in the trees.'

'I think I know him,' said Mr Satterthwaite.

'Do you? He is—interesting, isn't he?'

'Yes, he is interesting.'

There was a pause. Mr Satterthwaite was perplexed. There was something, he felt, that he ought to do—and he didn't know what it was. But surely—surely, it had to do with this girl. He said rather clumsily:

'Sometimes—when one is unhappy—one wants to get away—'

246

'Yes. That's true.' She broke off suddenly. 'Oh! I see what you mean. But you're wrong. It's just the other way round. I wanted to be alone because I'm happy.'

'Happy?'

'Terribly happy.'

She spoke quite quietly, but Mr Satterthwaite had a sudden sense of shock. What this strange girl meant by being happy wasn't the same as Madge Keeley would have meant by the same words. Happiness, for Mabelle Annesley, meant some kind of intense and vivid ecstasy . . . something that was not only human, but more than human. He shrank back a little.

'I—didn't know,' he said clumsily.

'Of course you couldn't. And it's not—the actual thing—I'm not happy yet—but I'm going to be.' She leaned forward. 'Do you know what it's like to stand in a wood—a big wood with dark shadows and trees very close all round you—a wood you might never get out of—and then, suddenly—just in front of you, you see the country of your dreams—shining and beautiful—you've only got to step out from the trees and the darkness and you've found it . . .'

'So many things look beautiful,' said Mr Satterthwaite, 'before we've reached them. Some of the ugliest things in the world look the most beautiful . . .'

There was a step on the floor. Mr Satterthwaite turned his head. A fair man with a stupid, rather wooden face, stood there. He was the man Mr Satterthwaite had hardly noticed at the dinner-table.

'They're waiting for you, Mabelle,' he said.

She got up, the expression had gone out of her face, her voice was flat and calm.

'I'm coming, Gerard,' she said. 'I've been talking to Mr Satterthwaite.'

She went out of the room, Mr Satterthwaite following. He turned his head over his shoulder as he went and caught the expression on her husband's face. A hungry, despairing look.

'Enchantment,' thought Mr Satterthwaite. 'He feels it right enough. Poor fellow—poor fellow.'

The drawing-room was well lighted. Madge and Doris Coles were vociferous in reproaches.

'Mabelle, you little beast—you've been ages.'

She sat on a low stool, tuned the ukelele and sang. They all joined in.

'Is it possible,' thought Mr Satterthwaite, 'that so many idiotic songs could have been written about My Baby?'

But he had to admit that the syncopated wailing tunes were stirring. Though, of course, they weren't a patch on the old-fashioned waltz.

The air got very smoky. The syncopated rhythm went on.

'No conversation,' thought Mr Satterthwaite. 'No good music. No *peace*.' He wished the world had not become definitely so noisy.

Suddenly Mabelle Annesley broke off, smiled across the room at him, and began to sing a song of Grieg's.

'My swan—my fair one . . .'

It was a favourite of Mr Satterthwaite's. He liked the note of ingenuous surprise at the end.

'Wert only a swan then? A swan then?'

After that, the party broke up. Madge offered drinks whilst her father picked up the discarded ukelele and began twanging it absent-mindedly. The party exchanged good-nights, drifted nearer and nearer to the door. Everyone talked at once. Gerard Annesley slipped away unostentatiously, leaving the others.

Outside the drawing-room door, Mr Satterthwaite bade Mrs Graham a ceremonious goodnight. There were two staircases, one close at hand, the other at the end of a long corridor. It was by the latter that Mr Satterthwaite reached his room. Mrs Graham and her son passed by the stairs near at hand whence the quiet Gerard Annesley had already preceded them.

'You'd better get your ukelele, Mabelle,' said Madge. 'You'll forget it in the morning if you don't. You've got to make such an early start.'

'Come on, Mr Satterthwaite,' said Doris Coles, seizing him boisterously by one arm. 'Early to bed—etcetera.'

Madge took him by the other arm and all three ran down the corridor to peals of Doris's laughter. They paused at the end to wait for David Keeley, who was following at a much more sedate pace, turning out electric lights as he came. The four of them went upstairs together.

*

Mr Satterthwaite was just preparing to descend to the dining-room for breakfast on the following morning, when there was a light tap on the door and Madge Keeley entered. Her face was dead white, and she was shivering all over.

'Oh, Mr Satterthwaite.'

'My dear child, what's happened?' He took her hand.

'Mabelle—Mabelle Annesley . . .'

'Yes?'

What had happened? What? Something terrible—he knew that. Madge could hardly get the words out.

'She—she hanged herself last night . . . On the back of her door. Oh! it's too horrible.' She broke down—sobbing.

Hanged herself. Impossible. Incomprehensible!

He said a few soothing old-fashioned words to Madge, and hurried downstairs. He found David Keeley looking perplexed and incompetent.

'I've telephoned to the police, Satterthwaite. Apparently that's got to be done. So the doctor said. He's just finished examining the—the—Good Lord, it's a beastly business. She must have been desperately unhappy—to do it that way—Queer that song last night. Swan song, eh? She looked rather like a swan—a black swan.'

'Yes.'

'Swan Song,' repeated Keeley. 'Shows it was in her mind, eh?'

'It would seem so—yes, certainly it would seem so.'

He hesitated, then asked if he might see—if, that is . . .

His host comprehended the stammering request.

'If you want to—I'd forgotten you have a *penchant* for human tragedies.'

He led the way up the broad staircase. Mr Satterthwaite followed him. At the head of the stairs was the room occupied by Roger Graham and opposite it, on the other side of the passage, his mother's room. The latter door was ajar and a faint wisp of smoke floated through it.

A momentary surprise invaded Mr Satterthwaite's mind. He had not judged Mrs Graham to be a woman who smoked so early in the day. Indeed, he had had the idea that she did not smoke at all.

They went along the passage to the end door but one. David Keeley entered the room and Mr Satterthwaite followed him.

The room was not a very large one and showed signs of a man's occupation. A door in the wall led into a second room. A bit of cut rope still dangled from a hook high up on the door. On the bed . . .

Mr Satterthwaite stood for a minute looking down on the heap of huddled chiffon. He noticed that it was ruched and pleated like the plumage of a bird. At the face, after one glance, he did not look again.

He glanced from the door with its dangling rope to the communicating door through which they had come.

'Was that open?'

'Yes. At least the maid says so.'

'Annesley slept in there? Did he hear anything?'

'He says—nothing.'

'Almost incredible,' murmured Mr Satterthwaite. He looked back at the form on the bed.

'Where is he?'

'Annesley? He's downstairs with the doctor.'

Agatha Christie

They went downstairs to find an Inspector of police had arrived. Mr Satterthwaite was agreeably surprised to recognize in him an old acquaintance, Inspector Winkfield. The Inspector went upstairs with the doctor, and a few minutes later a request came that all members of the house party should assemble in the drawing-room.

The blinds had been drawn, and the whole room had a funereal aspect. Doris Coles looked frightened and subdued. Every now and then she dabbed her eyes with a handkerchief. Madge was resolute and alert, her feelings fully under control by now. Mrs Graham was composed, as always, her face grave and impassive. The tragedy seemed to have affected her son more keenly than anyone. He looked a positive wreck this morning. David Keeley, as usual, had subsided into the background.

The bereaved husband sat alone, a little apart from the others. There was a queer dazed looked about him, as though he could hardly realize what had taken place.

Mr Satterthwaite, outwardly composed, was inwardly seething with the importance of a duty shortly to be performed.

Inspector Winkfield, followed by Dr Morris, came in and shut the door behind him. He cleared his throat and spoke.

'This is a very sad occurrence—very sad, I'm sure. It's necessary, under the circumstances, that I should ask everybody a few questions. You'll not object, I'm sure. I'll begin with Mr Annesley. You'll forgive my asking, sir, but had your good lady ever threatened to take her life?'

252

Mr Satterthwaite opened his lips impulsively, then closed them again. There was plenty of time. Better not speak too soon.

'I—no, I don't think so.'

His voice was so hesitating, so peculiar, that everyone shot a covert glance at him.

'You're not sure, sir?'

'Yes—I'm—quite sure. She didn't.'

'Ah! Were you aware that she was unhappy in any way?'

'No. I—no, I wasn't.'

'She said nothing to you? About feeling depressed, for instance?'

'I—no, nothing.'

Whatever the Inspector thought, he said nothing. Instead he proceeded to his next point.

'Will you describe to me briefly the events of last night?'

'We—all went up to bed. I fell asleep immediately and heard nothing. The housemaid's scream aroused me this morning. I rushed into the adjoining room and found my wife—and found her—'

His voice broke. The Inspector nodded.

'Yes, yes, that's quite enough. We needn't go into that. When did you last see your wife the night before?'

'I—downstairs.'

'Downstairs?'

'Yes, we all left the drawing-room together. I went straight up leaving the others talking in the hall.'

'And you didn't see your wife again? Didn't she say goodnight when she came up to bed?'

'I was asleep when she came up.'

'But she only followed you a few minutes later. That's right, isn't it, sir?' He looked at David Keeley, who nodded.

'She hadn't come up half an hour later.'

Annesley spoke stubbornly. The Inspector's eyes strayed gently to Mrs Graham.

'She didn't stay in your room talking, Madam?'

Did Mr Satterthwaite fancy it, or was there a slight pause before Mrs Graham said with her customary quiet decision of manner:

'No, I went straight into my room and closed the door. I heard nothing.'

'And you say, sir'—the Inspector had shifted his attention back to Annesley—'that you slept and heard nothing. The communicating door was open, was it not?'

'I—I believe so. But my wife would have entered her room by the other door from the corridor.'

'Even so, sir, there would have been certain sounds—a choking noise, a drumming of heels on the door—'

'No.'

It was Mr Satterthwaite who spoke, impetuously, unable to stop himself. Every eye turned towards him in surprise. He himself became nervous, stammered, and turned pink.

'I—I beg your pardon, Inspector. But I must speak. You are on the wrong track—the wrong track altogether. Mrs Annesley did not kill herself—I am sure of it. She was murdered.'

There was a dead silence, then Inspector Winkfield said quietly:

'What leads you to say that, sir?'

'I—it is a feeling. A very strong feeling.'

254

'But I think, sir, there must be more than that to it. There must be some particular reason.'

Well, of course there *was* a particular reason. There was the mysterious message from Mr Quin. But you couldn't tell a police inspector that. Mr Satterthwaite cast about desperately, and found nothing.

'Last night—when we were talking together, she said she was very happy. Very happy—just that. That wasn't like a woman thinking of committing suicide.'

He was triumphant. He added:

'She went back to the drawing-room to fetch her ukelele, so that she wouldn't forget it in the morning. That didn't look like suicide either.'

'No,' admitted the Inspector. 'No, perhaps it didn't.' He turned to David Keeley. 'Did she take the ukelele upstairs with her?'

The mathematician tried to remember.

'I think—yes, she did. She went upstairs carrying it in her hand. I remember seeing it just as she turned the corner of the staircase before I turned off the light down here.'

'Oh!' cried Madge. 'But it's here now.'

She pointed dramatically to where the ukelele lay on a table.

'That's curious,' said the Inspector. He stepped swiftly across and rang the bell.

A brief order sent the butler in search of the housemaid whose business it was to do the rooms in the morning. She came, and was quite positive in her answer. The ukelele had been there first thing that morning when she had dusted.

Inspector Winkfield dismissed her and then said curtly:

'I would like to speak to Mr Satterthwaite in private, please. Everyone may go. But no one is to leave the house.'

Mr Satterthwaite twittered into speech as soon as the door had closed behind the others.

'I—I am sure, Inspector, that you have the case excellently in hand. Excellently. I just felt that—having, as I say, a very strong feeling—'

The Inspector arrested further speech with an upraised hand.

'You're quite right, Mr Satterthwaite. The lady was murdered.'

'You knew it?' Mr Satterthwaite was chagrined.

'There were certain things that puzzled Dr Morris.' He looked across at the doctor, who had remained, and the doctor assented to his statement with a nod of the head. 'We made a thorough examination. The rope that was round her neck wasn't the rope that she was strangled with—it was something much thinner that did the job, something more like a wire. It had cut right into the flesh. The mark of the rope was superimposed on it. She was strangled and then hung up on the door afterwards to make it look like suicide.'

'But who—?'

'Yes,' said the Inspector. 'Who? That's the question. What about the husband sleeping next door, who never said goodnight to his wife and who heard nothing? I should say we hadn't far to look. Must find out what terms they were on. That's where you can be useful to us, Mr Satterthwaite. You've the *ongtray* here, and you can get

256

the hang of things in a way we can't. Find out what relations there were between the two.'

'I hardly like—' began Mr Satterthwaite, stiffening.

'It won't be the first murder mystery you've helped us with. I remember the case of Mrs Strangeways. You've got a *flair* for that sort of thing, sir. An absolute *flair*.'

Yes, it was true—he *had a flair*. He said quietly:

'I will do my best, Inspector.'

Had Gerard Annesley killed his wife? Had he? Mr Satterthwaite recalled that look of misery last night. He loved her—and he was suffering. Suffering will drive a man to strange deeds.

But there was something else—some other factor. Mabelle had spoken of herself as coming out of a wood—she was looking forward to happiness—not a quiet rational happiness—but a happiness that was irrational—a wild ecstasy . . .

If Gerard Annesley had spoken the truth, Mabelle had not come to her room till at least half an hour later than he had done. Yet David Keeley had seen her going up those stairs. There were two other rooms occupied in that wing. There was Mrs Graham's, and there was her son's.

Her son's. But he and Madge . . .

Surely Madge would have guessed . . . But Madge wasn't the guessing kind. All the same, no smoke without fire— Smoke!

Ah! he remembered. *A wisp of smoke curling out through Mrs Graham's bedroom door.*

He acted on impulse. Straight up the stairs and into her room. It was empty. He closed the door behind him and locked it.

Agatha Christie

He went across to the grate. A heap of charred fragments. Very gingerly he raked them over with his finger. His luck was in. In the very centre were some unburnt fragments—fragments of letters . . .

Very disjointed fragments, but they told him something of value.

'Life can be wonderful, Roger darling. I never knew . . . all my life has been a dream till I met you, Roger . . .'

'. . . Gerard knows, I think . . . I am sorry but what can I do? Nothing is real to me but you, Roger . . . We shall be together, soon.

'What are you going to tell him at Laidell, Roger? You write strangely—but I am not afraid . . .'

Very carefully, Mr Satterthwaite put the fragments into an envelope from the writing-table. He went to the door, unlocked it and opened it to find himself face to face with Mrs Graham.

It was an awkward moment, and Mr Satterthwaite was momentarily out of countenance. He did what was, perhaps, the best thing, attacked the situation with simplicity.

'I have been searching your room, Mrs Graham. I have found something—a packet of letters imperfectly burnt.'

A wave of alarm passed over her face. It was gone in a flash, but it had been there.

'Letters from Mrs Annesley to your son.'

She hesitated for a minute, then said quietly: 'That is so. I thought they would be better burnt.'

'For what reason?'

'My son is engaged to be married. These letters—if they had been brought into publicity through the poor girl's suicide—might have caused much pain and trouble.'

'Your son could burn his own letters.'

She had no answer ready for that. Mr Satterthwaite pursued his advantage.

'You found these letters in his room, brought them into your room and burnt them. Why? You were afraid, Mrs Graham.'

'I am not in the habit of being afraid, Mr Satterthwaite.'

'No—but this was a desperate case.'

'Desperate?'

'Your son might have been in danger of arrest—for murder.'

'Murder!'

He saw her face go white. He went on quickly:

'You heard Mrs Annesley go into your son's room last night. He had told her of his engagement? No, I see he hadn't. He told her then. They quarrelled, and he—'

'That's a lie!'

They had been so absorbed in their duel of words that they had not heard approaching footsteps. Roger Graham had come up behind them unperceived by either.

'It's all right, Mother. Don't—worry. Come into my room, Mr Satterthwaite.'

Mr Sattherwaite followed him into his room. Mrs Graham had turned away and did not attempt to follow them. Roger Graham shut the door.

'Listen, Mr Satterthwaite, you think I killed Mabelle. You think I strangled her—here—and took her along and hung her up on that door—later—when everyone was asleep?'

Mr Satterthwaite stared at him. Then he said surprisingly:

'No, I do not think so.'

'Thank God for that. I couldn't have killed Mabelle. I—I loved her. Or didn't I? I don't know. It's a tangle that I can't explain. I'm fond of Madge—I always have been. And she's such a good sort. We suit each other. But Mabelle was different. It was—I can't explain it—a sort of enchantment. I was, I think—afraid of her.'

Mr Satterthwaite nodded.

'It was madness—a kind of bewildering ecstasy . . . But it was impossible. It wouldn't have worked. That sort of thing—doesn't last. I know what it means now to have a spell cast over you.'

'Yes, it must have been like that,' said Mr Satterthwaite thoughtfully.

'I—I wanted to get out of it all. I was going to tell Mabelle—last night.'

'But you didn't?'

'No, I didn't,' said Graham slowly. 'I swear to you, Mr Satterthwaite, that I never saw her after I said goodnight downstairs.'

'I believe you,' said Mr Satterthwaite.

He got up. It was not Roger Graham who had killed Mabelle Annesley. He could have fled from her, but he could not have killed her. He had been afraid of her, afraid of that wild intangible fairy-like quality of hers. He had known enchantment—and turned his back on it. He had gone for the safe sensible thing that he had known 'would work' and had relinquished the intangible dream that might lead him he knew not where.

He was a sensible young man, and, as such, uninteresting to Mr Satterthwaite, who was an artist and a connoisseur in life.

He left Roger Graham in his room and went downstairs. The drawing-room was empty. Mabelle's ukelele lay on a stool by the window. He took it up and twanged it absent-mindedly. He knew nothing of the instrument, but his ear told him that it was abominably out of tune. He turned a key experimentally.

Doris Coles came into the room. She looked at him reproachfully.

'Poor Mabelle's uke,' she said.

Her clear condemnation made Mr Satterthwaite feel obstinate.

'Tune it for me,' he said, and added: 'If you can.'

'Of course I can,' said Doris, wounded at the suggestion of incompetence in any direction.

She took it from him, twanged a string, turned a key briskly—and the string snapped.

'Well, I never. Oh! I see—but how extraordinary! It's the wrong string—a size too big. It's an A string. How stupid to put that on. Of course it snaps when you try to tune it up. How stupid people are.'

'Yes,' said Mr Satterthwaite. 'They are—even when they try to be clever . . .'

His tone was so odd that she stared at him. He took

the ukelele from her and removed the broken string. He went out of the room holding it in his hand. In the library he found David Keeley.

'Here,' he said.

He held out the string. Keeley took it.

'What's this?'

'A broken ukelele string.' He paused and then went on: '*What did you do with the other one?*'

'The other one?'

'*The one you strangled her with*. You were very clever, weren't you? It was done very quickly—just in that moment we were all laughing and talking in the hall.

'Mabelle came back into this room for her ukelele. You had taken the string off as you fiddled with it just before. You caught her round the throat with it and strangled her. Then you came out and locked the door and joined us. Later, in the dead of night, you came down and—and disposed of the body by hanging it on the door of her room. And you put another string on the ukelele—*but it was the wrong string*, that's why you were stupid.'

There was a pause.

'But why did you do it?' said Mr Satterthwaite. 'In God's name, *why?*'

Mr Keeley laughed, a funny giggling little laugh that made Mr Satterthwaite feel rather sick.

'It was so very simple,' he said. 'That's why! And then— nobody ever noticed me. Nobody ever noticed what I was doing. I thought—I thought I'd have the laugh of them . . .'

And again he gave that furtive little giggle and looked at Mr Satterthwaite with mad eyes.

Mr Satterthwaite was glad that at that moment Inspector Winkfield came into the room.

It was twenty-four hours later, on his way to London, that Mr Satterthwaite awoke from a doze to find a tall dark man sitting opposite to him in the railway carriage. He was not altogether surprised.

'My dear Mr Quin!'

'Yes—I am here.'

Mr Satterthwaite said slowly: 'I can hardly face you. I am ashamed—I failed.'

'Are you sure of that?'

'I did not save her.'

'But you discovered the truth?'

'Yes—that is true. One or other of those young men might have been accused—might even have been found guilty. So, at any rate, I saved a man's life. But, she—she—that strange enchanting creature . . .' His voice broke off.

Mr Quin looked at him.

'Is death the greatest evil that can happen to anyone?'

'I—well—perhaps—No . . .'

Mr Satterthwaite remembered . . . Madge and Roger Graham . . . Mabelle's face in the moonlight—its serene unearthly happiness . . .

'No,' he admitted. 'No—perhaps death is not the greatest evil . . .'

He remembered the ruffled blue chiffon of her dress that had seemed to him like the plumage of a bird . . . A bird with a broken wing . . .

Agatha Christie

When he looked up, he found himself alone. Mr Quin was no longer there.

But he had left something behind.

On the seat was a roughly carved bird fashioned out of some dim blue stone. It had, possibly, no great artistic merit. But it had something else.

It had the vague quality of enchantment.

So said Mr Satterthwaite—and Mr Satterthwaite was a connoisseur.

CHAPTER 11

The World's End

Mr Satterthwaite had come to Corsica because of the Duchess. It was out of his beat. On the Riviera he was sure of his comforts, and to be comfortable meant a lot to Mr Satterthwaite. But though he liked his comfort, he also liked a Duchess. In his way, a harmless, gentlemanly, old-fashioned way, Mr Satterthwaite was a snob. He liked the best people. And the Duchess of Leith was a very authentic Duchess. There were no Chicago pork butchers in her ancestry. She was the daughter of a Duke as well as the wife of one.

For the rest, she was rather a shabby-looking old lady, a good deal given to black bead trimmings on her clothes. She had quantities of diamonds in old-fashioned settings, and she wore them as her mother before her had worn them: pinned all over her indiscriminately. Someone had suggested once that the Duchess stood in the middle of the room whilst her maid flung brooches at her haphazard. She subscribed generously to charities, and looked well after her tenants and dependants, but was extremely mean over small sums. She cadged lifts from her friends, and did her shopping in bargain basements.

The Duchess was seized with a whim for Corsica. Cannes bored her and she had a bitter argument with the hotel proprietor over the price of her rooms.

'And you shall go with me, Satterthwaite,' she said firmly. 'We needn't be afraid of scandal at our time of life.'

Mr Satterthwaite was delicately flattered. No one had ever mentioned scandal in connection with him before. He was far too insignificant. Scandal—and a Duchess—delicious!

'Picturesque you know,' said the Duchess. 'Brigands—all that sort of thing. And extremely cheap, so I've heard. Manuel was positively impudent this morning. These hotel proprietors need putting in their place. They can't expect to get the best people if they go on like this. I told him so plainly.'

'I believe,' said Mr Satterthwaite, 'that one can fly over quite comfortably. From Antibes.'

'They probably charge you a pretty penny for it,' said the Duchess sharply. 'Find out, will you?'

'Certainly, Duchess.'

Mr Satterthwaite was still in a flutter of gratification despite the fact that his role was clearly to be that of a glorified courier.

When she learned the price of a passage by Avion, the Duchess turned it down promptly.

'They needn't think I'm going to pay a ridiculous sum like that to go in one of their nasty dangerous things.'

So they went by boat, and Mr Satterthwaite endured

ten hours of acute discomfort. To begin with, as the boat sailed at seven, he took it for granted that there would be dinner on board. But there was no dinner. The boat was small and the sea was rough. Mr Satterthwaite was decanted at Ajaccio in the early hours of the morning more dead than alive.

The Duchess, on the contrary, was perfectly fresh. She never minded discomfort if she could feel she was saving money. She waxed enthusiastic over the scene on the quay, with the palm trees and the rising sun. The whole population seemed to have turned out to watch the arrival of the boat, and the launching of the gangway was attended with excited cries and directions.

'*On dirait,*' said a stout Frenchman who stood beside them, '*que jamais avant on n'a fait cette manoeuvre là!*'

'That maid of mine has been sick all night,' said the Duchess. 'The girl's a perfect fool.'

Mr Satterthwaite smiled in a pallid fashion.

'A waste of good food, I call it,' continued the Duchess robustly.

'Did she get any food?' asked Mr Satterthwaite enviously.

'I happened to bring some biscuits and a stick of chocolate on board with me,' said the Duchess. 'When I found there was no dinner to be got, I gave the lot to her. The lower classes always make such a fuss about going without their meals.'

With a cry of triumph the launching of the gangway was accomplished. A Musical Comedy chorus of brigands rushed aboard and wrested hand-luggage from the passengers by main force.

'Come on, Satterthwaite,' said the Duchess. 'I want a hot bath and some coffee.'

So did Mr Satterthwaite. He was not wholly successful, however. They were received at the hotel by a bowing manager and were shown to their rooms. The Duchess's had a bathroom attached. Mr Satterthwaite, however, was directed to a bath that appeared to be situated in somebody else's bedroom. To expect the water to be hot at that hour in the morning was, perhaps, unreasonable. Later he drank intensely black coffee, served in a pot without a lid. The shutters and the window of his room had been flung open, and the crisp morning air came in fragrantly. A day of dazzling blue and green.

The waiter waved his hand with a flourish to call attention to the view.

'Ajaccio,' he said solemnly. '*Le plus beau port du monde!*'

And he departed abruptly.

Looking out over the deep blue of the bay, with the snowy mountains beyond, Mr Satterthwaite was almost inclined to agree with him. He finished his coffee, and lying down on the bed, fell fast asleep.

At *déjeuner* the Duchess was in great spirits.

'This is just what will be good for you, Satterthwaite,' she said. 'Get you out of all those dusty little old-maidish ways of yours.' She swept a *lorgnette* round the room. 'Upon my word, there's Naomi Carlton Smith.'

She indicated a girl sitting by herself at a table in the window. A round-shouldered girl, who slouched as she sat. Her dress appeared to be made of some kind of brown sacking. She had black hair, untidily bobbed.

'An artist?' asked Mr Satterthwaite.

He was always good at placing people.

'Quite right,' said the Duchess. 'Calls herself one anyway. I knew she was mooching around in some queer quarter of the globe. Poor as a church mouse, proud as Lucifer, and a bee in her bonnet like all the Carlton Smiths. Her mother was my first cousin.'

'She's one of the Knowlton lot then?'

The Duchess nodded.

'Been her own worst enemy,' she volunteered. 'Clever girl too. Mixed herself up with a most undesirable young man. One of that Chelsea crowd. Wrote plays or poems or something unhealthy. Nobody took 'em, of course. Then he stole somebody's jewels and got caught out. I forget what they gave him. Five years, I think. But you must remember? It was last winter.'

'Last winter I was in Egypt,' explained Mr Satterthwaite. 'I had 'flu very badly the end of January, and the doctors insisted on Egypt afterwards. I missed a lot.'

His voice rang with a note of real regret.

'That girl seems to me to be moping,' said the Duchess, raising her *lorgnette* once more. 'I can't allow that.'

On her way out, she stopped by Miss Carlton Smith's table and tapped the girl on the shoulder.

'Well, Naomi, you don't seem to remember me?'

Naomi rose rather unwillingly to her feet.

'Yes, I do, Duchess. I saw you come in. I thought it was quite likely you mightn't recognize me.'

She drawled the words lazily, with a complete indifference of manner.

Agatha Christie

'When you've finished your lunch, come and talk to me on the terrace,' ordered the Duchess.

'Very well.'

Naomi yawned.

'Shocking manners,' said the Duchess, to Mr Satterthwaite, as she resumed her progress. 'All the Carlton Smiths have.'

They had their coffee outside in the sunshine. They had been there about six minutes when Naomi Carlton Smith lounged out from the hotel and joined them. She let herself fall slackly on to a chair with her legs stretched out ungracefully in front of her.

An odd face, with its jutting chin and deep-set grey eyes. A clever, unhappy face—a face that only just missed being beautiful.

'Well, Naomi,' said the Duchess briskly. 'And what are you doing with yourself?'

'Oh, I dunno. Just marking time.'

'Been painting?'

'A bit.'

'Show me your things.'

Naomi grinned. She was not cowed by the autocrat. She was amused. She went into the hotel and came out again with a portfolio.

'You won't like 'em, Duchess,' she said warningly. 'Say what you like. You won't hurt my feelings.'

Mr Satterthwaite moved his chair a little nearer. He was interested. In another minute he was more interested still. The Duchess was frankly unsympathetic.

'I can't even see which way the things ought to be,' she

complained. 'Good gracious, child, there was never a sky that colour—or a sea either.'

'That's the way I see 'em,' said Naomi placidly.

'Ugh!' said the Duchess, inspecting another. 'This gives me the creeps.'

'It's meant to,' said Naomi. 'You're paying me a compliment without knowing it.'

It was a queer vorticist study of prickly pear—just recognizable as such. Grey-green with splodges of violent colour where the fruit glittered like jewels. A swirling mass of evil, fleshy—festering. Mr Satterthwaite shuddered and turned his head aside.

He found Naomi looking at him and nodding her head in comprehension.

'I know,' she said. 'But it *is* beastly.'

The Duchess cleared her throat.

'It seems quite easy to be an artist nowadays,' she observed witheringly. 'There's no attempt to copy things. You just shovel on some paint—I don't know what with, not a brush, I'm sure—'

'Palette knife,' interposed Naomi, smiling broadly once more.

'A good deal at a time,' continued the Duchess. 'In lumps. And there you are! Everyone says: "How clever." Well, I've no patience with that sort of thing. Give me—'

'A nice picture of a dog or a horse, by Edwin Landseer.'

'And why not?' demanded the Duchess. 'What's wrong with Landseer?'

'Nothing,' said Naomi. 'He's all right. And you're all

right. The tops of things are always nice and shiny and smooth. I respect you, Duchess, you've got force. You've met life fair and square and you've come out on top. But the people who are underneath see the under side of things. And that's interesting in a way.'

The Duchess stared at her.

'I haven't the faintest idea what you're talking about,' she declared.

Mr Satterthwaite was still examining the sketches. He realized, as the Duchess could not, the perfection of technique behind them. He was startled and delighted. He looked up at the girl.

'Will you sell me one of these, Miss Carlton Smith?' he asked.

'You can have any one you like for five guineas,' said the girl indifferently.

Mr Satterthwaite hesitated a minute or two and then he selected a study of prickly pear and aloe. In the foreground was a vivid blur of yellow mimosa, the scarlet of the aloe flower danced in and out of the picture, and inexorable, mathematically underlying the whole, was the oblong pattern of the prickly pear and the sword motif of the aloe.

He made a little bow to the girl.

'I am very happy to have secured this, and I think I have made a bargain. Some day, Miss Carlton Smith, I shall be able to sell this sketch at a very good profit—if I want to!'

The girl leant forward to see which one he had taken. He saw a new look come into her eyes. For the first time she was really aware of his existence, and there was respect in the quick glance she gave him.

'You have chosen the best,' she said. 'I—I am glad.'

'Well, I suppose you know what you're doing,' said the Duchess. 'And I daresay you're right. I've heard that you are quite a connoisseur. But you can't tell me that all this new stuff is art, because it isn't. Still, we needn't go into that. Now I'm only going to be here a few days and I want to see something of the island. You've got a car, I suppose, Naomi?'

The girl nodded.

'Excellent,' said the Duchess. 'We'll make a trip somewhere tomorrow.'

'It's only a two-seater.'

'Nonsense, there's a dickey, I suppose, that will do for Mr Satterthwaite?'

A shuddering sigh went through Mr Satterthwaite. He had observed the Corsican roads that morning. Naomi was regarding him thoughtfully.

'I'm afraid my car would be no good to you,' she said. 'It's a terribly battered old bus. I bought it second-hand for a mere song. It will just get me up the hills—with coaxing. But I can't take passengers. There's quite a good garage, though, in the town. You can hire a car there.'

'Hire a car?' said the Duchess, scandalized. 'What an idea. Who's that nice-looking man, rather yellow, who drove up in a four-seater just before lunch?'

'I expect you mean Mr Tomlinson. He's a retired Indian judge.'

'That accounts for the yellowness,' said the Duchess. 'I was afraid it might be jaundice. He seems quite a decent sort of man. I shall talk to him.'

Agatha Christie

That evening, on coming down to dinner, Mr Satterthwaite found the Duchess resplendent in black velvet and diamonds, talking earnestly to the owner of the four-seater car. She beckoned authoritatively.

'Come here, Mr Satterthwaite, Mr Tomlinson is telling me the most interesting things, and what do you think?— he is actually going to take us on an expedition tomorrow in his car.'

Mr Satterthwaite regarded her with admiration.

'We must go in to dinner,' said the Duchess. 'Do come and sit at our table, Mr Tomlinson, and then you can go on with what you were telling me.'

'Quite a decent sort of man,' the Duchess pronounced later.

'With quite a decent sort of car,' retorted Mr Satterthwaite.

'Naughty,' said the Duchess, and gave him a resounding blow on the knuckles with the dingy black fan she always carried. Mr Satterthwaite winced with pain.

'Naomi is coming too,' said the Duchess. 'In her car. That girl wants taking out of herself. She's very selfish. Not exactly self-centred, but totally indifferent to everyone and everything. Don't you agree?'

'I don't think that's possible,' said Mr Satterthwaite, slowly. 'I mean, everyone's interest must go *somewhere*. There are, of course, the people who revolve round themselves—but I agree with you, she's not one of that kind. She's totally uninterested in herself. And yet she's got a strong character—there must be *something*. I thought at first it was her art—but it isn't. I've never met anyone so detached from life. That's dangerous.'

'Dangerous? What do you mean?'

'Well, you see—it must mean an obsession of some kind, and obsessions are always dangerous.'

'Satterthwaite,' said the Duchess, 'don't be a fool. And listen to me. About tomorrow—'

Mr Satterthwaite listened. It was very much his role in life.

They started early the following morning, taking their lunch with them. Naomi, who had been six months in the island, was to be the pioneer. Mr Satterthwaite went over to her as she sat waiting to start.

'You are sure that—I can't come with you?' he said wistfully.

She shook her head.

'You'll be much more comfortable in the back of the other car. Nicely padded seats and all that. This is a regular old rattle trap. You'd leap in the air going over the bumps.'

'And then, of course, the hills.'

Naomi laughed.

'Oh, I only said that to rescue you from the dickey. The Duchess could perfectly well afford to have hired a car. She's the meanest woman in England. All the same, the old thing is rather a sport, and I can't help liking her.'

'Then I could come with you after all?' said Mr Satterthwaite eagerly.

She looked at him curiously.

'Why are you so anxious to come with me?'

'Can you ask?' Mr Satterthwaite made his funny old-fashioned bow.

She smiled, but shook her head.

'That isn't the reason,' she said thoughtfully. 'It's odd . . . But you can't come with me—not today.'

'Another day, perhaps,' suggested Mr Satterthwaite politely.

'Oh, another day!' she laughed suddenly, a very queer laugh, Mr Satterthwaite thought. 'Another day! Well, we'll see.'

They started. They drove through the town, and then round the long curve of the bay, winding inland to cross a river and then back to the coast with its hundreds of little sandy coves. And then they began to climb. In and out, round nerve-shattering curves, upwards, ever upwards on the tortuous winding road. The blue bay was far below them, and on the other side of it Ajaccio sparkled in the sun, white, like a fairy city.

In and out, in and out, with a precipice first one side of them, then the other. Mr Satterthwaite felt slightly giddy, he also felt slightly sick. The road was not very wide. And still they climbed.

It was cold now. The wind came to them straight off the snow peaks. Mr Satterthwaite turned up his coat collar and buttoned it tightly under his chin.

It was very cold. Across the water, Ajaccio was still bathed in sunlight, but up here thick grey clouds came drifting across the face of the sun. Mr Satterthwaite ceased to admire the view. He yearned for a steam-heated hotel and a comfortable armchair.

Ahead of them Naomi's little two-seater drove steadily forward. Up, still up. They were on top of the world now. On either side of them were lower hills, hills sloping down to valleys. They looked straight across to the snow peaks. And the wind came tearing over them, sharp, like a knife. Suddenly Naomi's car stopped, and she looked back.

'We've arrived,' she said. 'At the World's End. And I don't think it's an awfully good day for it.'

They all got out. They had arrived in a tiny village, with half a dozen stone cottages. An imposing name was printed in letters a foot high.

'Coti Chiaveeri.'

Naomi shrugged her shoulders.

'That's its official name, but I prefer to call it the World's End.'

She walked on a few steps, and Mr Satterthwaite joined her. They were beyond the houses now. The road stopped. As Naomi had said, this was the end, the back of beyond, the beginning of nowhere. Behind them the white ribbon of the road, in front of them—nothing. Only far, far below, the sea . . .

Mr Satterthwaite drew a deep breath.

'It's an extraordinary place. One feels that anything might happen here, that one might meet—anyone—'

He stopped, for just in front of them a man was sitting on a boulder, his face turned to the sea. They had not seen him till this moment, and his appearance had the suddenness of a conjuring trick. He might have sprung from the surrounding landscape.

'I wonder—' began Mr Satterthwaite.

But at that minute the stranger turned, and Mr Satterthwaite saw his face.

'Why, Mr Quin! How extraordinary. Miss Carlton Smith, I want to introduce my friend Mr Quin to you. He's the most unusual fellow. You are, you know. You always turn up in the nick of time—'

He stopped, with the feeling that he had said something awkwardly significant, and yet for the life of him he could not think what it was.

Naomi had shaken hands with Mr Quin in her usual abrupt style.

'We're here for a picnic,' she said. 'And it seems to me we shall be pretty well frozen to the bone.'

Mr Satterthwaite shivered.

'Perhaps,' he said uncertainly, 'we shall find a sheltered spot?'

'Which this isn't,' agreed Naomi. 'Still, it's worth seeing, isn't it?'

'Yes, indeed.' Mr Satterthwaite turned to Mr Quin. 'Miss Carlton Smith calls this place the World's End. Rather a good name, eh?'

Mr Quin nodded his head slowly several times.

'Yes—a very suggestive name. I suppose one only comes once in one's life to a place like that—a place where one can't go on any longer.'

'What do you mean?' asked Naomi sharply.

He turned to her.

'Well, usually, there's a choice, isn't there? To the right or to the left. Forward or back. Here—there's the road behind you and in front of you—nothing.'

Naomi stared at him. Suddenly she shivered and began to retrace her steps towards the others. The two men fell in beside her. Mr Quin continued to talk, but his tone was now easily conversational.

'Is the small car yours, Miss Carlton Smith?'

'Yes.'

'You drive yourself? One needs, I think, a good deal of nerve to do that round here. The turns are rather appalling. A moment of inattention, a brake that failed to hold, and—over the edge—down—down—down. It would be—very easily done.'

They had now joined the others. Mr Satterthwaite introduced his friend. He felt a tug at his arm. It was Naomi. She drew him apart from the others.

'Who is he?' she demanded fiercely.

Mr Satterthwaite gazed at her in astonishment.

'Well, I hardly know. I mean, I have known him for some years now—we have run across each other from time to time, but in the sense of knowing actually—'

He stopped. These were futilities that he was uttering, and the girl by his side was not listening. She was standing with her head bent down, her hands clenched by her sides.

'He knows things,' she said. 'He knows things . . . How does he know?'

Mr Satterthwaite had no answer. He could only look at her dumbly, unable to comprehend the storm that shook her.

'I'm afraid,' she muttered.

'Afraid of Mr Quin?'

'I'm afraid of his eyes. He sees things . . .'

Something cold and wet fell on Mr Satterthwaite's cheek. He looked up.

'Why, it's snowing,' he exclaimed, in great surprise.

'A nice day to have chosen for a picnic,' said Naomi.

She had regained control of herself with an effort.

What was to be done? A babel of suggestions broke out. The snow came down thick and fast. Mr Quin made a suggestion and everyone welcomed it. There was a little stone Cassecroute at the end of the row of houses. There was a stampede towards it.

'You have your provisions,' said Mr Quin, 'and they will probably be able to make you some coffee.'

It was a tiny place, rather dark, for the one little window did little towards lighting it, but from one end came a grateful glow of warmth. An old Corsican woman was just throwing a handful of branches on the fire. It blazed up, and by its light the newcomers realized that others were before them.

Three people were sitting at the end of a bare wooden table. There was something unreal about the scene to Mr Satterthwaite's eye, there was something even more unreal about the people.

The woman who sat at the end of the table looked like a duchess—that is, she looked more like a popular conception of a duchess. She was the ideal stage *grande dame*. Her aristocratic head was held high, her exquisitely dressed hair was of a snowy white. She was dressed in grey—soft draperies that fell about her in artistic folds. One long white hand supported her chin, the other was holding a roll spread with *pâté de foie gras*. On her right was a man with a very white face, very black hair, and horn-rimmed spectacles. He was marvellously and beautifully dressed.

280

At the moment his head was thrown back, and his left arm was thrown out as though he were about to declaim something.

On the left of the white-haired lady was a jolly-looking little man with a bald head. After the first glance, nobody looked at him.

There was just a moment of uncertainty, and then the Duchess (the authentic Duchess) took charge.

'Isn't this storm too dreadful?' she said pleasantly, coming forward, and smiling a purposeful and efficient smile that she had found very useful when serving on Welfare and other committees. 'I suppose you've been caught in it just like we have? But Corsica is a marvellous place. I only arrived this morning.'

The man with the black hair got up, and the Duchess with a gracious smile slipped into his seat.

The white-haired lady spoke.

'We have been here a week,' she said.

Mr Satterthwaite started. Could anyone who had once heard that voice ever forget it? It echoed round the stone room, charged with emotion—with exquisite melancholy. It seemed to him that she had said something wonderful, memorable, full of meaning. She had spoken from her heart.

He spoke in a hurried aside to Mr Tomlinson.

'The man in spectacles is Mr Vyse—the producer, you know.'

The retired Indian judge was looking at Mr Vyse with a good deal of dislike.

'What does he produce?' he asked. 'Children?'

'Oh, dear me, no,' said Mr Satterthwaite, shocked by the mere mention of anything so crude in connection with Mr Vyse. 'Plays.'

'I think,' said Naomi, 'I'll go out again. It's too hot in here.'

Her voice, strong and harsh, made Mr Satterthwaite jump. She made almost blindly, as it seemed, for the door, brushing Mr Tomlinson aside. But in the doorway itself she came face to face with Mr Quin, and he barred her way.

'Go back and sit down,' he said.

His voice was authoritative. To Mr Satterthwaite's surprise the girl hesitated a minute and then obeyed. She sat down at the foot of the table as far from the others as possible.

Mr Satterthwaite bustled forward and button-holed the producer.

'You may not remember me,' he began, 'my name is Satterthwaite.'

'Of course!' A long bony hand shot out and enveloped the other's in a painful grip. 'My dear man. Fancy meeting you here. You know Miss Nunn, of course?'

Mr Satterthwaite jumped. No wonder that voice had been familiar. Thousands, all over England, had thrilled to those wonderful emotion-laden tones. Rosina Nunn! England's greatest emotional actress. Mr Satterthwaite too had lain under her spell. No one like her for interpreting a part—for bringing out the finer shades of meaning. He had thought of her always as an intellectual actress, one who comprehended and got inside the soul of her part.

He might be excused for not recognizing her. Rosina Nunn was volatile in her tastes. For twenty-five years of her life she had been a blonde. After a tour in the States she had returned with the locks of the raven, and she had taken up tragedy in earnest. This 'French Marquise' effect was her latest whim.

'Oh, by the way, Mr Judd—Miss Nunn's husband,' said Vyse, carelessly introducing the man with the bald head.

Rosina Nunn had had several husbands, Mr Satterthwaite knew. Mr Judd was evidently the latest.

Mr Judd was busily unwrapping packages from a hamper at his side. He addressed his wife.

'Some more *pâté*, dearest? That last wasn't as thick as you like it.'

Rosina Nunn surrendered her roll to him, as she murmured simply:

'Henry thinks of the most enchanting meals. I always leave the commissariat to him.'

'Feed the brute,' said Mr Judd, and laughed. He patted his wife on the shoulder.

'Treats her just as though she were a dog,' murmured the melancholy voice of Mr Vyse in Mr Satterthwaite's ear. 'Cuts up her food for her. Odd creatures, women.'

Mr Satterthwaite and Mr Quin between them unpacked lunch. Hard-boiled eggs, cold ham and Gruyère cheese were distributed round the table. The Duchess and Miss Nunn appeared to be deep in murmured confidences. Fragments came along in the actress's deep contralto.

'The bread must be lightly toasted, you understand? Then just a *very* thin layer of marmalade. Rolled up and put in the oven for one minute—not more. Simply delicious.'

'That woman lives for food,' murmured Mr Vyse. 'Simply lives for it. She can't think of anything else. I remember in *Riders to the Sea*—you know "and it's the fine quiet time I'll be having." I could *not* get the effect I wanted. At last I told her to think of peppermint creams—she's very fond of peppermint creams. I got the effect at once—a sort of far-away look that went to your very soul.'

Mr Satterthwaite was silent. He was remembering.

Mr Tomlinson opposite cleared his throat preparatory to entering into conversation.

'You produce plays, I hear, eh? I'm fond of a good play myself. *Jim the Penman*, now, that was a play.'

'My God,' said Mr Vyse, and shivered down all the long length of him.

'A tiny clove of garlic,' said Miss Nunn to the Duchess. 'You tell your cook. It's wonderful.'

She sighed happily and turned to her husband.

'Henry,' she said plaintively, 'I've never even *seen* the caviare.'

'You're as near as nothing to sitting on it,' returned Mr Judd cheerfully. 'You put it behind you on the chair.'

Rosina Nunn retrieved it hurriedly, and beamed round the table.

'Henry is too wonderful. I'm so terribly absentminded. I never know where I've put anything.'

'Like the day you packed your pearls in your sponge bag,' said Henry jocosely. 'And then left it behind at the hotel. My word, I did a bit of wiring and phoning that day.'

'They were insured,' said Miss Nunn dreamily. 'Not like my opal.'

A spasm of exquisite heartrending grief flitted across her face.

Several times, when in the company of Mr Quin, Mr Satterthwaite had had the feeling of taking part in a play. The illusion was with him very strongly now. This was a dream. Everyone had his part. The words 'my opal' were his own cue. He leant forward.

'Your opal, Miss Nunn?'

'Have you got the butter, Henry? Thank you. Yes, my opal. It was stolen, you know. And I never got it back.'

'Do tell us,' said Mr Satterthwaite.

'Well—I was born in October—so it was lucky for me to wear opals, and because of that I wanted a real beauty. I waited a long time for it. They said it was one of the most perfect ones known. Not very large—about the size of a two-shilling piece—but oh! the colour and the fire.'

She sighed. Mr Satterthwaite observed that the Duchess was fidgeting and seemed uncomfortable, but nothing could stop Miss Nunn now. She went on, and the exquisite inflections of her voice made the story sound like some mournful saga of old.

'It was stolen by a young man called Alec Gerard. He wrote plays.'

'Very good plays,' put in Mr Vyse professionally. 'Why, I once kept one of his plays for six months.'

'Did you produce it?' asked Mr Tomlinson.

'Oh, *no*,' said Mr Vyse, shocked at the idea. 'But do you know, at one time I actually thought of doing so?'

'It had a wonderful part in it for me,' said Miss Nunn. '*Rachel's Children*, it was called—though there wasn't anyone called Rachel in the play. He came to talk to me about it—at the theatre. I liked him. He was a nice-looking—and very shy, poor boy. I remember'—a beautiful far-away look stole over her face—'he bought me some peppermint creams. The opal was lying on the dressing-table. He'd been out in Australia, and he knew something about opals. He took it over to the light to look at it. I suppose he must have slipped it into his pocket then. I missed it as soon as he'd gone. There *was* a to-do. You remember?'

She turned to Mr Vyse.

'Oh, I remember,' said Mr Vyse with a groan.

'They found the empty case in his rooms,' continued the actress. 'He'd been terribly hard up, but the very next day he was able to pay large sums into his bank. He pretended to account for it by saying that a friend of his had put some money on a horse for him, but he couldn't produce the friend. He said he must have put the case in his pocket by mistake. I think that was a terribly weak thing to say, don't you? He might have thought of some-thing better than that . . . I had to go and give evidence. There were pictures of me in all the papers. My press agent said it was very good publicity—but I'd much rather have had my opal back.'

She shook her head sadly.

'Have some preserved pineapple?' said Mr Judd.

Miss Nunn brightened up.

'Where is it?'

'I gave it to you just now.'

Miss Nunn looked behind her and in front of her, eyed her grey silk pochette, and then slowly drew up a large purple silk bag that was reposing on the ground beside her. She began to turn the contents out slowly on the table, much to Mr Satterthwaite's interest.

There was a powder puff, a lip-stick, a small jewel case, a skein of wool, another powder puff, two handkerchiefs, a box of chocolate creams, an enamelled paper knife, a mirror, a little dark brown wooden box, five letters, a walnut, a small square of mauve crêpe de chine, a piece of ribbon and the end of a *croissant*. Last of all came the preserved pineapple.

'*Eureka*,' murmured Mr Satterthwaite softly.

'I beg your pardon?'

'Nothing,' said Mr Satterthwaite hastily. 'What a charming paper knife.'

'Yes, isn't it? Somebody gave it to me. I can't remember who.'

'That's an Indian box,' remarked Mr Tomlinson. 'Ingenious little things, aren't they?'

'Somebody gave me that too,' said Miss Nunn. 'I've had it a long time. It used always to stand on my dressing-table at the theatre. I don't think it's very pretty, though, do you?'

The box was of plain dark brown wood. It pushed open from the side. On the top of it were two plain flaps of wood that could be turned round and round.

'Not pretty, perhaps,' said Mr Tomlinson with a chuckle. 'But I'll bet you've never seen one like it.'

Mr Satterthwaite leaned forward. He had an excited feeling.

'Why did you say it was ingenious?' he demanded.

'Well, isn't it?'

The judge appealed to Miss Nunn. She looked at him blankly.

'I suppose I mustn't show them the trick of it—eh?' Miss Nunn still looked blank.

'What trick?' asked Mr Judd.

'God bless my soul, don't you know?'

He looked round the inquiring faces.

'Fancy that now. May I take the box a minute? Thank you.'

He pushed it open.

'Now then, can anyone give me something to put in it—not too big. Here's a small piece of Gruyère cheese. That will do capitally. I place it inside, shut the box.'

He fumbled for a minute or two with his hands.

'Now see—'

He opened the box again. It was empty.

'Well, I never,' said Mr Judd. 'How do you do it?'

'It's quite simple. Turn the box upside down, and move the left hand flap half-way round, then shut the right hand flap. Now to bring our piece of cheese back again we must reverse that. The right hand flap half-way round, and the left one closed, still keeping the box upside down. And now—Hey Presto!'

The box slid open. A gasp went round the table. The

cheese was there—but so was something else. A round thing that blinked forth every colour of the rainbow.

'*My opal!*'

It was a clarion note. Rosina Nunn stood upright, her hands clasped to her breast.

'My opal! How did it get there?'

Henry Judd cleared his throat.

'I—er—I rather think, Rosy, my girl, you must have put it there yourself.'

Someone got up from the table and blundered out into the air. It was Naomi Carlton Smith. Mr Quin followed her.

'But when? Do you mean—?'

Mr Satterthwaite watched her while the truth dawned on her. It took over two minutes before she got it.

'You mean last year—at the theatre.'

'You know,' said Henry apologetically. 'You *do* fiddle with things, Rosy. Look at you with the caviare today.'

Miss Nunn was painfully following out her mental processes.

'I just slipped it in without thinking, and then I suppose I turned the box about and did the thing by accident, but then—but then—' At last it came. 'But then Alec Gerard didn't steal it after all. Oh!'—a full-throated cry, poignant, moving—'How dreadful!'

'Well,' said Mr Vyse, 'that can be put right now.'

'Yes, but he's been in prison a year.' And then she startled them. She turned sharp on the Duchess. 'Who is that girl—that girl who has just gone out?'

'Miss Carlton Smith,' said the Duchess, 'was engaged to Mr Gerard. She—took the thing very hard.'

Mr Satterthwaite stole softly away. The snow had stopped. Naomi was sitting on the stone wall. She had a sketch book in her hand, some coloured crayons were scattered around. Mr Quin was standing beside her.

She held out the sketch book to Mr Satterthwaite. It was a very rough affair—but it had genius. A kaleidoscopic whirl of snowflakes with a figure in the centre.

'Very good,' said Mr Satterthwaite.

Mr Quin looked up at the sky.

'The storm is over,' he said. 'The roads will be slippery, but I do not think there will be any accident—now.'

'There will be no accident,' said Naomi. Her voice was charged with some meaning that Mr Satterthwaite did not understand. She turned and smiled at him—a sudden dazzling smile. 'Mr Satterthwaite can drive back with me if he likes.'

He knew then to what length desperation had driven her.

'Well,' said Mr Quin, 'I must bid you goodbye.'

He moved away.

'Where is he going?' said Mr Satterthwaite, staring after him.

'Back where he came from, I suppose,' said Naomi in an odd voice.

'But—but there isn't anything there,' said Mr Satterthwaite, for Mr Quin was making for that spot on the edge of the cliff where they had first seen him. 'You know you said yourself it was the World's End.'

He handed back the sketch book.

'It's very good,' he said. 'A very good likeness. But why—er—why did you put him in Fancy Dress?'

Her eyes met his for a brief second.

'I see him like that,' said Naomi Carlton Smith.

CHAPTER 12

Harlequin's Lane

Mr Satterthwaite was never quite sure what took him to stay with the Denmans. They were not of his kind—that is to say, they belonged neither to the great world, nor to the more interesting artistic circles. They were Philistines, and dull Philistines at that. Mr Satterthwaite had met them first at Biarritz, had accepted an invitation to stay with them, had come, had been bored, and yet strangely enough had come again and yet again.

Why? He was asking himself that question on this twenty-first of June, as he sped out of London in his Rolls Royce.

John Denman was a man of forty, a solid well-established figure respected in the business world. His friends were not Mr Satterthwaite's friends, his ideas even less so. He was a man clever in his own line but devoid of imagination outside it.

Why am I doing this thing? Mr Satterthwaite asked himself once more—and the only answer that came seemed to him so vague and so inherently preposterous that he almost put it aside. For the only reason that presented itself was the fact that one of the rooms in the house (a comfortable well-appointed house), stirred his curiosity. That room was Mrs Denman's own sitting-room.

It was hardly an expression of her personality because, so far as Mr Satterthwaite could judge, she had no personality. He had never met a woman so completely expressionless. She was, he knew, a Russian by birth. John Denman had been in Russia at the outbreak of the European war, he had fought with the Russian troops, had narrowly escaped with his life on the outbreak of the Revolution, and had brought this Russian girl with him, a penniless refugee. In face of strong disapproval from his parents he had married her.

Mrs Denman's room was in no way remarkable. It was well and solidly furnished with good Hepplewhite furniture—a trifle more masculine than feminine in atmosphere. But in it there was one incongruous item: a Chinese lacquer screen—a thing of creamy yellow and pale rose. Any museum might have been glad to own it. It was a collector's piece, rare and beautiful.

It was out of place against that solid English background. It should have been the key-note of the room with everything arranged to harmonize subtly with it. And yet Mr Satterthwaite could not accuse the Denmans of lack of taste. Everything else in the house was in perfectly blended accord.

He shook his head. The thing—trivial though it was—puzzled him. Because of it, so he verily believed, he had come again and again to the house. It was, perhaps, a woman's fantasy—but that solution did not satisfy him as he thought of Mrs Denman—a quiet hard-featured woman, speaking English so correctly that no one would ever have guessed her a foreigner.

The car drew up at his destination and he got out, his mind still dwelling on the problem of the Chinese screen. The name of the Denman's house was 'Ashmead', and it occupied some five acres of Melton Heath, which is thirty miles from London, stands five hundred feet above sea level and is, for the most part, inhabited by those who have ample incomes.

The butler received Mr Satterthwaite suavely. Mr and Mrs Denman were both out—at a rehearsal—they hoped Mr Satterthwaite would make himself at home until they returned.

Mr Satterthwaite nodded and proceeded to carry out these injunctions by stepping into the garden. After a cursory examination of the flower beds, he strolled down a shady walk and presently came to a door in the wall. It was unlocked and he passed through it and came out into a narrow lane.

Mr Satterthwaite looked to left and right. A very charming lane, shady and green, with high hedges—a rural lane that twisted and turned in good old-fashioned style. He remembered the stamped address: ASHMEAD, HARLEQUIN'S LANE—remembered too, a local name for it that Mrs Denman had once told him.

'Harlequin's Lane,' he murmured to himself softly. 'I wonder—'

He turned a corner.

Not at the time, but afterwards, he wondered why this time he felt no surprise at meeting that elusive friend of his: Mr Harley Quin. The two men clasped hands.

'So *you're* down here,' said Mr Satterthwaite.

'Yes,' said Mr Quin. 'I'm staying in the same house as you are.'

'Staying there?'

'Yes. Does it surprise you?'

'No,' said Mr Satterthwaite slowly. 'Only—well, you never stay anywhere for long, do you?'

'Only as long as is necessary,' said Mr Quin gravely.

'I see,' said Mr Satterthwaite.

They walked on in silence for some minutes.

'This lane,' began Mr Satterthwaite, and stopped.

'Belongs to me,' said Mr Quin.

'I thought it did,' said Mr Satterthwaite. 'Somehow, I thought it must. There's the other name for it, too, the local name. They call it the "Lovers' Lane". You know that?'

Mr Quin nodded.

'But surely,' he said gently, 'there is a "Lovers' Lane" in every village?'

'I suppose so,' said Mr Satterthwaite, and he sighed a little.

He felt suddenly rather old and out of things, a little dried-up wizened old fogey of a man. Each side of him were the hedges, very green and alive.

'Where does this lane end, I wonder?' he asked suddenly.

'It ends—*here*,' said Mr Quin.

They came round the last bend. The lane ended in a

piece of waste ground, and almost at their feet a great pit opened. In it were tin cans gleaming in the sun, and other cans that were too red with rust to gleam, old boots, fragments of newspapers, a hundred and one odds and ends that were no longer of account to anybody.

'A rubbish heap,' exclaimed Mr Satterthwaite, and breathed deeply and indignantly.

'Sometimes there are very wonderful things on a rubbish heap,' said Mr Quin.

'I know, I know,' cried Mr Satterthwaite, and quoted with just a trace of self-consciousness: '*Bring me the two most beautiful things in the city, said God.* You know how it goes, eh?'

Mr Quin nodded.

Mr Satterthwaite looked up at the ruins of a small cottage perched on the brink of the wall of the cliff.

'Hardly a pretty view for a house,' he remarked.

'I fancy this wasn't a rubbish heap in those days,' said Mr Quin. 'I believe the Denmans lived there when they were first married. They moved into the big house when the old people died. The cottage was pulled down when they began to quarry the rock here—but nothing much was done, as you can see.'

They turned and began retracing their steps.

'I suppose,' said Mr Sattertwaite, smiling, 'that many couples come wandering down this lane on these warm summer evenings.'

'Probably.'

'Lovers,' said Mr Satterthwaite. He repeated the word thoughtfully and quite without the normal embarrassment of the Englishman. Mr Quin had that effect upon him. 'Lovers . . . You have done a lot for lovers, Mr Quin.'

The other bowed his head without replying.

'You have saved them from sorrow—from worse than sorrow, from death. You have been an advocate for the dead themselves.'

'You are speaking of yourself—of what *you* have done— not of me.'

'It is the same thing,' said Mr Satterthwaite. 'You know it is,' he urged, as the other did not speak. 'You have acted—through me. For some reason or other you do not act directly—yourself.'

'Sometimes I do,' said Mr Quin.

His voice held a new note. In spite of himself Mr Satterthwaite shivered a little. The afternoon, he thought, must be growing chilly. And yet the sun seemed as bright as ever.

At that moment a girl turned the corner ahead of them and came into sight. She was a very pretty girl, fair-haired and blue-eyed, wearing a pink cotton frock. Mr Satterthwaite recognized her as Molly Stanwell, whom he had met down here before.

She waved a hand to welcome him.

'John and Anna have just gone back,' she cried. 'They thought you must have come, but they simply had to be at the rehearsal.'

'Rehearsal of what?' inquired Mr Satterthwaite.

'This masquerade thing—I don't quite know what you'll call it. There is singing and dancing and all sorts of things in it. Mr Manly, do you remember him down here? He had quite a good tenor voice, is to be Pierrot, and I am Pierrette. Two professionals are coming down for the dancing—Harlequin and Columbine, you know. And then there is a big chorus of girls. Lady Roscheimer is so keen on training village girls to sing. She's really getting the thing up for that. The music is rather lovely—but very modern— next to no tune anywhere. Claude Wickam. Perhaps you know him?'

Mr Satterthwaite nodded, for, as has been mentioned before, it was his *métier* to know everybody. He knew all about that aspiring genius Claude Wickam, and about Lady Roscheimer who had a *penchant* for young men of the artistic persuasion. And he knew all about Sir Leopold Roscheimer who liked his wife to be happy and, most rare among husbands, did not mind her being happy in her own way.

They found Claude Wickam at tea with the Denmans, cramming his mouth indiscriminately with anything handy, talking rapidly, and waving long white hands that had a double-jointed appearance. His short-sighted eyes peered through large horn-rimmed spectacles.

John Denman, upright, slightly florid, with the faintest possible tendency to sleekness, listened with an air of bored attention. On the appearance of Mr Satterthwaite, the musician transferred his remarks to him. Anna Denman sat behind the tea things, quiet and expression-less as usual.

Mr Satterthwaite stole a covert glance at her. Tall, gaunt, very thin, with the skin tightly stretched over high cheek bones, black hair parted in the middle, a skin that was weather-beaten. An out of door woman who cared nothing for the use of cosmetics. A Dutch Doll of a woman, wooden, lifeless—and yet . . .

He thought: 'There *should* be meaning behind that face, and yet there isn't. That's what's all wrong. Yes, all wrong.' And to Claude Wickam he said: 'I beg your pardon? You were saying?'

Claude Wickam, who liked the sound of his own voice, began all over again. 'Russia,' he said, 'that was the only country in the world worth being interested in. They experimented. With lives, if you like, but still they experimented. Magnificent!' He crammed a sandwich into his mouth with one hand, and added a bite of the chocolate éclair he was waving about in the other. 'Take,' he said (with his mouth full), 'the Russian Ballet.' Remembering his hostess, he turned to her. What did *she* think of the Russian Ballet?

The question was obviously only a prelude to the important point—what Claude Wickam thought of the Russian Ballet, but her answer was unexpected and threw him completely out of his stride.

'I have never seen it.'

'What?' He gazed at her open-mouthed. 'But—surely—'

Her voice went on, level and emotionless.

'Before my marriage, I was a dancer. So now—'

'A busman's holiday,' said her husband.

'Dancing.' She shrugged her shoulders. 'I know all the tricks of it. It does not interest me.'

'Oh!'

It took but a moment for Claude to recover his aplomb. His voice went on.

'Talking of lives,' said Mr Satterthwaite, 'and experimenting in them. The Russian nation made one costly experiment.'

Claude Wickam swung round on him.

'I know what you are going to say,' he cried. 'Kharsanova! The immortal, the only Kharsanova! You saw her dance?'

'Three times,' said Mr Satterthwaite. 'Twice in Paris, once in London. I shall—not forget it.'

He spoke in an almost reverent voice.

'I saw her, too,' said Claude Wickam. 'I was ten years old. An uncle took me. God! I shall never forget it.'

He threw a piece of bun fiercely into a flower bed.

'There is a statuette of her in a museum in Berlin,' said Mr Satterthwaite. 'It is marvellous. That impression of fragility—as though you could break her with a flip of the thumb nail. I have seen her as Columbine, in the Swan, as the dying Nymph.' He paused, shaking his head. 'There was genius. It will be long years before such another is born. She was young too. Destroyed ignorantly and wantonly in the first days of the Revolution.'

'Fools! Madmen! Apes!' said Claude Wickam. He choked with a mouthful of tea.

'I studied with Kharsanova,' said Mrs Denman. 'I remember her well.'

'She was wonderful?' said Mr Satterthwaite.

'Yes,' said Mrs Denman quietly. 'She was wonderful.'

Claude Wickam departed and John Denman drew a deep sigh of relief at which his wife laughed.

Mr Satterthwaite nodded. 'I know what you think. But in spite of everything, the music that that boy writes *is* music.'

'I suppose it is,' said Denman.

'Oh, undoubtedly. How long it will be—well, that is different.'

John Denman looked at him curiously.

'You mean?'

'I mean that success has come early. And that is dangerous. Always dangerous.' He looked across at Mr Quin. 'You agree with me?'

'You are always right,' said Mr Quin.

'We will come upstairs to my room,' said Mrs Denman. 'It is pleasant there.'

She led the way, and they followed her. Mr Satterthwaite drew a deep breath as he caught sight of the Chinese screen. He looked up to find Mrs Denman watching him.

'You are the man who is always right,' she said, nodding her head slowly at him. 'What do you make of my screen?'

He felt that in some way the words were a challenge to him, and he answered almost haltingly, stumbling over the words a little.

'Why, it's—it's beautiful. More, it's unique.'

'You're right.' Denman had come up behind him. 'We bought it early in our married life. Got it for about a tenth of its value, but even then—well, it crippled us for over a year. You remember, Anna?'

'Yes,' said Mrs Denman, 'I remember.'

'In fact, we'd no business to buy it at all—not then. Now, of course, it's different. There was some very good lacquer going at Christie's the other day. Just what we need to make this room perfect. All Chinese together. Clear out the other stuff. Would you believe it, Satterthwaite, my wife wouldn't hear of it?'

'I like this room as it is,' said Mrs Denman.

There was a curious look on her face. Again Mr Satterthwaite felt challenged and defeated. He looked round him, and for the first time he noticed the absence of all personal touch. There were no photographs, no flowers, no knick-knacks. It was not like a woman's room at all. Save for that one incongruous factor of the Chinese screen, it might have been a sample room shown at some big furnishing house.

He found her smiling at him.

'Listen,' she said. She bent forward, and for a moment she seemed less English, more definitely foreign. 'I speak to you for you will understand. We bought that screen with more than money—with love. For love of it, because it was beautiful and unique, we went without other things, things we needed and missed. These other Chinese pieces my husband speaks of, those we should buy with money only, we should not pay away anything of ourselves.'

Her husband laughed.

'Oh, have it your own way,' he said, but with a trace of irritation in his voice. 'But it's all wrong against this English background. This other stuff, it's good enough of its kind, genuine solid, no fake about it—but mediocre. Good plain late Hepplewhite.'

She nodded.

'Good, solid, genuine English,' she murmured softly.

Mr Satterthwaite stared at her. He caught a meaning behind these words. The English room—the flaming beauty of the Chinese screen . . . No, it was gone again.

'I met Miss Stanwell in the lane,' he said conversationally. 'She tells me she is going to be Pierrette in this show tonight.'

'Yes, said Denman. 'And she's awfully good, too.'

'She has clumsy feet,' said Anna.

'Nonsense,' said her husband. 'All women are alike, Satterthwaite. Can't bear to hear another woman praised. Molly is a very good-looking girl, and so of course every woman has to have their knife into her.'

'I spoke of dancing,' said Anna Denman. She sounded faintly surprised. 'She is very pretty, yes, but her feet move clumsily. You cannot tell me anything else because I know about dancing.'

Mr Satterthwaite intervened tactfully.

'You have two professional dancers coming down, I understand?'

'Yes. For the ballet proper. Prince Oranoff is bringing them down in his car.'

'Sergius Oranoff?'

The question came from Anna Denman. Her husband turned and looked at her.

'You know him?'

'I used to know him—in Russia.'

Mr Satterthwaite thought that John Denman looked disturbed.

'Will he know you?'

'Yes. He will know me.'

She laughed—a low, almost triumphant laugh. There was nothing of the Dutch Doll about her face now. She nodded reassuringly at her husband.

'Sergius. So he is bringing down the two dancers. He was always interested in dancing.'

'I remember.'

John Denman spoke abruptly, then turned and left the room. Mr Quin followed him. Anna Denman crossed to the telephone and asked for a number. She arrested Mr Satterthwaite with a gesture as he was about to follow the example of the other two men.

'Can I speak to Lady Roscheimer. Oh! it is you. This is Anna Denman speaking. Has Prince Oranoff arrived yet? What? *What?* Oh, my dear! But how ghastly.'

She listened for a few moments longer, then replaced the receiver. She turned to Mr Satterthwaite.

'There has been an accident. There would be with Sergius Ivanovitch driving. Oh, he has not altered in all these years. The girl was not badly hurt, but bruised and shaken, too much to dance tonight. The man's arm is broken. Sergius Ivanovitch himself is unhurt. The devil looks after his own, perhaps.'

'And what about tonight's performance?'

'Exactly, my friend. Something must be done about it.'

She sat thinking. Presently she looked at him.

'I am a bad hostess, Mr Satterthwaite. I do not entertain you.'

'I assure you that it is not necessary. There's one thing though, Mrs Denman, that I would very much like to know.'

'Yes?'

'How did you come across Mr Quin?'

'He is often down here,' she said slowly. 'I think he owns land in this part of the world.'

'He does, he does. He told me so this afternoon,' said Mr Satterthwaite.

'He is—' She paused. Her eyes met Mr Satterthwaite's. 'I think you know what he is better than I do,' she finished.

'I?'

'Is it not so?'

He was troubled. His neat little soul found her disturbing. He felt that she wished to force him further than he was prepared to go, that she wanted him to put into words that which he was not prepared to admit to himself.

'*You* know!' she said. 'I think you know most things, Mr Satterthwaite.'

Here was incense, yet for once it failed to intoxicate him. He shook his head in unwonted humility.

'What can anyone know?' he asked. 'So little—so very little.'

She nodded in assent. Presently she spoke again, in a queer brooding voice, without looking at him.

'Supposing I were to tell you something—you would not laugh? No, I do not think you would laugh. Supposing, then, that to carry on one's'—she paused—'one's trade, one's profession, one were to make use of a fantasy—one were to pretend to oneself something that did not exist—that one were to imagine a certain person . . . It is a pretence, you understand, a make believe—nothing more. But one day—'

'Yes?' said Mr Satterthwaite.

He was keenly interested.

'The fantasy came true! The thing one imagined—the impossible thing, the thing that could not be—was real! Is

305

that madness? Tell me, Mr Satterthwaite. Is that madness—
or do you believe it too?'

'I—' Queer how he could not get the words out. How
they seemed to stick somewhere at the back of his throat.

'Folly,' said Anna Denman. 'Folly.'

She swept out of the room and left Mr Satterthwaite
with his confession of faith unspoken.

He came down to dinner to find Mrs Denman entertaining a guest, a tall dark man approaching middle age.

'Prince Oranoff—Mr Satterthwaite.'

The two men bowed. Mr Satterthwaite had the feeling
that some conversation had been broken off on his entry
which would not be resumed. But there was no sense of
strain. The Russian conversed easily and naturally on those
objects which were nearest to Mr Satterthwaite's heart. He
was a man of very fine artistic taste, and they soon found
that they had many friends in common. John Denman
joined them, and the talk became localized. Oranoff
expressed regret for the accident.

'It was not my fault. I like to drive fast—yes, but I am
a good driver. It was Fate—chance'—he shrugged his
shoulders—'the masters of all of us.'

'There speaks the Russian in you, Sergius Ivanovitch,'
said Mrs Denman.

'And finds an echo in you, Anna Mikalovna,' he threw
back quickly.

Mr Satterthwaite looked from one to the other of the
three of them. John Denman, fair, aloof, English, and
the other two, dark, thin, strangely alike. Something rose

in his mind—what was it? Ah! he had it now. The first Act of the Walküre. Siegmund and Sieglinde—so alike—and the alien Hunding. Conjectures began to stir in his brain. Was this the meaning of the presence of Mr Quin? One thing he believed in firmly—wherever Mr Quin showed himself—there lay drama. Was this it here—the old hackneyed three-cornered tragedy?

He was vaguely disappointed. He had hoped for better things.

'What has been arranged, Anna?' asked Denman. 'The thing will have to be put off, I suppose. I heard you ringing the Roscheimers up.'

She shook her head.

'No—there is no need to put it off.'

'But you can't do it without the ballet?'

'You certainly couldn't have a Harlequinade without Harlequin and Columbine,' agreed Anna Denman drily. 'I'm going to be Columbine, John.'

'You?' He was astonished—disturbed, Mr Satterthwaite thought.

She nodded composedly.

'You need not be afraid, John. I shall not disgrace you. You forget—it was my profession once.'

Mr Satterthwaite thought: 'What an extraordinary thing a voice is. The things it says—and the things it leaves unsaid and means! I wish I knew . . .'

'Well,' said John Denman grudgingly, 'that solves one half of the problem. What about the other? Where will you find Harlequin?'

'I *have* found him—there!'

She gestured towards the open doorway where Mr Quin had just appeared. He smiled back at her.

'Good lord, Quin,' said John Denman. 'Do you know anything of this game? I should never have imagined it.'

'Mr Quin is vouched for by an expert,' said his wife. 'Mr Satterthwaite will answer for him.'

She smiled at Mr Satterthwaite, and the little man found himself murmuring:

'Oh, yes—I answer for Mr Quin.'

Denman turned his attention elsewhere.

'You know there's to be a fancy dress dance business afterwards. Great nuisance. We'll have to rig you up, Satterthwaite.'

Mr Satterthwaite shook his head very decidedly.

'My years will excuse me.' A brilliant idea struck him. A table napkin under his arm. 'There I am, an elderly waiter who has seen better days.'

He laughed.

'An interesting profession,' said Mr Quin. 'One sees so much.'

'I've got to put on some fool pierrot thing,' said Denman gloomily. 'It's cool anyway, that's one thing. What about you?' He looked at Oranoff.

'I have a Harlequin costume,' said the Russian. His eyes wandered for a minute to his hostess's face.

Mr Satterthwaite wondered if he was mistaken in fancying that there was just a moment of constraint.

'There might have been three of us,' said Denman, with a laugh. 'I've got an old Harlequin costume my wife made

308

me when we were first married for some show or other.'
He paused, looking down on his broad shirt front. 'I don't
suppose I could get into it now.'

'No,' said his wife. 'You couldn't get into it now.'

And again her voice said something more than mere
words.

She glanced up at the clock.

'If Molly doesn't turn up soon, we won't wait for her.'

But at that moment the girl was announced. She was
already wearing her Pierrette dress of white and green, and
very charming she looked in it, so Mr Satterthwaite reflected.

She was full of excitement and enthusiasm over the
forthcoming performance.

'I'm getting awfully nervous, though,' she announced,
as they drank coffee after dinner. 'I know my voice will
wobble, and I shall forget the words.'

'Your voice is very charming,' said Anna. 'I should not
worry about it if I were you.'

'Oh, but I do. The other I don't mind about—the dancing,
I mean. That's sure to go all right. I mean, you can't go
very far wrong with your feet, can you?'

She appealed to Anna, but the older woman did not
respond. Instead she said:

'Sing something now to Mr Satterthwaite. You will find
that he will reassure you.'

Molly went over to the piano. Her voice rang out, fresh
and tuneful, in an old Irish ballad.

'Sheila, dark Sheila, what is it that you're seeing?
What is it that you're seeing, that you're seeing in the fire?'

'*I see a lad that loves me—and I see a lad that leaves me,*
And a third lad, a Shadow Lad—and he's the lad that
   grieves me.'

The song went on. At the end, Mr Satterthwaite nodded vigorous approval.

'Mrs Denman is right. Your voice is charming. Not, perhaps, very fully trained, but delightfully natural, and with that unstudied quality of youth in it.'

'That's right,' agreed John Denman. 'You go ahead, Molly, and don't be downed by stage fright. We'd better be getting over to the Roscheimers now.'

The party separated to don cloaks. It was a glorious night and they proposed to walk over, the house being only a few hundred yards down the road.

Mr Satterthwaite found himself by his friend.

'It's an odd thing,' he said, 'but that song made me think of you. *A third lad—a Shadow Lad*—there's mystery there, and wherever there's mystery I—well, think of you.'

'Am I so mysterious?' smiled Mr Quin.

Mr Satterthwaite nodded vigorously.

'Yes, indeed. Do you know, until tonight, I had no idea that you were a professional dancer.'

'Really?' said Mr Quin.

'Listen,' said Mr Satterthwaite. He hummed the love motif from the Walküre. 'That is what has been ringing in my head all through dinner as I looked at those two.'

'Which two?'

'Prince Oranoff and Mrs Denman. Don't you see the

310

difference in her tonight? It's as though—as though a shutter had suddenly been opened and you see the glow within.'

'Yes,' said Mr Quin. 'Perhaps so.'

'The same old drama,' said Mr Satterthwaite. 'I am right, am I not? Those two belong together. They are of the same world, think the same thoughts, dream the same dreams . . . One sees how it has come about. Ten years ago Denman must have been very good-looking, young, dashing, a figure of romance. And he saved her life. All quite natural. But now—what is he, after all? A good fellow—prosperous, successful—but—well, mediocre, Good honest English stuff—very much like that Hepplewhite furniture upstairs. As English—and as ordinary—as that pretty English girl with her fresh untrained voice. Oh, you may smile, Mr Quin, but you cannot deny what I am saying.'

'I deny nothing. In what you see you are always right. And yet—'

'Yet what?'

Mr Quin leaned forward. His dark melancholy eyes searched for those of Mr Satterthwaite.

'Have you learned so little of life?' he breathed.

He left Mr Satterthwaite vaguely disquieted, such a prey to meditation that he found the others had started without him owing to his delay in selecting a scarf for his neck. He went out by the garden, and through the same door as in the afternoon. The lane was bathed in moonlight, and even as he stood in the doorway he saw a couple enlaced in each other's arms.

For a moment he thought—

311

And then he saw. *John Denman and Molly Stanwell.* Denman's voice came to him, hoarse and anguished.

'I can't live without you. What are we to do?'

Mr Satterthwaite turned to go back the way he had come, but a hand stayed him. Someone else stood in the doorway beside him, someone else whose eyes had also seen.

Mr Satterthwaite had only to catch one glimpse of her face to know how wildly astray all his conclusions had been.

Her anguished hand held him there until those other two had passed up the lane and disappeared from sight. He heard himself speaking to her, saying foolish little things meant to be comforting, and ludicrously inadequate to the agony he had divined. She only spoke once.

'Please,' she said, 'don't leave me.'

He found that oddly touching. He was, then, of use to someone. And he went on saying those things that meant nothing at all, but which were, somehow, better than silence. They went that way to the Roscheimers. Now and then her hand tightened on his shoulder, and he understood that she was glad of his company. She only took it away when they finally came to their destination. She stood very erect, her head held high.

'Now,' she said, 'I shall dance! Do not be afraid for me, my friend. I shall dance.'

She left him abruptly. He was seized upon by Lady Roscheimer, much bediamonded and very full of lamentations. By her he was passed on to Claude Wickam.

'Ruined! Completely ruined. The sort of thing that always

happens to me. All these country bumpkins think they can dance. I was never even consulted—' His voice went on—went on interminably. He had found a sympathetic listener, a man who *knew*. He gave himself up to an orgy of self-pity. It only ended when the first strains of music began.

Mr Satterthwaite came out of his dreams. He was alert, once more the critic. Wickam was an unutterable ass, but he could write music—delicate gossamer stuff, intangible as a fairy web—yet with nothing of the pretty pretty about it.

The scenery was good. Lady Roscheimer never spared expense when aiding her protégés. A glade of Arcady with lighting effects that gave it the proper atmosphere of unreality.

Two figures dancing as they had danced through time immemorial. A slender Harlequin flashing spangles in the moonlight with magic wand and masked face . . . A white Columbine pirouetting like some immortal dream . . .

Mr Satterthwaite sat up. He had lived through this before. Yes, surely . . .

Now his body was far away from Lady Roscheimer's drawing-room. It was in a Berlin Museum at a statuette of an immortal Columbine.

Harlequin and Columbine danced on. The wide world was theirs to dance in . . .

Moonlight—and a human figure. Pierrot wandering through the wood, singing to the moon. Pierrot who has seen Columbine and knows no rest. The Immortal two vanish, but Columbine looks back. She has heard the song of a human heart.

Pierrot wandering on through the wood . . . darkness . . . his voice dies away in the distance . . .

The village green—dancing of village girls—pierrots and pierrettes. Molly as Pierrette. No dancer—Anna Denman was right there—but a fresh tuneful voice as she sings her song 'Pierrette dancing on the Green'.

A good tune—Mr Satterthwaite nodded approval. Wickham wasn't above writing a tune when there was a need for it. The majority of the village girls made him shudder, but he realized that Lady Roscheimer was determinedly philanthropical.

They press Pierrot to join the dance. He refuses. With white face he wanders on—the eternal lover seeking his ideal. Evening falls. Harlequin and Columbine, invisible, dance in and out of the unconscious throng. The place is deserted, only Pierrot, weary, falls asleep on a grassy bank. Harlequin and Columbine dance round him. He wakes and sees Columbine. He woos her in vain, pleads, beseeches . . .

She stands uncertain. Harlequin beckons to her to be gone. But she sees him no longer. She is listening to Pierrot, to his song of love outpoured once more. She falls into his arms, and the curtain comes down.

The second Act is Pierrot's cottage. Columbine sits on her hearth. She is pale, weary. She listens—for what? Pierrot sings to her—woos her back to thoughts of him once more. The evening darkens. Thunder is heard . . . Columbine puts aside her spinning wheel. She is eager, stirred . . . She listens no longer to Pierrot. It is her own music that is in the air, the music of Harlequin and Columbine . . . She is awake. She remembers.

A crash of thunder! Harlequin stands in the doorway. Pierrot cannot see him, but Columbine springs up with a glad laugh. Children come running, but she pushes them aside. With another crash of thunder the walls fall, and Columbine dances out into the wild night with Harlequin.

Darkness, and through it the tune that Pierrette has sung. Light comes slowly. The cottage once more. Pierrot and Pierrette grown old and grey sit in front of the fire in two armchairs. The music is happy, but subdued. Pierrette nods in her chair. Through the window comes a shaft of moonlight, and with it the motif of Pierrot's long-forgotten song. He stirs in his chair.

Faint music—fairy music . . . Harlequin and Columbine outside. The door swings open and Columbine dances in. She leans over the sleeping Pierrot, kisses him on the lips . . .

Crash! A peal of thunder. She is outside again. In the centre of the stage is the lighted window and through it are seen the two figures of Harlequin and Columbine dancing slowly away, growing fainter and fainter . . .

A log falls. Pierrette jumps up angrily, rushes across to the window and pulls the blind. So it ends, on a sudden discord . . .

Mr Satterthwaite sat very still among the applause and vociferations. At last he got up and made his way outside. He came upon Molly Stanwell, flushed and eager, receiving compliments. He saw John Denman, pushing and elbowing his way through the throng, his eyes alight with a new flame. Molly came towards him, but, almost unconsciously, he put her aside. It was not her he was seeking.

'My wife? Where is she?'

'I think she went out in the garden.'

It was, however, Mr Satterthwaite who found her, sitting on a stone seat under a cypress tree. When he came up to her, he did an odd thing. He knelt down and raised her hand to his lips.

'Ah!' she said. 'You think I danced well?'

'You danced—as you always danced, Madame Kharsanova.'

She drew in her breath sharply.

'So—you have guessed.'

'There is only one Kharsanova. No one could see you dance and forget. But why—why?'

'What else is possible?'

'You mean?'

She had spoken very simply. She was just as simple now. 'Oh! but you understand. You are of the world. A great dancer—she can have lovers, yes—but a husband, that is different. And he—he did not want the other. He wanted me to belong to him as—as Kharsanova could never have belonged.'

'I see,' said Mr Satterthwaite. 'I see. So you gave it up?'

She nodded.

'You must have loved him very much,' said Mr Satterthwaite gently.

'To make such a sacrifice?' She laughed.

'Not quite that. To make it so light-heartedly.'

'Ah, yes—perhaps—you are right.'

'And now?' asked Mr Satterthwaite.

Her face grew grave.

'Now?' She paused, then raised her voice and spoke into the shadows.

'Is that you, Sergius Ivanovitch?'

Prince Oranoff came out into the moonlight. He took her hand and smiled at Mr Satterthwaite without self-consciousness.

'Ten years ago I mourned the death of Anna Kharsanova,' he said simply. 'She was to me as my other self. Today I have found her again. We shall part no more.'

'At the end of the lane in ten minutes,' said Anna. 'I shall not fail you.'

Oranoff nodded and went off again. The dancer turned to Mr Satterthwaite. A smile played about her lips.

'Well—you are not satisfied, my friend?'

'Do you know,' said Mr Satterthwaite abruptly, 'that your husband is looking for you?'

He saw the tremor that passed over her face, but her voice was steady enough.

'Yes,' she said gravely. 'That may well be.'

'I saw his eyes. They—' he stopped abruptly.

She was still calm.

'Yes, perhaps. For an hour. An hour's magic, born of past memories, of music, of moonlight—That is all.'

'Then there is nothing that I can say?' He felt old, dispirited.

'For ten years I have lived with the man I love,' said Anna Kharsanova. 'Now I am going to the man who for ten years has loved me.'

Mr Satterthwaite said nothing. He had no arguments left. Besides it really seemed the simplest solution. Only—only, somehow, it was not the solution he wanted. He felt her hand on his shoulder.

'I know, my friend, I know. But there is no third way. Always one looks for one thing—the lover, the perfect, the eternal lover . . . It is the music of Harlequin one hears. No lover ever satisfies one, for all lovers are mortal. And Harlequin is only a myth, an invisible presence . . . unless—'

'Yes,' said Mr Satterthwaite. 'Yes?'

'Unless—his name is—Death!'

Mr Satterthwaite shivered. She moved away from him, was swallowed up in the shadows . . .

He never knew quite how long he sat on there, but suddenly he started up with the feeling that he had been wasting valuable time. He hurried away, impelled in a certain direction almost in spite of himself.

As he came out into the lane he had a strange feeling of unreality. Magic—magic and moonlight! And two figures coming towards him . . .

Oranoff in his Harlequin dress. So he thought at first. Then, as they passed him, he knew his mistake. That lithe swaying figure belonged to one person only— Mr Quin . . .

They went on down the lane—their feet light as though they were treading on air. Mr Quin turned his head and looked back, and Mr Satterthwaite had a shock, for it was not the face of Mr Quin as he had ever seen it before. It was the face of a stranger—no, not quite a stranger. Ah! he had it now, it was the face of John Denman as it might have looked before life went too well with him. Eager, adventurous, the face at once of a boy and a lover . . .

Her laugh floated down to him, clear and happy . . . He looked after them and saw in the distance the lights of a little cottage. He gazed after them like a man in a dream.

He was rudely awakened by a hand that fell on his shoulder and he was jerked round to face Sergius Oranoff. The man looked white and distracted.

'Where is she? Where is she? She promised—and she has not come.'

'Madam has just gone up the lane—alone.'

It was Mrs Denman's maid who spoke from the shadow of the door behind them. She had been waiting with her mistress's wraps.

'I was standing here and saw her pass,' she added.

Mr Satterthwaite threw one harsh word at her.

'Alone? Alone, did you say?'

The maid's eyes widened in surprise.

'Yes, sir. Didn't you see her off?'

Mr Satterthwaite clutched at Oranoff.

'Quickly,' he muttered. 'I'm—I'm afraid.'

They hurried down the lane together, the Russian talking in quick disjointed sentences.

'She is a wonderful creature. Ah! how she danced tonight. And that friend of yours. Who is he? Ah! but he is wonderful—unique. In the old days, when she danced the Columbine of Rimsky Korsakoff, she never found the perfect Harlequin. Mordroff, Kassnine—none of them were quite perfect. She had her own little fancy. She told me of it once. Always she danced with a dream Harlequin—a man who was not really there. It was Harlequin himself, she said, who came to dance with her. It was that fancy of hers that made her Columbine so wonderful.'

Mr Satterthwaite nodded. There was only one thought in his head.

'Hurry,' he said. 'We must be in time. Oh! we must be in time.'

They came round the last corner—came to the deep pit and to something lying in it that had not been there before, the body of a woman lying in a wonderful pose, arms flung wide and head thrown back. A dead face and body that were triumphant and beautiful in the moonlight.

Words came back to Mr Satterthwaite dimly—Mr Quin's words: *'wonderful things on a rubbish heap'* . . . He understood them now.

Oranoff was murmuring broken phrases. The tears were streaming down his face.

'I loved her. Always I loved her.' He used almost the same words that had occurred to Mr Satterthwaite earlier in the day. 'We were of the same world, she and I. We had the same thoughts, the same dreams. I would have loved her always . . .'

'How do you know?'

The Russian stared at him—at the fretful peevishness of the tone.

'How do you know?' went on Mr Satterthwaite. 'It is what all lovers think—what all lovers say . . . There is only one lover—'

He turned and almost ran into Mr Quin. In an agitated

320

manner, Mr Satterthwaite caught him by the arm and drew him aside.

'It was *you*,' he said. 'It was *you* who were with her just now?'

Mr Quin waited a minute and then said gently:

'You can put it that way, if you like.'

'And the maid didn't see you?'

'The maid didn't see me.'

'But *I* did. Why was that?'

'Perhaps, as a result of the price you have paid, you see things that other people—do not.'

Mr Satterthwaite looked at him uncomprehendingly for a minute or two. Then he began suddenly to quiver all over like an aspen leaf.

'What is this place?' he whispered. 'What is this place?'

'I told you earlier today. It is *My* lane.'

'A Lovers' Lane,' murmured Mr Satterthwaite. 'And people pass along it.'

'Most people, sooner or later.'

'And at the end of it—what do they find?'

Mr Quin smiled. His voice was very gentle. He pointed at the ruined cottage above them.

'The house of their dreams—or a rubbish heap—who shall say?'

Mr Satterthwaite looked up at him suddenly. A wild rebellion surged over him. He felt cheated, defrauded.

'But *I*—' His voice shook. '*I* have never passed down your lane . . .'

'And do you regret?'

Mr Satterthwaite quailed. Mr Quin seemed to have

loomed to enormous proportions . . . Mr Satterthwaite had a vista of something at once menacing and terrifying . . . Joy, Sorrow, Despair.

And his comfortable little soul shrank back appalled.

'Do you regret?' Mr Quin repeated his question. There was something terrible about him.

'No,' Mr Satterthwaite stammered. 'N-no.'

And then suddenly he rallied.

'But I see things,' he cried. 'I may have been only a looker-on at Life—but I see things that other people do not. You said so yourself, Mr Quin . . .'

But Mr Quin had vanished.